Hood Misfits Volume 1:

Carl Weber Presents

Hood Misfits Volume 1:

Carl Weber Presents

Brick & Storm

www.urbanbooks.net

Urban Books, LLC
97 N18th Street
Wyandanch, NY 11798

ISBN 13: 978-1-60162-625-7
ISBN 10: 1-60162-625-8

First Trade Paperback Printing September 2014
Printed in the United States of America

10 9 8 7 6 5 4 3

Distributed by Kensington Publishing Corp.
Submit Wholesale Orders to:
Kensington Publishing Corp.
C/O Penguin Group (USA) Inc.
Attention: Order Processing
405 Murray Hill Parkway
East Rutherford, NJ 07073-2316
Phone: 1-800-526-0275
Fax: 1-800-227-9604

Acknowledgment

First and foremost, we'd like to thank all the readers who've been rocking with us from day one. From the moment *Hood Misfits* hit the market, you guys have come out in full support, and it hasn't wavered. So, we'd like to take a moment to thank Dymetra LaChey Miller (always with us no matter what), Lenika Winfield (always down to ride with B&S), Jazz Nicole, Erica Martinez (Queen DOA. LOL), Laura Hughes (all the way from the UK), Lawrence Huggins (you introduced us to the world), The 556 Chicks Book Club (Tiffany, Benita, and yes you, Monika, every last one of you), Sharlene Smith, Tasha Bynum (your commentary is hilarious), Danielle Green, Christina Jones, Krisha DeShawn (you crack us up too, mama), Carla Towns, Shawnda Hamilton, Rara Nichole, Lizzy King, Athea Cranford, Teana Foggie, Tee Elyse, and so many more. If we forgot to name you, charge our heads and not our hearts. To Brenda Hampton, thank you for believing in us then taking that chance on a set of newbies. We promise to always make you proud by giving our best at all times. There are so many more of our supporters that we would love to thank, but we're going to run out of room if we do. LOL. Much love to all of you, and we hope you continue to rock with us as we'll continue to try our hardest to bring you our best. And whatever you do, never forget, Every Nigga Gotta Agenda.

E.N.G.A. fam.

Prologue

Shit was real out there in the street. You understand me? What I'd learned in the last two weeks would stay with me for the rest of my life. Ray-Ray is my name. I was sixteen years old, and I had been sold to a pimp by my father. I worked hard all my life not to lead the life my parents had. They'd made sure of it too. My father had been a two-bit hustler and a con man. My mother was no better. She'd been a whore since birth, damn near. Her mother had sold her to the highest bidder at age ten. She'd tried heroin by age twelve and had snorted coke by fourteen. My father was twenty years older than she was, and she had me at fifteen. He was her pimp, and she was his bottom bitch.

There were days I'd watched my father beat my mother until she couldn't stand anymore. Then, there were days I'd seen my mother stab my father—yes, it happened more than one time—and one day I thought she'd killed him. But, no, not my old man. Hell naw. There was no way he would let a woman snuff him out. When he got home from the hospital, he beat her again, and by the end of the night, they were snorting coke together and getting drunk. That was the kind of love they had. That was my fuckin' life, and although I saw them do these things, most times they would make me go to my room or send me to the mall so I wouldn't be too much in their business.

Everything was everything, until my father ran up on the wrong nigga. He sent my mother to be a distraction, like always. Even with the abuse of drugs and alcohol, at age thirty-one, Shanna Willington was still a bad bitch. I think it was because my grandmamma was Italian and granddaddy was right out of Africa that my mama looked as good as she did. She was five eight and light-skinned with long jet-black hair that cascaded down to her ass. Both she and I could fit in the same clothes, perfect size tens. Yes, a bitch was bad at sixteen because of my parents' genes. Only difference between me and my mama was, I was as black as the night was long. My skin was so chocolate, they said my mama didn't think I was her baby at first. Not until I opened my eyes and looked just like my daddy. People said I looked just like Raymond Jenkins, which was why my nickname was Ray-Ray.

Don't get it twisted. Yeah, my parents were criminals, but they loved the hell out of me. I know you're asking, How yo' daddy love you and he sold you to a pimp? Because, bitch, he didn't do that shit intentionally. Let me stop running my mouth and tell you what went down. Better yet, let me show you the movie, like the way my life had played out for me.

Episode One: Taken

"All warfare is based on deception."
—SUN TZU

Ray-Ray

"Mama, what's going on?" I asked with tears in my eyes.

No matter how many times I'd seen my mama frightened, I'd never seen the total look of terror and panic in her eyes. Her skin was fire-red, and her eyes watered to the point where I was sure her vision was blurry.

"Shut up, Ray-Ray. Just cut them open and dump them, baby. Please."

She was working frantically as we dumped ounces of pure white coke into the toilet. I was going so fast, the sharp knife in my hand had cut me. I didn't understand why we were dumping the goods when the Feds weren't at the door. Yeah, somebody was banging on the door, but I knew it wasn't the Feds, judging by the way my father was pleading for the people on the other side of the door to give him some time.

"We fucked up, Ray. We did, baby. We fucked—"

She couldn't even get the words out before the front door of our house came flying off its hinges. My mama jumped up, her chest heaving up and down like she was having an asthma attack. Her mouth was moving but nothing would come out.

"Come on, Dame. Man, look, man . . . let me—"

My daddy's words got cut short when the sound of gunshots rent the air, and he was silent for a brief moment. I jumped up, ready to run out to see if he was dead, but my mama stopped me, snatched me back into the bathroom, and silently closed the door.

"Shhhh!" she ordered me as she moved me back. "Get in the shower and lay down. Don't move, Ray-Ray. Don't say shit, baby. Understand?"

My mama looked at me, I mean, really looked at me for the first time in my sixteen years. I saw all of the things that she feared, all of her worries, all of her anxiety. For the first time, she looked older than thirty-one.

"Mama, please, don't leave me," I cried.

"No, Ray-Ray. No. No fuckin' tears," she aggressively whispered. "You never shed one gotdamned tear, you hear me? Never let these niggas see your fear. They feed on that shit. Understand? Dry those fuckin' tears now." She then reached to cup the back of my neck and lay her forehead on mine.

My eyes widened, and we listened on in horror as my father's agony rent the apartment.

"Aw, man. Fuck! Come on, Dame, just give me time," Daddy pleaded. "I'll get yo' shit back to you, nigga. Just give me time."

Then I heard his voice. He sounded like he could be your savior, but in reality, he was your executioner.

"Fuck, nigga! You gone steal my shit then try to sell me my own work back?"

I assumed that was Dame.

"Look, man, I fucked up, a'ight. I fucked up. We been boys, Dame. I looked out for you when your pops caught it back in the day. Come on, man."

"Where's your bitch?" Dame asked.

My mother held me tighter and stared into my eyes. She'd told me not to cry, but her tears were flowing freely.

"I'm so sorry, baby," she said to me. "Please forgive me and Raymond. We fucked up, baby."

"Sh-she ain't here," my daddy lied. "I sent her to get the product."

"See? You see this shit, my niggas? Even on his death bed, this nigga lying. Go find her."

My mother stood quickly, kissed my lips, and then forced me to lie down in the tub. She then quickly unscrewed the lightbulb in the bathroom.

"Stay there," she told me then grabbed the knife she had been using to cut the coke bricks open.

Both of us still had the powder on our hands, fear in our breaths, and death in our eyes. We listened on as they ransacked our house. Silently, I was wishing, hoping, and praying that they didn't find me or my mama. I was praying, as bad as it may sound, that they would just kill my daddy and be gone. But the look on my mama's face said the end was near. She knew what was coming.

Suddenly, the door to the bathroom swung open. Mama didn't even have time to swing the knife. Somebody yanked her by her long black hair and slung her out of the bathroom into the hall. I almost screamed when he kicked her in her stomach then punched her, but I slapped my hand over my mouth and inched down into the tub. I tried to lay flat like a plank. I was grateful then that the bathroom was dark.

"Aye, yo, Dame, we found the bitch and some of your shit," the guy said, his voice deep and raspy as if he had smoked too many cigarettes.

I couldn't see his face, but I would remember that voice.

He dragged my mama kicking and screaming from the bathroom, taunting her. "Shut up, bitch."

There was a loud smack, and then my mother screamed. Items crashed to the floor. I could only assume she had fallen over something. What I heard next made my heart stop.

POP!

My daddy's yells when they shot my mama chilled me to the bone.

"Aww God. Oh fuck, Dame! Oh shit, baby. Shanna, baby, I'm—"

"Shut up, nigga," the raspy voice growled out behind another gunshot.

My daddy's agonizing shriek pierced the air again. I couldn't stand it anymore. I wanted to see my parents, needed to see them, even if they were dead. Before my common sense kicked in, I hopped from the tub, screaming and sobbing, then ran to the front room, falling over my mother's dead body. Her eyes were wide open with a bullet hole between them.

"No, mama! No!" I cried, trying to cradle her in my arms.

Her body was limp, heavy. The weight of death was suffocating me. Through hazy and burning eyes I looked at my daddy. He was still clinging to life. I'd never seen my father cry before. Had never seen him weak, but in that moment I knew he was at his weakest.

"Dun"— He coughed, spat up blood as it bubbled in his throat— "don't kill my baby," he begged with his last breath.

"Pick that bitch up, Trigga," Dame said.

I looked up at the man through blurry vision. I couldn't really make him out. There were about twelve other men in our home. It was overkill. Did he really need all of those men to kill my mama and daddy?

Trigga snatched me up by the back of my hair and then made me kneel in front of him. I couldn't see his face, just felt the aggressiveness in his hold on me. The tight grip on the back of my hair was already giving me a headache. I tried to snatch away to no avail. I almost fell face first into his steel-toe Timberlands. Trigga snatched me back up, and I tried to fight back. My mama would want me to fight back. My daddy always babied me, but my mama told me to fight. I had to fight for my mama.

I started to kick, scream, and yell, bucking my body, trying to get away. I arched my back and reached behind me to claw at his face. I got him too, just enough to try to dig his eyes out for my mama. "Get off of me!" I screamed out, kicking my legs and bucking like a horse.

I could make out some of the faces of the niggas in the room. Could hear them laughing at me clawing at the man's eyes. Half of them were supposed to be my daddy's boys, was supposed to be his friends, have his fuckin' back. Pookie, Slammer, Janky, all those niggas was just breaking bread with my mama and daddy, and laughing about how they had come up.

Rage took away my senses. I swung my hand in a backward motion at the nigga who had a hold on me, trying to hit him in his dick. He was quicker and stronger than me, and used his big foot to take my legs from under me, taking me down to the floor face first. His knee in my back made me scream out louder. I could feel the blood oozing from my nose. My daddy had always told me niggas in the street didn't care for you.

"They don't give a fuck. You hear me, Ray-Ray? Niggas ruthless as fuck, baby girl," he'd said as he used his pinky nail to sniff coke up his nose.

He was right. The big muthafucka on me was sure to kill me.

See, real niggas didn't care about raping no chick when it came to their money being fucked up. They didn't waste time with pussy when there was bloodlust.

"Sit this nigga up so he can see Trigga cap his daughter," Dame barked out then took a seat on our leather sofa.

All I could see was his expensive-clad feet. He had on Italian leather dress shoes that looked fresh from the shoemaker.

I could hear movement as Dame's henchmen moved to sit my father up.

Daddy breathed out, "Don . . . don't kill . . . my . . . baby, Dame."

"Fuck you, nigga!" Dame responded. "You already know the move, Trigga."

Oh God, my life was about to end. Somebody would walk in and find me, my mama, and my daddy dead on the floor.

"Dame, please . . ." My daddy choked as he tried to talk.

I heard the gun click back. I squeezed my eyes shut tight, hot tears rolling down my face.

Daddy's sobbing voice finally found its way out. "Waittttt. She's a virgin. Use her." He coughed. "Don't kill her. Pussy . . . fresh money."

"Yo, yo, Trigga, wait a minute, my nigga. I think Ray just sold me his daughter's virgin pussy."

There was an awkward silence, and then Dame and his henchmen burst into a fit of laughter, all of them except the one with his knee in my back.

"You really bargaining your daughter's pussy for your life, nigga?" Dame asked.

"Don't kill her" was all my father could get out.

"Finish him," Dame ordered.

My body jerked when the shot rang out. I didn't know who had shot my daddy, just like I didn't know who'd shot my mama. When I opened my eyes, my daddy was laying right in front of me, his lifeless eyes wide just like mama's. The last look in them begged my forgiveness.

Trigga

"Stop fuckin' struggling," I growled low next to li'l shawty's ear, my knee dug deep into her back as I pressed her hard, her cheek sandwiched between my foot and the floor.

I licked my lips in a scowl before looking up at my boss Dame. I pushed my hand against li'l shawty's head to keep her there and waited for my next command, gun ready to bust at any moment. This shit was my birthday present—my rise as Dame's main killer—and the shit had me on a rush.

All around me was niggas thirsty for my new position, and fuck if I was gonna let another nigga take my shit. So, I kneeled there, holding down the shawty who fucked up my face with that shit she pulled. Bitch cut under my right eye good. I knew I was gonna have a scar there, but I didn't care; I just wasn't digging how shawty got at me. The broad had to be stupid. She should have stayed where she was, and her life would have been much better, but that was her bad. Now her bitch-ass parents' debt was hers. And she was still fighting me. I hated when I had to introduce people to who I was.

Every nigga had a sob story, had the tiniest violin playing and shit, waiting to spill their secrets like bitches. I didn't. My life was simple as it was, and this broad was about to find that out. My name was Trigga. My finger was always itching to grip that Glock, and my right hook ready to connect to any nigga's jaw. I didn't mess around and play games. I had no time for that shit. So I sat and waited for the command from the boss.

Life in "the trap" was like that. Li'l shawty was tapping on my black box, reminding me of that shit. Like I said, it was my birthday. A nigga eighteen now. People in my past would say I was a man now, but that shit ain't true. I became a man the day my mom handed me a Glock and told me to take down the killers who'd snuffed both my parents out. Yeah, simple as that. Who I was then died, and Trigga came out of the shadows. A li'l nigga educated by a revolutionary NGE/New Black Panther from Brooklyn and his Assata Shakur protégé wife, both of whom went to one of those HBCUs around here in ATL but lived in the trap. Yeah, Trigga got education but was raised on the streets of the trap. Went from house to house once my parents got popped. Stopped caring about my situation when I touched the blood of my pops, mom, and little sister. Stopped caring when I watched my mom get raped by some niggas who wanted what my pops had. Had took him down just to get her.

Yeah, in that shit, my pops taught me a man who was king was never a nigga unless he wanted to be, and a king always took care of his throne to survive. My throne was gone the moment they got popped, so I had to survive by becoming a nigga. Feel me? My moms taught me that day that a queen was a jaguar and a jaguar could never be made pussy. She lived that truth even as she got ran through and then, in turn, snuffed a couple of them niggas out as she lay choking in her own blood. I finished off the rest I could get to as she schooled me on her and pops' rules in surviving the game. She told me where their stash of paper was hidden with her and my pops' book of thoughts then she took her last breath. Her glossy amber eyes were the last thing I remembered.

I took it and hid all that shit before five-O ran through. I watched as they lined the place with that dust and said my parents were drug runners.

People forgot about my fam and me. My name disappeared that day, and I became Trigga.

I watched in silence as they threw me in the system, where I went from home to home until I met Dame. You know, same story every little black kid got. In my black box was all that shit. All emotions died in those moments. I was ten then. So, like I said, every nigga got a sob story, but mine never made me cry, so I ain't got shit to sob over.

Dame gave his approval from behind me. "Trigga nigga, good look. Now pick that pussy up, and let's roll out. I got better shit to do."

"So we ain't cappin the bitch?" one of the homies asked.

Nigga was sweating and shit, dick print visible, and it pissed me off. Sloppy killers always got caught and snitched, and this fool was just that type. He killed 'cause shit made his dick hard. Sewer-ass niggas like him always had to find some way to get his, and by the way he was sweating and shit, it looked like he needed to get him some molly too. Weak-ass niggas, I swear.

I yanked hard and lifted li'l shawty's head to slam it hard against the floor, knocking her out easily. Then I picked her up, threw her over my shoulder, and locked eyes on Dame.

"Did I say cap that bitch yet? No, I didn't. Let's be out. Got uses for that pussy," Dame said and walked out.

My eyes narrowed, I pulled my fitted down to shield my eyes, reached back to tuck my short locks into my hoodie, and pulled it over my head. As we walked out the apartment, I made a mental note to come back and holler at each broad and nigga in the complex that may have wanted to talk. Everyone knew that you didn't fuck with Dame and you didn't fuck with his product. This broad's people had done just that. Never take from the hand that feed you. Feel me? That was a straight OG rule right there.

Throwing her in the back seat, I watched some of the niggas grab their dicks the moment li'l shawty's legs fell apart and showed her pink panties. Typical-ass niggas. Pussy always on their minds no matter where they could get it. Me? Fuck that shit! My pussy knew where to stay and knew not to be fucked with outside of me. I stayed getting my dick wet, so being hungry for random pussy, especially fresh pussy, wasn't even on my mind. My throne was on my mind.

My throne always equaled staying tight in the street, my money, my kills, and then pussy. Ain't no order to that shit either.

"Ey yo, pretty boy Trigga, we got some shit ready for tonight for your day." TooTight, another nigga in the crew, flashed his gold and laughed while watching me. "Li'l nigga going to get mad pussy and dough, right?"

Nigga always called me pretty boy, because of my brown skin. Broads stayed thirsty from that alone. They said I had eyes that look lined with eyeliner or some shit. I hated when they said that crap, but it always made their pussies wet at the same time. Said my brown skin looked like red clay and you know the broads loved my short locks and smile. They loved the way I licked my lips and rubbed my jaw too. So, yeah, a nigga was pretty to them. Always had me pullin' pussy for Dame and the crew. Always. But TooTight's words went over my head as he asked me again.

So, I said nothing. Why? Because I didn't talk. But I did smirk and swipe at my nose, closing the door to the car behind me. Yeah, party was going to be swagged out, but I couldn't give two shits about it really. I just wanted my cash and wanted to push more product. Was done with school, so I had to hit up my block on the regular now to push out Dame's goods. Yeah, a nigga had his high-school diploma. I really don't know why I cared about that, just reminded me of what my pops always put in my head, I guess. Either way, it kept me close to anyone that needed some dust, as well as our enemies on the street.

Climbing into the car, I dropped my head back as the other goon niggas started clapping at the mouth, talking 'bout dumb shit. This was the time I usually always go into my black box and pull out the teachings of my pops and one of the books on being a samurai that I found in his closet. But right now, that shit wasn't even possible. Niggas kept talking, asking me about when I was going to get inked up.

I mean, I didn't know how many fuckin' times I had to tell them that shit wasn't happening. I mean, I thought about that shit, but my mind was always ten steps ahead of niggas. What was the quickest way to be ID'd in the black streets of ATL? Ink. You got ink that stands out and shows, then how you gonna hide in the hood? Naw. I wasn't going to do any visible shit, and if I did, you would have to get up on me to ID that shit. That wasn't going to happen.

I sat back and just laughed as they asked me questions, like bitches.

"Yo, li'l homie is getting inked up just right tonight. My gift," Dame said to us from the front.

Of course he would throw his weight around. *Damn!*

When Dame said something, it was law around the *A*, and since I didn't feel like hearing that nigga's mouth, I had to oblige. Now I had to think about how to do the shit smart. I mean, yeah, I had an idea of what kind of ink I wanted to get—something dealing with who I was—which made me smile inwardly. I knew getting a tat went against everything I'd just said, but I had to show loyalty to Dame's word or he would start to fuck with me. It was all good though because I was a different kind of nigga. So, what I got would be something I drew—two shackles on my wrists with the chains disappearing into my veins. That was it. They'd think it was some hood shit. I didn't care. It would be what I wanted it to be.

So the day came close to night, and li'l shawty started whimpering on my lap. We had run some product all the while she laid in the back of the ride tied up, blindfolded, and gagged. Every time I got in, I made sure to knock her out with a quick squeeze near her neck and behind her head, something I learned in my pop's book that I had been practicing. Made shit easier in these situations, and I didn't want another Band-Aid on the side of my eye.

The trap was thick with niggas and bitches in the streets. As we made it to Dame's spot, we got out and flanked him, watching for any enemy that might try to get at dude. My fingers began to itch, which let me know we were being watched. The situation got so tense, it had me pacing with one hand in my pocket, and the other tugging on my fitted hat.

Behind me, I heard, "What you see, Trigga, nigga?"

I said nothing because I was in my zone. I'd learned how to listen to the streets long ago after being homeless and hiding from DFCS, Division of Family and Children Services. It was a certain vibe you got when you knew shit was about to pop off. Some didn't listen to that shit, but I did. Stepping backwards, I slapped the top of the car to tell the driver to get Dame in the house.

Walking slowly to the locking gates, I tilted my head up at a set of young cats watching from across the street and adjusted my Glock before yelling behind me, "Nothing, my nigga. You know how shit gets."

"*Hahaha*. Yeah, that's why Dame got you where you at, li'l nigga. Forgot how you read the Trap," some random nigga said to me.

Walking backwards, I moved past the new niggas that ain't know about me and how I worked without saying shit and went inside. One of the rules of the street was, you always protect the boss. Protect him and you protect that profit you may get later. How did you turn your back and trust that everything was good in the crib? You didn't. That was how niggas got taken out, turning their backs with guns always pointed their way.

Inside, I heard li'l shawty screaming again and fighting. I threw back my hood and rubbed my hands together. Wasn't my place to even check on that shit. I was just the gun, not the right hand. So as she screamed, I watched her kick and slam her balled fist against Big Jake's broad shoulders. I knew that shit had to hurt her because he was one solid fat-ass nigga. All his beef was nothing but muscle, which people didn't know, but I did. See, we niggas in the streets always had to have an ace. Mine was my mind, my eyes, and my always clean-shot takedowns.

Big Jake was making people think he was a big, dumb, fat-ass nigga that always had to eat. He was the body-guard, and I always trained with that nigga on the low to get our strength up. See, he was the one who told Dame to get me when I met them in the streets long ago. Back then I was just a runner with good eyes who could tell when people were ready to gun for them. That was how I got in, and me and Big Jake had been like extended fam always. Nothing more than just a cool dude.

Anyway, I dropped back on the couch and watched as li'l shawty planted her feet against Big Jake's chest, push-ing, and swinging. She balled her fists up and connected them to each side of his skull. Big Jake laughed at each blow.

Something about her fight reminded me of some old shit. I kept my amber gaze on her, following and laughing when Big Jake dropped her on the floor with a loud bang. The broad's body bowed up then went straight as a board when her head hit the wall, her dark hair covering the wooden floor.

Kicking my feet up on the table, pushing weed, and empty cans out of the way, I kept watching while she fought and tried to kick at Big Jake, until he picked her up by her head and threw her into the closet and locked the door. Laughter had me dropping my head back against the couch and picking up the game controller to start up some Madden.

This side of the bossman's property was for his goons. Here we did whatever the fuck we liked, which was why there was shit everywhere. That irritated me. No matter the fuckin' way I grew up, a nigga still liked to have at least a spot where it was clean and roaches and shit weren't trying to come through and say whaddup. Bossman was the same, so though shit was everywhere, it wasn't dirty to the point of roaches and mice.

"What you laughing at, nigglet?" Big Jake's booming voice rumbled behind me.

Shrugging my shoulder, I reached into my pocket and pulled out some candy. Just as I popped it in my mouth, the other niggas in the house came into the room.

"A big-ass bear getting fucked up by some pussy." I smirked.

"Little nigglet, you should talk. She got you too. Get the fuck up and get ready for this party," Big Jake boomed.

I laughed as he gripped me by my hoodie and threw me off the couch.

The party. I had forgot about it that fast. Bossman Dame was serious about this shit, so I knew I had to get ready. We all did. That meant the street pussy he always called in to clean the house was already working on one side of the house and about to come this way. All I had at Dame's was a backpack and some shoes, so I needed to go to my own place, which was over an abandoned firehouse.

"A'ight, Big Jake," I threw at him, still laughing, "hit you up later."

My eyes locked on the closet where I heard pleading, screaming, and clawing. Shit had nothing to do with me, so I kept it trill and walked out.

Hours later, I walked back to the crib dressed in dark sagging jeans, tan Tims, and a black leather and jean hoodie with a black tee underneath it. The streets were hyped about my big day. Honestly, I didn't care, but it was dope to see Dame's place spilling with pussy and people from all over simply for my birthday. I wasn't allowed to deal in Dame's crib, so I couldn't look at any of these cats as money for the night. That was one fucked-up thing about it.

"Hey, Trigga," several sweet female voices said around me.

I rubbed my chin and licked my lips as my eyes ran over curve-hugging leggings that left a plump pussy-print then upward toward titties that made me want to touch. I tilted my chin up, and shawties surrounded me, crooking their fingers for me to bend down so they could press their pillow-soft lips on my cheeks. My dimples settled in my cheeks, causing more pussy to surround me. Of course, a nigga was in heaven right then.

Hands played in my shoulder-length locks, running over my chests, and some even slipped into my sagging jeans to feel how much of a man I was. Dropping my hands over asses aplenty, I smelled wet pussy the moment they learned my dick game was on ten.

"Ohhh, happy birthday, Trigga! You gonna come get some of this pussy, huh?" one of the chicks asked.

As I smirked, Dame appeared behind me and said, "Later. Let this little nigga get into the party first."

If anybody was a pretty boy, it was that nigga—light bright damn-near white nigga with light eyes that always had chicks on some swooning shit. Bitches had no idea what they were getting themselves into when they flocked to that nigga. Everyone stepped away from me and went to him, giggling and flirting, flipping their hair and laying kisses on his lips and cheeks.

"You ready for all this pussy around here, li'l nigga?" Dame asked.

Like I said, I was a selective talker, so I nodded, rubbing my hands together, and gave a smirk, which Dame understood as gloating.

"A'ight then, li'l nigga, quit talking wit' ya chest and enjoy this party. Hit me up in five so you can get inked and your dick sucked." Dame laughed, slapping the pretty asses around him.

Dame didn't give a damn about nothing but his, and I had to respect it. But a lot of his mannerism just didn't make sense to me. At times he could get real stupid over pussy and product, but that was the game.

I moved through the dancing bodies in the house. Everyone was grinding, groping, and probably fuckin', thanks to the product and liquid running through, and all of it was for me, but really in the name of Dame.

As I got deeper into the house, I walked past the closet that shawty was in. I wondered what he had done with her, if she got popped or not. Either way, she wasn't in the closet anymore.

Music thumped around me, and I bobbed my head to the tunes while grinding up on two women. Everyone who knew me knew not to offer me any product or drink.

I always kept a level head in this game and never dove into using my own shit. Just another OG rule I knew I never wanted to break. Which was why I always had my own weed. I lit up and let the broads around me get kush off of it.

Time passed and everything was icing. The crew niggas grabbed me up and took me upstairs, where I sat down with Starry, the baddest tattooist in the game, and one of Dame's former bitches. Baby had the look of Blac Chyna, but with black hair. She sat on her knees, a pillow under her, waiting on me, dressed in only a red thong and bra that pushed up her caramel titties. No lie, her plump lips made my dick hard as some of her chicks led me into the room. I saw Dame nod and then walk out the bedroom closing the door as I was stripped naked and sat on the bed. Bad bitches surrounded me and I let Starry know what I wanted, which she digged. Pulling out a drawing I did, she glanced at it once, before having me lean back on the bed.

With pussy surrounding me left and right, my shit sprung up rigid hard, only to get swallowed and throated. Any tension I had melted away with the kush I'd inhaled and with my dick being swallowed then dunked into the finest pussy in the game. The sound of the tattoo gun on my wrists then forearms had me in purple haze as sex scented the air and, "*Ohhh*, Trigga . . ." flooded my ears.

Ray-Ray

When I opened my eyes, the room started to spin. I knew I was no longer in a closet because there was light. The bed I was laying on was soft, almost like a cloud. The lower part of my back hurt from where that nigga had put his knee, and my neck hurt from that big burly grizzly bear-looking nigga sending me head first into the wall. Shit, my whole body hurt.

I could hear music and feel the bass thumping from the speakers. The first thing I would have done was try to run away, but I couldn't even sit up straight. Where was I? How would I get away? I couldn't front like a bitch wasn't terrified. I was so scared, I was shaking, but when I realized I was only in my bra and panties, my senses quickly came together.

I jumped up from the bed and grabbed between my legs like I had a dick. Everything felt normal. I didn't want to be raped or none of that shit. I didn't want a nigga's dick in me who I didn't know shit about. I looked around the room in a panic. It wasn't what I was expecting. The marble floors, decked-out bedroom suite, bay windows with attached balcony, and flowing sheer panels to the windows told me I was in place of money. The walls were cream colored and trimmed in gold, and an expensive-looking rug lay at the foot of the bed.

I did notice the room had another queen-sized bed in there. That was how big it was. To the left was a big walk-in closet. I knew that because someone had left the door open. There were all kinds of expensive shit in there—clothes, shoes, purses, belts, lace-front wigs. There was another closed door. I could hear two people behind it oohing and aahing; it sounded like they were having sex.

I could hear chicks in the next room screaming out something about Trigga, the muthafucka who had knocked me out. He was on my hit list. I'd kill his ass too. Just like I was going to kill the muthafucka with the deep, raspy voice. And I was going to murk whoever the fuck Dame was.

Yeah, my mama and daddy were foul as fuck in their dealings, but they'd sheltered me from the shit most times. Other times, I made myself disappear, reading a book or jumping ahead in my homework studies. My daddy always told me keep my head in my books and out their business. Which was what I did.

As I thought about my mama and my daddy, my fear was replaced with anger. I dropped my weak body back down to the bed and placed my head between my legs. The tears started, and they wouldn't stop. I cried loudly and didn't care who heard me. I didn't think they could hear me over the loud-ass music anyway.

"Oh shit," a female's voice said after I heard the bathroom door swing open.

"What?" a male's voice asked.

"This new bitch is up. Dame wanted me to make sure she bathed and put some clothes on. You know that nigga like his new pussy fresh for him," the woman said.

"But I ain't even bus' yet."

"Nigga, put ya dick away and get the fuck out. Let me handle daddy's business, or else I'ma tell 'im you dipping and ain't tipping."

The dude sucked his lips and grumbled something about her playing with his dick later.

I slowly lifted my head and took in the woman, who looked older than me. Light-skin with a long blonde weave that hung down her back, she had an abundance of ass, but not nearly enough titties. She looked like a stripper. The red leather catsuit she had on hugged her pussy and made it sit out like a moose knuckle. Her berry-colored lips were plush, and her makeup was done like she was prepping for a photo shoot or some shit. I could tell she had blue contacts in her almond-shaped eyes. She was pretty, and when she smiled at me, I almost felt safe. Almost. But I knew this game. A smiling face could mean your death around these parts.

The dude stumbled from the bathroom wiping white powder from his nose. He then turned a bottle of Henny to his ashy black lips. That nigga was straight-up ugly. The nappy twists on top of his head looked like dried worms. He cut his bloodshot eyes over at me.

"Damn, Sasha. Who dat?" he asked, motioning his head my way.

"Don't worry about it, nigga," Sasha snapped. "Now get the fuck out before Dame has Trigga body you."

"You saying that shit like a nigga scared of Trigga or some shit. That nigga can get got just like any other muthafucka. He ain't invincible."

Sasha rolled her eyes and then turned to snatch the door open, shoving whoever he was out the heavy mahogany door.

"Stupid niggas." She sucked her teeth. "Anyway, bitch, get up and follow me to the bathroom."

She started to walk back to where her and leather lips had come from, like she hadn't just called me a bitch.

"My name is Ray-Ray."

She scoffed then jerked her head back like she had been slapped. "I don't give a fuck what your name is, bitch! Get yo' black ass in here so you can shower. By the time Dame and them niggas get finish wit' yo' ass, yo' name gon' be whatever the fuck he want it to be anyway."

I stood with my fist balled. At this point, I no longer gave a damn where I was or who she was. I wasn't gonna be anybody's bitch. "Call me a bitch again," I dared her.

She dropped her folded arms and tilted her head to the side with a smirk that said she was amused or maybe she thought me to be a joke.

She smacked her lips, rolled her eyes, and chuckled. "It's always you new young hoes that gotta make a bitch show her hand."

I didn't say anything as we stared one another down. All I could think about was that I was in a new place and alone. I had nobody, so it was me against the world. Daddy may have babied me most times, but when he did school me on fighting, he always taught me to attack before being attacked. I already knew I had to fight. I had to let people know that I was no punk.

We played that staring game for a few more seconds before she shook her head and gave a *tsk* sound with her mouth.

She looked like she was going to go to the bathroom, and I made the mistake of taking my eyes off her. Next thing I knew, she yanked me by my hair and threw me on the floor. I kicked and swung back, but she had the upper hand. She straddled her big ass on me and started hammering me with closed fists back to back.

I brought both arms up to protect myself as best I could. I admit, for the most part, I was a little scared. I had even thought about just lying there and letting her beat me to death, but then, out of nowhere, I could have sworn I heard my mother in my ear., *You better get up and get this black bitch off you. You don't let no bitch try to steal your beauty. This ugly-ass ho trying to fuck yo' face up because you the new competition. Get the fuck up and handle yo' shit, Ray-Ray.*

I didn't know where my strength came from, but I screamed out, uncovered my face, and dug my nails so deep in that bitch's face that she yelled and fell back. When that ho fell over, I jumped up quick as ever and went to work on her face. I grabbed a fistful of her weave, yanked her head down, and started upper-cutting that bitch. I dragged her ass across the room, and every time she tried to get up, I yanked her head down harder. All I heard were her screams.

As I dragged her, I slipped and fell backwards on a table that I didn't see, sending lamps crashing to the floor. I kept her hair in my hand though, and then used my feet to kick her in the stomach to keep her from getting back on top of me, but she still got some hits in.

"Bitch, let my fuckin' hair go! I'ma kill you, ho!" she screamed.

By then the door had come flying open, and I could hear men and women yelling that a fight was going on.

"Oh shit. My nigga, we got us one," a male yelled.

I could hear Trinidad James playing, but I was focused on keeping that big, tall Amazon bitch off of me.

"Fuck you, bitch!" I yelled back and kicked her in her stomach as I banged the back of her head.

She twisted and turned, trying to get her footing. One of her fists landed in my jaw, another in my stomach, knocking the wind out of me, but I didn't let that bitch's weave go. I tried to yank that shit from the scalp.

"Ahahahahaha! Oh shit, Dame. Yo' bitches in here tearing it down, my nigga!"

There was that deep, raspy voice again. That broke my attention. I turned toward the door trying to see the man who had helped killed my parents. Big mistake. Sasha straddled me again and got a few good hits in my face, but I kept swinging on that ho. She tried to lean in to choke me, but I wasn't about to let her choke me out. I'd been knocked unconscious too many times already. As she leaned in, her almost nonexistent titty fell out. I latched on and bit down so hard I was sure I drew blood.

"Ahhhh! Ahhhh!" Sasha screamed. "This ho biting me. Dough Boy, come get this bitch."

I kept biting, yanking her weave from the root, and she kept screaming and punching. Feet rushed into the room. I saw Timberland boots and the one with the raspy voice she'd called Dough Boy, who tried pulling her off me.

The guy in the Timberland boots came my way and snatched me up. By the time I saw the blade coming for my face, it was almost too late. As I threw my hands up, Dough Boy yanked Sasha back and the blade fell from her.

Since the one they called Trigga was the only one I'd seen in Timberland boots, I figured it was he who'd grabbed me. His hard body was pressed against my back.

My eyes trained on the blade that had fallen to the floor, I kicked and swung my elbows back and forth trying to get away from Trigga. I didn't even realize my bra had been ripped off. Sasha's blood was in my mouth, and blood also leaked from her face.

"Aye, li'l shawty, calm yo' ass down," he said to me in a low growl.

It was the same tone of voice he'd used earlier. Something about the way he said those words chilled me, made me stop struggling against his hold. I believed he was the one that kept knocking me out before. I didn't want to be put to sleep again, not in this place.

He had a strong arm wrapped around my waist. I looked down at his wrists and saw a fresh tattoo. They looked like chains, slave chains. That nigga was weird. People had gathered in the room. More girls in different kinds of catsuits, but mostly red-and-white, filed in. Their outfits made them stand out from the rest of the half-naked women around.

When the girls in the catsuits all moved away and huddled into a corner with the look of fear in their eyes, I knew Dame was near.

His expensive shoes were the first things I saw. Then the cream-colored linen suit with the shirt open, showing his white wifebeater and chiseled chest. He was tall, at least six four, and light like Sasha. He was mixed with something. What? I didn't know. A low-cut Caesar with deep waves adorned his head, razor-shaped to perfection.

Hazel eyes cast a mean glare from me to Sasha and then from Sasha to me.

There was a grimace on his face that said he wasn't happy at all. The look was mean, evil, like he was about to snap and kill us both without hesitation.

The voices that had been loud just moments before were now so quiet, I could hear my heartbeat in my ears.

I could never say that he wasn't fine as hell because he was. Even to my young eyes. But there was a fear in the room, especially over those women huddled against the wall that said his good looks also came with ruthlessness.

"Sasha, what the fuck is going on in here?" Dame asked in a coarse voice.

"This li'l raggedy bitch you done brought in—"

Dame moved to stand in front of her quick as lightning. "You forget who the fuck you talking to?"

She swallowed and cast her glance down to the floor then back up at him, one hand over her exposed breasts.

"No, Daddy, I didn't," she said, her voice much softer. "I was trying to get the new girl ready like you said and she attacked me."

"I did not! You saggy-titty bitch!" I spat.

I didn't understand how a woman with hardly any titties had sagging ones. I could hear a few of the dudes laughing, looking from her chest to mine.

"Shut up!" Dame barked at me as he pointed.

I snapped back, "You shut up!"

Judging by the way the women by the wall widened their eyes, I could tell I'd said the wrong thing.

My reward? Trigga tossed me so hard over the bed, I fell to the floor and hit my head against another wall.

I heard a few chuckles from some niggas standing around. By the time, I opened my eyes to look up, Dame was coming toward me with a look on his face that almost made me piss myself. I knew if he was going to hit me, then I was going to feel it deep in my bones.

My eyes skirted between Dame and the blade. I was too far away now.

Trigga stopped him. "You got some bosses downstairs, right, Bossman. Don't let li'l shawty keep you away from your business. Take care of that later."

The devil was in that man's eyes. Something in the way he glared at me told me I would pay for what I had said to him. One way or another I'd pay for my disrespect.

"Gina, get this bitch to another room," Dame ordered. "Let's see if you can handle the simple task of getting her to shower and dress."

A girl in a white catsuit came forward. She was timid. Like she was afraid to move the wrong way for fear of what Dame would do to her. Gina was almost as dark as me, and slim, and she had long braids down past her ass. She looked like she could be Kelly Rowland's twin sister. Her big doe-like eyes were wide as she chewed on her bottom lip.

She walked over and kneeled a little to help me. She whispered, "You gon' have to learn how to talk to him, or he's going to kill you."

It was almost like her lips didn't move. I felt at ease with her. She was scared like me. Young like me too.

"Janay, call the doc and have him look at Sasha." Dame scowled down at Sasha. "You still gon' make me my money tonight. You understand me?"

"But, Daddy, I'm fucked up."

"Who the fuck you talking to?"

Dame backhanded her so hard, every woman and even some niggas gasped. I swear her neck was broken in two places. More blood poured from her nose like a faucet.

I remember Daddy hitting Mama like that a couple times.

I almost felt sorry for the bitch as she fell to the floor like a rag doll. Almost.

Dame drew back and smacked her again.

Sasha screamed out then stopped as soon as the noise had left her mouth. It was like Dame had enforced a rule of no screaming when he smacked the shit out of you.

"Get the fuck up! Since you want to talk back like you run shit, stand up and take this ass-whupping like you can run my shit."

Dame's lips were tight, his eyes narrowed. He'd been embarrassed in front of his house, first by me, the new girl, and then by Sasha, who should have known better.

Her whimpers and the way she was backing away in terror bothered me.

Trigga cut his eyes over at me. It was like he was warning me in some way, but I couldn't tell. His eyes were blank; the boy carried no emotions. It was just the way he slowly turned to look at me that made me feel like he was trying to tell me something.

I didn't have time to think on that though. Gina rushed me from the room so fast, we were almost running. She shoved her way through the crowd, and once we were in the clear, we hightailed it down the hall. The smell of beer, liquor, and weed assaulted my senses. I almost got a contact high just passing down the hall.

Gina took me to another room, closed the door, and locked it. She checked all the doors and windows then the two walk-in closets.

"Damien, be having some fucked-up people in here sometimes. Gotta make sure we safe, is all," she told me. "Guess you know my name is Gina. Daddy don't like when we fight because he says it fucks with his money—and nobody fucks with Daddy's money."

I just listened as she talked. I thought she could have potential to help me with my plan when the time came.

She walked into a small closet and then came back out with towels and Dove Body Wash. "You have to wash in this stuff, 'cuz he likes the smell of Dove," she said. "Never wash yo' pussy in nothing else or he will flip.

"You might as well get ready to get yo' ass whupped for talking to him like that too. He ain't gon' let that shit slide. He never do."

As she talked she kept grabbing stuff and handing it to me—butter cream lotion, new red lace thongs with the bra to match, and a red dress that looked more like a shirt.

Gina's voice sounded like it had wisdom, but I could tell she was still young in the mind, by the way she acted.

"What's all this stuff?" I asked.

"His favorite color is red. You gon' have to wear red now to show him that, although you pissed him off, you down for the game."

"*Game*? What game?"

"He put you in that room with Sasha. That means you 'bout to be a new part of his team of elite bitches. We his hoes—We sell pussy and shake ass to make him his money."

"What the fuck!" I tossed all the shit she had given me to the floor. "I ain't about to sell no pussy for no nigga!"

Gina shook her head. "That's what *you* think, but once Dame has you on his turf, you gon' do what the fuck he wants you to do, by choice or by force. You don't want it by force, trust me. I seen what they do to bitches 'round here. You ain't gotta go that route."

"No. I'm better than that. My mama didn't raise me to be no ho."

"Girl, please. Your mama was the biggest ho 'round here. She brought most of us to Dame for a fee. How the hell you think I got here? I been doing this shit since I was sixteen. Yo' mama Shanna the Great, is what they call her 'round here. Why? Because she gave great head, had great pussy, and brought Dame the greatest pussy to sell. There gon' be a lot of niggas lining up too by yo' little tight snatch. Niggas already spreading rumors you a virgin and shit. Dame had been wanting yo' ass for a long time anyway. But your mama would kill a nigga talking 'bout getting yo' little ass. Yo' daddy would too, but not quick as yo' mama would.

"Now that Dame gotchu, ain't no fuckin' turning back. You gon' sell some pussy, or he gon' get one of these niggas, probably Trigga's crazy ass, to leave you stanking. Now, you can sell some pussy and live, or refuse and die." She started picking the stuff up from the floor.

Sixteen? My mama brought her here when she was only sixteen? I was sixteen and I just couldn't imagine being forced to sell myself.

Gina extended her arm out to me, but I refused to take the items. I moved away from her and grabbed the bath towel to wipe Sasha's blood from my lips. I went to sit on the bed.

The wind against my nipples reminded me that my bra was gone. I used my arms to cover them.

"See, I'm trying to help you. Don't get fucked up like most these bitches 'round here. I'm only eighteen and I done been doped up, raped, beat up, and all. They brought two new girls in here after me, and I tried to help 'em because them other bitches ain't gon' help you. Them bitches like Sasha jealous as fuck, and they gon' do what-ever to keep you down. 'Cuz them hoes don't be wanting you getting they bread. Daddy be a dick most times, but he take real good care of us in here. We get money, trips, cars, clothes, shoes, the best of everything—as long as we do what he says. But them last two bitches they brought in here didn't make it. One OD'd and the other one got missing. This nigga named Micah—he be getting rid of bodies for Dame—took her out of here, and we ain't seen her since. We all know what the fuck that mean. Don't get missing, because you can't close your eyes and pretend you somewhere else while letting a nigga fuck you."

I heard her, but I didn't care what she said. I knew that I'd rather die than let random niggas fuck me for money. Money that I couldn't even fuckin' keep? No way in hell. I couldn't imagine having to suck indiscriminate dick just because another nigga said you had to. I didn't care about none of that shit. All I had on my mind was how to kill the niggas that killed my parents.

Trigga

Gotdamn broads are fuckin' crazy. This shit always happened with new pussy. Naw, shit like this always happened with *any* pussy, period. Broads turning on each other, acting like chickens, cluck-clucking and shit, being disrespectful and shit.

Damn, that new broad was stupid as fuck. You wanted to live, then you had to act like you did—Get in the game. I didn't get broads at all.

A nigga knew immediately what to do. I ain't have not one fuckin' person there to hold my hand as soon as I hit the streets and ended up in foster homes with trill-ass goons. Niggas got it all twisted. You fight smart, not stupid as fuck.

Now I was standing with my arms over my chest in front of some Latin Kings trying to explain why some chickens interrupted the deal, two big tall-ass machete-looking goons eyeing me, trying to shake a nigga down.

Check it, I may have been young, but no nigga of any race, creed, or ethnicity could make me fear a damn thing. Not anymore. So I wasn't fazed by it as I stared at those cats eye to eye. I was a tall nigga too. Now what?

"My bad. We had some shit to take care of, but we're not tryin'a take up your time, sirs," I calmly stated in Spanish.

See, only reason I was there was to communicate, because I knew their dialect, and to put bullets in their skulls if they fucked up. I'd had a Spanish foster mom who'd adopted me into her world for a while, until she died, so it wasn't shit for me to sit down and break bread with these niggas. Now because of tricks getting catty, Dame was on some other shit and not there. So I had to take care of business for him until he got back.

"No problemo, kid. We see you gentlemen like to waste time. Let's go, family. Don't contact us, we'll contact you," their leader nonchalantly spoke up to me in Spanish. His dark eyes assessed me before he stood and brushed his Italian suit to the side and snuffed out his Cuban.

From head to toe, dude had on all black. From the black diamonds in his ears to the blacked-out diamond watch on his wrist, the nigga was on some designer dope shit. I wasn't into labels, but his style was cold. Nigga probably would have every bitch in the place tryin'a hit. He was always smiling and running his hands over his low waves.

Dude looked like he was a nigga and Latino, so he had an almond-brown complexion with dark eyes that almost matched mine. His jaw was covered in a goatee that ran up into his fade, and he wore black designer glasses that framed his angular face. Nigga looked like he was some NFL player too, so I knew this cat was getting pussy left and right.

Immediately my jaw clenched in anger as they were leaving. *Fuckin' bitches messing with my gwap. I need to fix this shit pronto.*

Stepping forward, I held up my hands and signaled Janky, one of the house niggas, to bring in some of the product. "Trust me, time is of the essence, but you also know patience can be rewarding."

I watched the Latin Kings study me to see if I was bullshitting while I spoke to them in Spanish. I knew any other day this would have worked, but fuck, big bosses had shit to do, money to make, and they didn't have time to play around.

The leader said, "I like you, Trigga, so let me school you—When you are about your money, you don't let your money sit and stall. Do you want business with us?"

I knew Dame would be pissed if I didn't try to save this deal anyway I could. "Yes, we invited you in and mean you nothing but respect."

"Then answer me one more question. You stand here bullshitting me, my friend, while you have us standing waiting for product we know you don't have?"

Inwardly, a nigga was tilting his head to the side. *Is he for real?* All I could do was stand there with a blank face and not reveal my hand.

Stepping forward, the leader held his hand up, telling his guards to step back. He dropped his voice as he said to me, "I like you. You're about your honor, kid. If you survive this game, you come to us, we'll take care of you. But right now, I'm giving you some drop, because you all have twenty-four hours before you give us our shit, or it's lights out."

I opened my mouth to respond, but he kept talking.

"Tell me why your nigga behind you is sweating bullets. I tell you why—I think you have a problem with your family, my friend. And it's a bad look. Especially since the streets are talking about our stash being stolen. We found our boys dead, the ones who were going to exchange with you. Just the fact that we are still invited here lets me know your boss ain't know shit, but he's not here to talk business. No good. So step back and shake my hand. Tell your family we are good, and tell your boss you have twenty-four hours to make shit right, or we're gunning for you."

I stepped back and reached for his tattooed almond-colored hand, and he gripped mine as he flipped to English. Smiling, he tucked a Cuban in my jacket.

That broad is bad luck. First, her people stole from us then the Latin Kings know about that shit and giving us twenty-four hours to give him bodies, or we're done?

The night had turned out to be lame as fuck. Like he'd told me, it looked like niggas was playing games in house, clearly since that broad's pops use to be Dame's right hand. He knew all the close intel. Something more was going on.

The leader coolly walked out with his goons.

I kicked the table over as Drake's music blared.

"Ey yo, Trigga, why the fuck they leaving, man?" Janky nervously asked.

I didn't have time for that shaken-ass nigga's questions, so I walked out, heading to Dame to tell him what up. As I walked up the stairs, I realized that I needed to snatch up Janky so he could relay what he watched. Taking the stairs back down, I heard voices in the back of the kitchen.

"Yo, I'm telling you," Janky's voice rushed out. "Them Mexican-ass niggas know it was us. They know, man, and I think they told Trigga, homie."

My eyes narrowed as I listened quietly from a shadowed nook of the hallway, my arms crossed.

"Those fuckas don't know shit, trust me," Slammer said. "You know how we handled that shit for Ray and Shanna. They died with our truth, so we good, man. Now chill the fuck out and quit shaking, nigga."

As I continued listening, some drunk-ass nigga came thriller-walking into the hallway outta nowhere. OG was leaning to the side, dragging his left foot, ticking and shit, swiping at his nose as he sang to the music and drowned out the rest of what was being said. I almost punched the drunk-ass old head in his throat.

The niggas were foul. Turned on the family and caused this shit. Immediately, my fingers started twitching. Everything in me was ready to pop those niggas, but since it was my birthday, I thought, *Why not do that shit in style?*

Listening in, I quickly moved back to the stairway and hollered for Janky. Nigga came in the blink of an eye, and I almost spat on the fool.

"Ey, yo, just letting you know, we did good with them Kings. Everything is good, just need to tell Bossman. You good?" I watched that shaky-ass nigga walk on the side of me. I never let a nigga walk behind me. You never knew what a nigga was capable of. Feel me?

"Damn! For real? That's chill, man. I need to learn some of that Spanglish or some shit, so I can be better ears."

Chuckling low, I just kept walking. Bitches strolled by trying to get our attention, but my focus was on this lame-ass nigga.

"You know what, homie, since you cool and shit, I got you. I'll teach you some shit. You know you got to know the streets, all levels of them. Feel me? Otherwise, grimy niggas start taking and playing in ya shit." I cut my eyes low at him.

He laughed nervously. "Yeah, bro. You know that shit would be 'ppreciated."

"Oh yeah, you know I'm down for my fam. Ey yo, I couldn't find Slammer. Hit that nigga on his cell and tell him to come here. Bossman is gonna need you both to help handle that new bird."

Janky glanced at me for a moment and then hit his cell. Right as we stood outside of Bossman's door, Slammer walked up nodding, his eyes red as fuck from the many blunts he had hit. In one hand he had a cup of what I knew was some 'yurp, and in the other hand, nigga was smashing a piece of chicken.

Cutting my eyes at him, I played the game, reaching out to give him dap, as we all walked into Dame's office. The sound of my brown Tims hitting the mahogany floor filled the room. Nigga one and nigga two started cutting up, laughing, as they shared the blunt that Slammer had tucked behind his ear.

Dame stood outside on his iron balcony, his hands sprawled out over the railing as he looked down at the front of his massive digs.

I scanned the decked-out office. I knew he had watched the Latin Kings leave out, and due to the fact that nigga was already pissed over pussy, their leaving was about to turn the rest of my party and the deal sour.

"You handle that shit, Trigga?" he asked, his back still turned away from us. Nigga knew we were there without ever turning around.

"No doubt, Bossman, I handled it. Tried to get them to stay for you, but you know how they do?" I calmly responded, moving to sit on the arm of the couch in his office.

Behind me was some crazy-ass artwork. A lot of it I dug. Some of it was just lame as fuck, like the picture of the dog man fuckin' some chair made to look like a bitch pussy. Crazy fuckin' shit, I tell you.

I casually brushed off my Tims, while Janky and Slammer kept cracking simple-ass jokes about some shit at the party. Bossman was silent as death. I knew he was thinking about all the shit that went down.

Janky choked out, "And when those bitches fucked up the top level, that shit was crackin'. Bossman put them paws on Sasha. Shit was fuckin' hilarious."

"Yo, yeah, he did. Didn't you, Dame? How you gonna show that new pussy you boss?" Slammer took a deep drink of his 'yurp.

I kept quiet just watching. I knew it was some shit you could say around Bossman and other shit you just couldn't. While they thought they were pumpin' Dame's ego, niggas couldn't even see that they were pissing him off more. I sat back ready to see shit go down.

"That's why you two motherfuckas are here. That new pussy you two so into right now is about to learn whose fuckin' roof this is." Dame cracked his knuckles as he strolled in, heading to his desk. He picked up the two Cubans I had sat on his desk. Rubbing the cigar between his hands, he looked at me.

Janky said, "Ey, Bossman, I'm down with whatever. What you need? Need us to stomp that ho?"

"Yeah, man, we can take care of that bitch in more ways than one. 'Bout time to drag her bitch ass through the house and introduce her to everyone. Right, man?" Slammer laughed, giving Janky dap.

Through it all, Dame just rested against his desk. Crossing his arms over his white beater, he glanced at the two brothers.

"Good looking out. Just reminded me of some shit. Yeah, drag that bitch through the house and introduce her to the basement," Dame stated.

Adjusting my jacket, I inwardly shook my head. *Damn! Li'l shawty fucked up that bad?* She was about to get herself into some shit. No one—no female, no nigga—wanted to go to the basement.

I couldn't give two shits if I went again. To get my spot, I had to experience that shit myself anyway, so it wasn't shit for me but a cakewalk to prove my worth. Now li'l shawty was about to experience some shit that her young virginal pussy was never going to probably make it through without breaking. I saw that shit firsthand with Gina. Shawty was something slick, until she was forced down there. Then she came out broken to the point that she sometimes was like a kid still. Fucked-up shit, but that was the streets.

"Oh shit. Yeah, Dame, man! The basement. Fuck that little trick up just right," Janky spat.

Dame took slow puffs off his cigar then reached for his shot of Rémy, an evil grin spread across his face. He gave a jagged laugh. "You know my rules—you don't fuck with Daddy unless I'm fuckin' you. Feel me?"

Everyone laughed except me. I just sat back and listened.

"You two niggas will take that bitch down below, introduce her to the game, and get her ready for me like I fuckin' been saying all night. See, loyalty is bond. I don't fuck with cats that can't get with that shit, and right now that bitch is about to learn that law," Dame growled, throwing his glass at the wall.

Everyone watched it shatter on the floor and then murmured in agreement. Music droned on from the Geto Boys, hitting me with my theme song, while Slammer and Janky spoke with Bossman.

Janky started talking again, his chest all poked out, flossing his pride. "Yeah, man, loyalty is bond. We got you always, Bossman."

This nigga. My fingers began to itch, aching to get the feel of cold steel in my palm as I bobbed my head to the track.

I tried to play the shit out, to bust them out in front of boss man, but when Slammer's ol' greasy-chicken, grinning ass started flapping at the gums, talking about, "Right, and that bitch is gonna learn," it only pissed me the fuck off more and had a nigga doing like he was at that moment.

Running a hand over my short locks, I pushed off the arm of the couch, playing like I really was into all the shit they were saying, and then all I heard was, "Trigga, yo! The fuck!"

Two bullets each from my nine landed in the middle of their skulls, and my knife slashed out to run across their throats. A nigga moved like a panther that got loose in the streets. Fast and quiet. No emotions and no need to get my hands dirty. I was what I was made to be, a killer. All day, every day, taking down niggas like those two made my mental hard.

Blood hit me like rain. Neither nigga knew what hit them. They'd reached for Glocks too late, gasping for air and staring at death the moment the bullet cut through their brains.

I looked down at the two big muthafuckas that lay at me feet.

"You die, muthafucka," boomed on the speakers down below. The rhythm made their pools of blood vibrate with the song.

Kicking my Tims into the side of each fallen nigga, I wiped a hand down my face, kneeled down to wipe my blade on their clothes, and moved to sit back on the couch. I dropped my foot on the arm of the couch and wiped my Tims off.

"I'll foreva be a trigga-happy nigga," I crooned with a lethal smirk. I glanced up at my boss with blank eyes. "Yeah, loyalty is bond, Bossman, and them two niggas are foul as fuck."

Dame watched me in amusement. He knew it was why he hired me and moved me up in ranks after schooling me so many years. I was good at my shit, and he had no issue with me playing with my kills.

"Motherfucka, call the cleaners and get your ass off my couch, little nigga. Tell me what you found out."

Quickly standing, I walked over to his desk and hit the com, calling for select niggas and bitches he had on his payroll to clean up any mess.

"Latin Kings gave us twenty-four hours to give them bodies. These niggas right here are the gifts. They played us, Bossman. It was them, Ray, Shanna, and some other nigga, I couldn't hear his name, who took from home, man."

Crossing his arms over his chest, Dame walked to Janky and Slammer then dropped to one knee to crush his fists into their skulls. Each hit, he cursed, and gripped their heads, slamming them into the floor.

As he did so, I broke down how I heard it all and why I didn't get to learn the rest. Bloodshot-red eyes looked up at me in the screwed-up face of a man who was nothing but evil.

I stood my ground, waiting to hear what he had to say.

"Party is fuckin' over! Deliver these muthafuckas to the Kings, get my shit back on line, Trigga. And change out these muthafuckin' floors. Now my shit is fucked up! Get my office clean! Fuck! Bitches fucked up my goods, now I'm gonna fuck up theirs."

This was where I took my pop's teachings and chilled my spirit. Like, how the fuck this nigga gonna come at me on some bullshit, talking about, clean his shit? Clean his shit? This nigga OCD and shit was kicking in, in this moment? Did he forget I just told him these two pussy-ass bitches turned game on him? *Fuck outta here.*

Exhaling, I walked over to where Dame once stood over those niggas, niggas he'd stomped before walking out of his office, kicking over a table.

Pushing Janky's smashed face that held the blank stare of death on it, I dropped down to pick the niggas up while the cleaners came in to handle their business. Damn fucked-up birthday. Feel me? And now I wanted some chicken on top of that shit.

I threw Janky's heroin-skinny ass over my shoulder and walked to the door, where I saw Gina hovering in the hall, pointing the cleaners to the office.

This broad really thought I couldn't catch that she was being nosy. *Damn! Why are broads stupid in this house?* I mean, she was sexy as fuck, used to think right, but after her trip to the basement, shawty wasn't all there anymore.

Brushing past her, I watched her turn her back to me, but not before she saw me tap two fingers against Janky's leg, showing her the deuces then the middle. That was our sign of knowledge.

Walking down the stairs, I dropped my voice while she pretended she was pointing people away. I said to her, "Bitches always end up in the 'underworld.'"

Ray-Ray

I jumped up when Gina came rushing into the room. I didn't know what time it was. I hadn't seen the outside of the place since I had been tossed in that closet. Gina looked like she had just seen a ghost.

"You done fucked up, girl," she said with wide eyes.

She was looking at me, but at times it was like she was looking past me, like she was staring at a ghost or some shit.

"What I do?" I asked her. "I been in here the whole time. I ain't done or said shit to nobody."

Finally, she looked at me, genuinely looked in my eyes. "That crazy nigga sending you to the basement."

"The basement? Can't be worse than being locked in a closet."

"You gonna wish he locked yo' ass in the closet. I tried to tell you to calm down, girl."

Maybe I didn't get what she was saying, but going to the basement meant he was locking me away, so it couldn't have been any worse than being locked in that fuckin' closet.

"It's just a fuckin' basement, Gina."

"It ain't just no damn basement. When bitches get sent to the basement, sometimes they don't come back out that muthafucka."

That had my attention. I walked closer to her. The stuff she had tried to hand me before still lay haphazardly on the king-sized bed. The room itself was just as caked-out as the last one I had been in. Only, this room was made to appear like it belonged to some princess. There were even porcelain dolls decoratively sitting about. I had figured it was Gina's room, since she knew it in and out and because of her, sometimes, kid-like disposition.

"Whatchu mean?" I asked her.

Her eyes darted back and forth, and then she brought a closed fist to the side of her head. She started to pace the floor as she mumbled the words, "No, no, no," over and over again.

"Don't go to the basement. You shoulda showered and put them damn clothes on like I told you. You shoulda not have fought with that bitch Sasha. Big-booty Amazon bitch got me sent to the basement. They fuck bitches up bad in the underworld, baby."

She said all of that as she walked a hole in the cashmere rug at the foot of her bed.

"Niggas, lots of niggas, fuck you in the basement, beat you, drug you. They fuck hoes up in the underworld. And Trigga said—"

There's that name again. "Trigga said what?" I asked her.

My hands covered my breasts as I followed her then grabbed her arm to make her stop pacing. All I still had on was my pink cotton panties. I didn't know who had taken my clothes off or where they had put them. And I didn't want to put no damn clothes on that man wanted me to.

"Trigga said bitches always end up in the underworld. That mean Daddy done put word out that you free game. No telling how many niggas gon' be down there waiting on you. Sasha is just as grimy as these niggas. Bitch stuck a pipe up my pussy 'cuz I ain't wanna eat hers. Daddy had told her to break me in, but I ain't wanna eat that bitch rancid cunt. I mean, I'll sex women, but her pussy looked like dried prunes with stray coconut hair. How that bitch light skin with a burnt pussy?"

If what she had said about the basement hadn't damn near scared me stiff, I would have laughed my fat ass clear off. But fear had me shaking. I mean, I started shaking like I was about to have a seizure.

I heard movement out in the hall and backed away from the door, scared that niggas was coming to get me.

Once the commotion died down, I started to look around for some sort of weapon to keep on me.

"You ain't got no blades up in here, Gina? Like you strip, right, you ain't got nothing on you to protect you from niggas out there?" I asked in a panic.

"Naw. Daddy takes care of me. I get my own bodyguard. Big Jake. You know the cute big dude?"

She said that in a dreamy way, like she liked him or something.

I nodded. "Yeah, he threw me in the closet."

"You lucky then. If Big Jake put you there, he wasn't gon' let nobody fuck wit' yo'. And you still kinda lucky 'cuz Trigga warned me so I could tell you. Trigga don't like none of these niggas in here really. Him and Big Jake hang tight. Trigga always brings me my favorite Happy Meal and stuff, if I don't piss him off. Sometimes I do though, but he don't call me out my name, like Dough Boy. You don't wanna get hooked up wit' Dough Boy."

I still had yet to know what he looked like beyond a glimpse. But I knew that fuckin' voice, and before my time here was up, I was going to kill that muthafucka. "I don't really know who he is."

"You don't wanna know that nigga either. He likes using his big retarded dick as a weapon. You know, like that nigga didn't want no pussy from me. He just rammed the shit up my ass. He a fuckin' faggot on the down low I bet. He likes beating on bitches too much."

After a while I just drowned Gina out. I had to figure out a way to get myself a weapon. I wasn't gon' be taken there without nothing in my hand to fight with. If I died or some shit, I'd die fighting.

I asked her, did she think I could take a shower.

She told me, "Smelly pussy ain't selling pussy, and if you going to the basement, ain't no need to wash ya cunt."

That scared the hell out of me even more.

She locked me in her room when it was time to eat dinner. She said Dame always fed them good because he wanted them at their best, since they were his prime stock.

"I'll let you know when shit's about to get hell for you. Most of these niggas talk around me 'cuz they think I'm stupid. I'll try to get you a heads-up."

I didn't see Gina for the rest of the night. I stayed awake for fear of being tossed in the basement. And I was hungry. I could smell the food wafting through the house. I sat in a corner with my back to the wall and facing the door. Anytime somebody walked back, I jumped up.

That went on for two days. I still didn't see Gina. Nobody brought me any food. I drank water from the faucet in her bathroom and pretended it was my mama's lasagna and my daddy's corn bread. I was starting to smell a little bit, but not as much as I wished. I was getting weak because of no food, but I tried to do the exercises I'd always seen my daddy do to stay alert. Push-ups, jumping jacks, shadowboxing. I found a white sports bra that fit, and I put it on to cover my titties. Then I found a pair of sweats too.

On the second day Gina rushed into the room then dragged me into the closet. She looked different. Her long braids were in two pigtails, and she had a bag on her shoulder. She was dressed in booty shorts that exposed her ass cheeks, and a ripped top that showcased her big breasts and small waist. And she wore tall army-like boots on her pigeon-toed feet.

"You starting to stink. That's good," she calmly said as she rushed to open the book bag. She started taking out fried chicken, steak, mac and cheese, bread, and water.

I snatched up everything before she could say it was mine. I tore into the fried chicken and ripped the top from the container of mac and cheese.

"Daddy gon' fuck me up for feeding you. Nigga got cameras everywhere in this house, probably got some shit in here too." She then looked up, like she was trying to scope where one would be. She then stood and quickly turned the light.

"Thank you," I was able to get out between mouthfuls of food.

"Don't thank me, Ray-Ray. I'm only feeding you 'cuz they coming for yo' ass soon. Heard niggas jawing." She giggled. "I learned that word from Trigga and Big Jake. *Jawing* means niggas standing 'round yapping gums like bitches. All excited over pussy, like they ain't had it. That's what Trigga was saying. He ain't like these other niggas. He smart, Ray-Ray. You need to try to get him to talk to you."

"Fuck him!" I spat. "He was there when they killed my mama and daddy. Fuck him! I'ma kill that nigga too."

Gina laughed like she was having a fit. Even though it was dark in the closet, I could see her fall back laughing.

"Girl, you ain't killing Trigga. That nigga crazy, lightning quick. He could kill you before you blinked. Yo' ass better off trying to kill that fake bitch, Sasha. She mad as fuck at you right now, but, naw, you ain't killing Trigga. You know he killed Janky and Slammer two days ago, right? Daddy said he shot them niggas then sliced their throats before they bodies even hit the fuckin' ground."

I listened to what she said as I gulped water down. *Was he the one that killed my mama and my daddy? I didn't know, but I was gonna kill everybody in the room when it happened. So he had killed Janky and Slammer, huh? Why not Pookie? Why he ain't kill that nigga too?* I looked up at Gina when she stood.

"I gotta go give Daddy his afternoon massage. He be pissed when I'm late," she said, like this life was normal. "I do it every day, and when he's really satisfied with me, he gives me extra stuff."

I mean, I knew my mama and daddy lived the life, but they ain't let me live it. They did drugs and shit and tried to kill each other around me, but they loved me too much to pimp me. Mama said she would never do to me what her mama had done to her—Make her suck a nigga's dick at ten. Daddy said wasn't no nigga gon' be pimping his daughter, making her sell her pussy to the highest bidder. I wanted to believe the only reason he gave me to Dame was to keep him from killing me. I wished he would have let them kill me.

"Got somethin' you need in that bag, Ray-Ray. Don't leave nothing in the bag." Gina then left me there.

I was eating like a damn pig. I didn't even know if the shit was good. All I knew was, it felt good going down my throat. As I chewed on a piece of steak, I reached into the bag. I pulled out some peach cobbler and then looked into the bag again. When I didn't see anything, I wondered why Gina told me not to leave nothing in the bag. I shrugged then used my hand to start eating the cobbler. Shit was still hot, but I was starving.

When I stuck my hand in the second time, I yelped, dropped the bowl, and hopped up. I flipped the light on to see blood dripping from my left hand. "Shit!" I had sliced my finger. I grabbed a shirt from the hanger to wrap around my hand.

But I took my attention back to the container with the peach cobbler; I dumped it all out then saw the gift Gina had left me—three razor blades. I thanked that dense-in-the-head girl as I rushed to swoop them up. I was about to run to the bathroom to wash them until I remembered what she had said about the cameras.

I picked up the cobbler container and rushed to the bath-room to fill it with water then I brought it back to the closet and washed the sticky mess off them. Once done, I tried to decide how I was going to hide them on me.

My mama had showed me how to hide a blade under my tongue. I prayed I remembered and didn't cut my shit off. The other two I hid in my bra, hoping I would be able to get to them when time called for it.

From there I just waited. I paced the room floor back and forth like Gina had done just days before, but nobody came. I got tired and was feeling sluggish from all the food I'd scarfed down, so I took a seat in the corner that I occupied. Before I knew it, I'd fallen asleep.

When I came to, four niggas were rushing in the room. I tried to fight, but they had caught me sleeping. I managed to kick one right in his dick as he came for me. He yelped out and fell to his knees.

"Yo, grab that li'l bitch!" Dough Boy yelled out. "How the fuck it take fo' of y'all niggas for a sixteen-year-old ho?"

I knew it wasn't gon' do much good, since four of them had come for me, but I would always fight for my life. When one picked me up from behind, I kicked my leg out to kick Pookie in the face. I kicked that ugly bumpy-face fool so hard, his teeth cut my bare foot. That nigga was gon' pay for snitching out my folks too. I tried to do it again, but another nigga grabbed my right foot.

I could hear Dough Boy laughing at the door.

I finally got a good look at him. He was five eleven, tops, and rocking cornrows that stopped just below his neck. He was dark like me, with beady eyes that showed sinister thinking, and his big greasy lips protruded from his face, reminding me of a platypus.

When the niggas who had grabbed me carried me through the door, I wanted to spit in that nigga face, but couldn't because of the blade in my mouth.

I spotted Gina hiding in a corner, peeking at the chaos. Big Jake shook his head and turned to walk the other way.

For some reason, I was looking for Trigga. He was always around somewhere. There was no party going on, and everyone had come up the stairs to watch me being dragged to the basement.

Sick muthafuckas! The whole fuckin' house was sick.

I caught a movement out the corner of my eye and saw Sasha slink forward from the room I was in first, a smirk on her face. She had gotten that weave fixed, and her makeup hid the bruises. She was decked out in a pink two-piece jumpsuit and pink Nike Shox on her feet. I wished like hell I could get my feet loose and kick that bitch in her face.

"Let's see how tough you are now, *bitch!*" she quipped, emphasizing on the *bitch*, just to fuck with me.

I saw countless faces of women: black, white, Latino, Asian, and other ethnicities too. A few looked like they felt sorry for me, while the rest gave shakes of the head, with looks that said I was getting what I deserved.

I had almost pissed on myself from being so scared.

Then I heard my mama's voice again. Seen her face just like she was right in front of me.

"Fight these niggas, baby. Don't give up shit. If they want it, make 'em kill you for it. It's yours. Ain't naan nigga got a right to take it. Kill yo'self if you have to. Better than this shit."

Right then I decided I wasn't going to the underworld. *Fuck that!*

I started kicking and bucking again. Managed to free one of my hands. I reached into my mouth and grabbed the blade. First thing I did was slice at the nigga's face who was holding my left side, Pookie. I sliced right down the side of his face.

He yelped out, "Ahhh, fuck! Shit! This bitch cut me!" He fell against the wall, hands trying to stop the bleeding.

That caused him to drop his hold on me, and the other niggas to drop me to the floor. I hit with a hard thud.

I jumped up and sliced at another nigga, catching his face. I swung wildly with the blade, not giving a fuck about cutting myself in the process. That didn't stop the others from grabbing at me though. I screamed out as I swung, but they kept coming.

I started praying. I ain't ever prayed a day before in my life, but I did then.

Next thing I knew, I heard Dame's booming voice. "Can't none of you niggas handle this little bitch?"

Blood was everywhere, on the floor, on the walls. I'd cut up at least four niggas.

By now, most of the girls had run off.

Dame's cold gaze turned my way. I knew I was fucked. I knew that, because he charged at me.

I got my footing and then tried to run away, but his big hand in the back of my hair stopped me. My blade fell to the floor, but I couldn't run no more, so I had to fight.

He jerked my body around, and my fists started flying. I already knew I'd made a mistake as soon as my fists connected with his face.

"No, no, Ray-Ray. You never hit Daddy."

I knew it was Gina's voice, without even seeing her.

Dame let my hair go, and because I was trying to pull away anyway, it caused me to fly backwards, but I didn't fall.

His upper lip twitched, and his hazel eyes turned to ice. He drew back and punched me square in the jaw, and I felt teeth loosen and fall out, saw the blood leap from my mouth, and felt my world come to a halt, all before crashing to the floor. I was halfway dead in my head.

I was being moved. I knew I was going to the basement for sure now. *I tried, Mama,* I thought. *I tried.* My head was heavy; I couldn't even hold that shit up.

"Put that bitch in my room!" Dame ordered. "I need a whole new set of fuckin' niggas. Is Trigga the only son of a bitch I count on around this muthafucka? How has one bitch been able to fuck up half my team in three fuckin' days? I should have Trigga body all you muthafuckas! And clean my muthafuckin' hall! Clean the fuck up! Clean this shit! Now!"

My body was tossed on the floor at the foot of a colossal bed. I was in and out of consciousness. Didn't know how long I would live after that hit. All I knew was, I didn't want to be hit again.

"Muthafuckin' fuckin' up my shit I paid my hard-earned money for. I'ma show you, bitch," I heard Dame say as he slammed the door to his room. Then I heard his belt buckle loosen.

I started to moan as I tried to crawl away. It was going to happen. I was going to be raped. I heard the light swoosh of the belt leaving the loops of his pants.

I closed my eyes. I would have tried to talk if my mouth could function. But, I swear, that nigga had broken my jaw. When he yanked the sweats I had on down to my ankles, and then my underwear, I just laid there, accepting what was about to happen.

However, I was wrong about being raped. I was about to be beaten.

The first lash of the belt came down on my back, and I found my voice. What was left of it, I used it to cry out.

"That's what the fuck wrong with yo' ass—Your daddy didn't ever beat the fuck outta you! Got you walking around my shit thinking you run some shit, bitch."

WACK! WACK! WACK!

The belt pounded my back, butt, and thighs.

"Fuckin' up my walls and shit like you done made me some fuckin' money to cover the shit."

I shrieked as each hit tore into my skin. It felt like electricity was shooting up my spine. Anyone within a twenty-mile radius could have probably heard me crying.

Dame was right. My daddy had never put a hand on me. Neither had my mama. I was a good kid. I listened to them. They didn't have to hit me ever.

One hit came across the back of my head. *WACK!*

Another one to the side of my face. *WACK!*

I grabbed a hold of his pant leg, trying to wrap myself between them, to get away from the belt, but he kept hitting me, beating me like he had a mission to engrave the holes of the leather belt into my skin.

I caught a glimpse of his face, and it was twisted in a demonic kind of way. That nigga looked like the devil to me at that point. He was as crazy as Gina said he was.

I didn't know how long he beat me. Eventually, I blacked out.

Trigga

Two days had passed, and a nigga was tired as fuck. Bossman Dame had me running the streets hard, after taking down Janky and Slammer. I wasn't sure what was up with him, outside of being pissed that his rep was fucked up with the LKs, as well as his money. But I was good with it, because I was out of the madhouse. Yeah, that's what I called it.

Ever since that new broad came into the place and shook up the crazy, every nigga and bitch in there, except for the ones who I know had minds like mine, had been on edge, mean-mugging everyone and causing some shit, especially Sasha. The old bitch, thinking she was the head bitch in charge, was popping off at the mouth at any chance she could when Dame wasn't around.

After the party, and after I had dumped those two niggas, I had heard through my sources, Gina and Big Jake, that Dame had fucked up the new broad. But it was how he did it that made me laugh. Chick stayed fighting, which I could respect in some sense, and she cut up all the niggas Dame had put on her. Of course that pissed off Dame more, especially since he didn't get to take her to the basement, or what some niggas called the underworld.

Like I said, I had my dealing in there. Naw, I ain't ever in my young life rape not one chick. I wasn't even being about that shit, but the way Dame had that shit set up, even niggas could get fucked up by getting branded, beat the fuck up or, for some of those prison niggas that were about the life down there, fucked in the ass and the mouth.

Me, I just got strung up and beat. It happened when I was mad young and still learning how to run for Dame. Got shortchanged some *dinero*, and it ended up falling back on me.

Yeah, I saw bitches raped, beat, burned, cut, pipes up pussy and asshole, all kinds of shit. At thirteen, I knew already not to fuck up to the point of being handed to some prison niggas. Was I scared? Fuck, nah. But I like shitting normal, so I knew not to ever have to go down there. Feel me?

Anyway, like I was saying, my ears and eyes stayed in the street, so everyone was talking about my party and everything that had been going down after that.

Two days, I went in and out of the house doing me, running product, trying to speak to the Latin Kings again, watching Dame's right hand, Dough Boy, move money around. I was a killer, but after having Dame's back and snuffing out those two niggas, Dame fucked around and told me to shadow Dough Boy, learn how to move the money and shit. Yeah, I was a happy nigga, and I was a watchful nigga.

Gina hit me up in our own slick way, letting me know what went down with that new crazy broad. She handed me one of those small Mickey D's Happy Meal fry containers that had two blades in it and a blunt. In code that meant, a nigga got cut up, but li'l shawty survived. The rest of the details, I learned from Big Jake the next day while we were out fuckin' around grabbing some shit for the Bossman in the streets.

The thing about Big Jake was, homie was like twenty-one and should have been in the NFL but got shot right before his big tryouts. Any other nigga would be hating life, but not Big Jake. He took that shit and used it to get him where he was now.

Homie had me laughing and rolling when he told me how Bossman sounded when he saw all those niggas on the ground cut up, grabbing their faces and shit. Said nigga sounded like a cat hitting scalding water. Yo, I died laughing right then and there. He said niggas were heated like bitches, crying and shit over gashes, at the way li'l shawty busted their faces.

The scar under my eye twitched, reminding me that li'l shawty was something like a jaguar. My mom's words came back to me, and I had to respect that.

We shit-talked for a bit, and I let him know that li'l shawty was crazy, seemed to be a lot like her moms.

I remembered Shanna. She was nice to me when I came into the house. Used to make these bomb reverse chocolate chip cookies—caramel-based with chocolate chips in it. I didn't know how she did that shit, but it was *fiyah*. She would also bring me some Trinidadian and Jamaican food to the house and make sure I got a big plate, saying I needed to get some muscles and shit, and learn about my people.

Yeah, she was a boss bitch, but when no one was really checking for her, she always took care of me. She said, since I ain't have no momma, she'd be that 'cuz I was so young and cute to her. I ain't ever tell no one that, but Big Jake knew 'cuz she treated him the same way. We was Shanna's house sons, and she took care of us good.

That was why I was eager to go to her house that day. Shit fucked with my mental that she was in the mix like that. Ain't wanna see her go like that, on some real shit, but it was whatever. People do what they gotta. I just got no love for them once loyalty is broken.

***

The slamming of my car door had me turning off my iPod as I listened to *The Art of War* by Sun Tzu.

"A'ight, li'l nigga," Dough Boy said to me. "Take us to the LKs. That's the next drop."

Nigga quickly pulled out a blunt that smelled as if it had lived in a piece of dead ass that baked in the ATL heat for four months and two days. Shit pissed me off. Disrespectful muthafucka right there. Especially when he spilled his Four Loko on my seats.

See, I always took care of my shit. The day I got enough paper from Dame to get me a ride, I got me one and made sure to take care of that shit and only use it for drops. The moment this punk-ass nigga got in my ride was the moment I realized how he thought about me. I was gonna fuck him up over the disrespect he was throwing at me.

We rolled through Dame's territory, pausing to check on some drops, and hit up the niggas that were our eyes in the street. We turned out of the west side of the Trap, so we could hit that highway.

Dough Boy rolled down his window and hollered at me to slow down the ride. "Ey yo. little nigga, you see that?" he literally screamed. "You see all one, two, three, four of those jiggly asses? Damn, son, slow this shit down."

Now what did I say about niggas making pussy priority before money? Fuck niggas.

I sat there listening as he tried to spit some lame-ass game, asking one of the shawties, "'S up, mama? Where you from?"

Some kinda cute mixed ghetto-booty chick rolled her eyes as her other cute girls laughed, iggin' that coon-ass nigga.

"Yo, you know you hear a nigga. I said, What it is, yo? So wassup? Can a nigga just beat dem guts?"

Right there I almost slammed the brakes on my ride. Was that nigga for real? Did he really just quote some trap music? Fuck outta here.

I turned to look at the back of this nigga's fitted cap. This motherfucka was leaning out of the window of my Escalade, slamming his hands on the side of the door to get attention. I leaned forward to grab his whack ass, but the sound of the chicks going off on him then pausing to smile, lean down to look past him and giggle, made him sit back and glare at me.

"Oh my God! Girl, is that Trigga?"

"When this fine nigga get a ride like this?"

"Heyyyyyy, Trigga!!"

I nodded at each dime.

I almost laughed my ass off when Dough Boy glared at me and growled, "Fuck them bitches! We ain't got time for some weak-ass pussy. Let's go, li'l nigga."

Rolling out of Zone 1 was my main priority, but busting this nigga's ego made this trip even better.

It took nothing to get to the Kings' location. I was ready for Dough Boy's lame ass to get out my ride, so I quickly parked and brushed out my ride.

"Ey, li'l nigga, you still pissed about me pissing in that bottle in your ride and spilling it? I said my bad." He laughed then went to the door where I stood.

"Fuck you, nigga! You did that shit to be funny. I shoulda made your lame ass drink that shit," I purposely mumbled, keeping my hoodie low while I looked down at my feet. I knew that would irritate him, so I ignored him as he got in my face.

"What you say, li'l dumb nigga? You don't talk much, do you? Fuck is wrong with you? Like you on some special-ed shit." He laughed. "Only good for being a goon, huh? 'Cuz I'm not getting why Dame brought you in anyway. Any nigga can shoot." He threw his blunt on the ground before banging on the door with his fist.

I really was about hating this nigga right here.

See, every hood nigga thought he was invincible, me included, but unlike them, I didn't believe it. This nigga right here was going to get his real soon, and it might be by me.

Iggin' that coon-face nigga, I peeped the same twin machete-looking cats as they stood in the middle of two oak-carved Spanish doors. Each one looked us over, and we held our arms out to be searched before being let in.

Inside the place was pretty dope. The head of the LKs lived decked-out in a mansion in Sandy Springs, which was why we were using my ride. I didn't have a hood-nigga car. Had me a simple all-black Escalade with tinted window and normal rims, so I could blend in wherever I went in the *A* and not be trailed by five-O.

All around us was some regal rich-nigga shit. Shit that said, "I'm new to this money game, so I had to have everything and all." I laughed to myself, looking around, expecting to see some Scarface shit with the motto "The world is mine" etched in glass somewhere, but I didn't.

What I did see was a set of pretty broads from all backgrounds walking down the grand staircase. Each one had a dress on so tight, I could see their nipples poking out for show. Their dresses were so short, at the angle I was, all I saw were pretty slits. Some had those smiling slits— you know, the type that said come suck and lick me—just poking out.

Damn! Those broads were bad bitches, each and everyone one of them. Hair looked real, so I could tell he wasn't down with some fake-ass weave. Each broad's breasts jiggled when they moved, right along with their asses, so I knew that shit was real too.

"*Amigos*, come follow my dolls, and we'll discuss some things." Armando, the head of the LKs, walked down the stairs, stopping in the middle of his broads, which he named dolls.

Today, he was wearing a black Italian suit with a teal button-down. I could tell that nigga was strapped up, by the way his jacket moved. Following his broads—although each one had only a drop of clothes and was almost bare-ass naked— as my eyes watched the plentiful asses in front of me, I could tell they also had Glocks strapped in smart ways on their bodies.

I respected that a lot. Get your tricks familiar with a Glock and no nigga could ever tell if your goons were niggas or bitches. Bossman Dame needed to get on that, but his pride was too fucked up because he knew his broads would smoke his ass the moment they got a Glock in their hands. If I had some bad bitches, they'd be like Armando's.

Each exit in the place was burned in my mind as we walked through the mansion. Paintings covered the walls, all better than that half-dog, half-bike painting Dame had on his wall. The shit was better, but I knew the leader was about his rich tip. Which, to me, meant he still wasn't shit. Hiding behind money just to look good.

I listened and then sat down in the middle of a sexy chocolate broad, who had her hair up in a ponytail that sat on the top of her head, and a caramel-brown chick, her hair down with bangs that cut close to covering her eyes. These two were some sexy-ass broads, who I wouldn't mind getting my dick wet with.

When the broad with the ponytail sat on my lap, I watched as her teal dress slid up to show me her thick thighs. My dick got hard at the feel of her cushion on top of me. Yeah, Armando was trying to distract me with pussy, and it was kind of working, but not totally. I was very much paying attention to everything and memorizing everyone and everything in the room with us as Dough Boy spoke with him.

Something was going down that wasn't feeling right with me. I smirked when the caramel drop began kissing on the side of my neck. Yeah, she was in a white minidress, her thighs, ass, and creamy titties asking to be kissed on.

Armando and Dough Boy seemed to be having some private conversation of the minds. Dough Boy brought out a stash of ducats and handed it to him. Told him that Dame had his back.

But if you weren't used to watching for small shit, like I was, you wouldn't have seen Armando slipping Dough Boy additional money.

Both niggas turned my way.

Armando glanced at me then smiled. "You like my dolls, *amigo*? Remember what we spoke on? Any time, you are welcome. I've been watching you in the streets, my man, and your word is bond. Anyway, sit back, enjoy yourselves, and tell Dame we'll speak again later, to get this problem fixed. We appreciate the drop, Trigga, we really do. *Adiós*, I have other important manners to take care of. *Mamacitas*, take care of them."

Sliding both hands on the thighs of the two broads all on me, I gave him a wide grin, not saying a thing, all the while my mind on some other shit.

Dame's house was falling down all around him. His shit was beyond weak now, and too many niggas were turning on him. Nigga's law was slowly washing away in the streets. This meant that any of us that was his hands in the street was going to catching some shit too.

"Get off that slow-ass nigga. He can't handle no bitches like you two. You two should be over here. All of you should." Dough Boy smirked, rubbing his hands together.

I only laughed when the two ignored him and slid down my body to let me out. I knew they heard about me because one whispered so in my ear. They wanted to see if my dick was true to the game. I wasn't going to tell them now. Fuck I look like? So I let them see.

Dough Boy narrowed his eyes at me and walked off, pulling a couple of broads with him. There was going to be some problems if Dough Boy disrespected any of Armando's dolls like he loved to do to Dame's broads.

I swear I caught the nigga one day getting his dick sucked by some nigga on the street. It wasn't shit to me. If he liked to do that, then do that, but don't get pissed at me because your lame ass is gay. He still was a lame-ass nigga, and I planned on letting him know just that real soon.

Right now, my dick was being swallowed as I pushed the chocolate dime down on her back. Spreading her legs wide, I tilted my head to the side just to see if she had a pussy that smiled, and sure enough, that tongue was poking out at me asking me to suck and lick it, which I did. Her cream tasted like Henny and sugar. Damn, she was tasty! I wasn't down with drinking personally, but I had tasted some before, and right now, this dime had me thirsty.

The way she worked her hips against my mouth had my dick staying hard as the pretty caramel drop stayed sucking me off.

Caramel momma moaned, licking my dick on the side, playing with my nuts, like she was in heaven. She squeezed my tip in a way that had me bucking. Never had some shit done like this one was doing me. When she parted her pretty thighs, pulling up her skirt, I moved my mouth off my Chocolate Kisses slit and turned my head to look at the bare, golden pussy in front of me. This dime was glistening. And I liked that she had a condom in her hand rolling in on my sensitive dick while sliding me inside her.

My mouth dropped open in a "Whoa!" the moment she swallowed me deep. Her pussy was still tight, and the way she gripped my locks let me know she was digging the way I filled her up. I grunted and dug my hips upward, shifting some, to go back to sucking off the chocolate pussy that was tugging on me to make her come again.

Later, I was definitely thanking Armando for his gifts. The sound of me slapping the Jell-O-soft ass on top of me had both broads giggling.

Damn! A simple nigga would be lost in all this glory, but trust, I wasn't.

Though everything was damn good, I still was checking Dough Boy. He had pushed his broads in a corner and was fuckin' them off. Every time they tried to turn to ride him, he flipped them and rimmed they ass. Some made it work for them by bouncing that shit back and letting it slap against his thighs. The others, you could tell, were not into that type of fuckin' by how rigid they got. Dough Boy was a fucked-up nigga.

An hour later, we both ended up back at Dame's. I was happy to get that nigga outta my ride as I drove off.

I headed out of the hood to switch my ride off with a low-riding caddy I had fixed up that was in the garage my pop's used to own, which fell to me. I only trusted Big Jake to be there. He lived in the loft and wanted to open a car shop there, which I was down for. You always had to have a plan B in the game. I learned that from some of the OGs in the street, and ours would be that shop which we'd run under different names.

Back at Dame's, I walked into the mansion fresh from my shower. I rubbed my jaw and smiled as some of his broads giggled and flirted with me. They said they liked that I was growing a beard. I had just gotten lined up, so it was real nice.

I smacked plenty of asses, my way of saying thank you, while they commented on my dark baggy jeans, grey hoodie shirt, and the black jacket I sported over it.

My locks spilled around my face, and one of the chicks stopped me to quickly pull it back and braid it. I knew immediately that it was Gina. I saw in one hand that she had a plastic bag with Band-Aid, and a first-aid kit. *Must be for li'l shawty.* The fact that I saw gauzes too made my jaw clench. *Dame must have really went in on her.* "Thank you, baby," I muttered low.

See, she was about one of the only few chicks I really said anything to. The rest, I grinned and let them feel like I was checking for them.

Gina gave a childlike giggle and walked away to the right of me, heading down the hallway. I chuckled when her walk became sexier, and she made her plump ass switch when Big Jake stepped into view.

I knew since day one of Gina being brought here that she was feeling Big Jake. He had been nice to her, so nice, that Dame didn't even know that he popped her cherry just so she could have something special before he ruined her.

Yeah, sometimes shit had to go that way just to protect some dimes. Too many of our women were being lost in the game to muthafuckas like Dame and Armando. Made to go crazy and lose their thrones, forgetting that they were queens. My mom and pops used to school me on that all of the time, and now I was living it every day. Just how shit went.

I headed up to Dame's. I knocked on the door and waited. Nigga liked to be extra a lot of the time and have us waiting for up to twenty minutes.

Luckily for me, Dough Boy was rocking out of the room with a grin on his face, and Sasha was following him. Bitch looked like she had swallowed some sour dick.

I inwardly laughed. That meant Dame had gifted her to Dough Boy and she was 'bout to get rimmed in.

"Damn, Trigga! Fuck you looking at dee-a-dee ass?" Dough Boy bucked at me then stood back laughing and grabbing my hand to give me dap. "Just playing, little nigga. Took you long enough. Might want to holla at the Boss quickly. He got shit to do. One."

Sasha's rusty laughter flowed over Dough Boy's shoulder.

I cut my eyes at both of them and sucked my teeth.

Dough Boy yanked hard on Sasha's hand, making her stumble while she turned to follow him. "Come on," he barked, and she flipped her dried blonde husked weave over her shoulder and tried to switch in a pair of plastic clear stripper shoes.

Ho was only twenty-five, but the bitch looked sixty. *Fuckin' shame.*

I knocked on the door again and heard Dame yell to me, "Yeah."

After pushing in, I closed the door and moved to stand in front of Dame's desk. He sat bowed forward rubbing his temples. Paper, money in envelopes, blunts, dust, and other shit was spread out everywhere. I checked that his hazel eyes were dark and bloodshot. His Caesar cut was looking raggedy, and he sat wearing jeans with a beater, something he typically didn't do much of. Nigga looked like his kingdom was falling. Guess he finally was waking up.

"What do you want, Trigga?" he asked, without looking up at me. "You got some more intel for me?"

I had a lot on my mind, and everything that was going down now had me stepping to the big boss. "Yeah, look. I think it's time you start cleaning house. Your kingdom is falling, Bossman. Everyone in the street is talking shit about you and yours, and we all starting to get disrespected."

Pausing, I balled my fists at my side, making sure to stay on guard just in case this nigga tried to pop me.

Dame slid back in his chair, locking eyes on me. His large hand laid on top of the gun that was in front of him then he moved it to pull out a piece of paper and threw it at me.

"You think I'm stupid? I got eyes everywhere, nigga. I know and I trust your word since day one of raising you. So what else new you got to tell me?"

Licking my lips, I relaxed enough to cross my arms over my chest. It was true. Since coming into his house, I had started from the bottom and got to where I was now by being schooled by him. So, the fact that he trusted me showed that he knew my loyalty was bond.

"The LKs keep trying to get at me," I told him. "And I think they already got your nigga. You know me, I mean no disrespect, but fuck it! I'm about loyalty, so that shit that's going on ain't cool, because it's affecting your house and those still loyal to you, man. I know you see it. Some of these new niggas you got are lame as fuck and not strong to hold down this camp. You need to clean house."

Dame sat in silence, his neck tense with nerves, his vessels bulking out. The moment his fingers clenched the surface of his desk, I swiftly moved out the way as it went flying.

"Get your Glocks ready!" he roared out loud. "Like you said, it's time for a shakeup." He kicked the desk and smashed a glass door with his chair.

Ray-Ray

Seven days I'd been in that place. The welt on my face was going down.

I was locked in Gina's room. She took care of me. I didn't know what I would have done without that girl. Yeah, she was dense as fuck, but she had proved to be smarter than me. She was surviving, and I was barely living after Dame damn-near beat me to death. Once she had nursed me back to consciousness, she had been with me nonstop. She brought me food and even picked up the two teeth Dame had knocked out and saved them for me. I laughed at it. I didn't know why she'd done that, but I thanked her anyway.

I stood and looked at my body in her full-length mirror. There I was, sixteen with no parents. I was thankful my skin was dark; otherwise the bruises and cuts would have looked much worse. I had some cuts under my breasts from where I had put the razors, and my full, thick chocolate thighs had lumps of welts all over them, front and back.

First time Gina had gotten me into the shower and turned the water on, I screamed like hell. Shit burned me. Then she put some shit she called turpentine on me along with alcohol and peroxide. I think she got a kick out of having a real life doll. She even trimmed my pussy then waxed it too. Removed all the hair from my whole body. It probably would have hurt if I hadn't been out of my mind during it.

She had said a few of the niggas I'd cut was hoping Dame let them have another go at me.

My eyes watered and glazed over as I stared at myself. I missed my mama and my daddy so much. I cried a lot at night. I was always scared I was going to have to fight again. I was tired of fighting.

You hear me, Mama? I'm tired of fighting right now.

I just wanted my old life back. I wanted my old friends. I wanted to go to school again. I wanted to read my books and pretend I could be a writer one day. I wanted to dress in my fresh gear and roam the mall with my bestie, Dominique.

Fresh tears rolled down my cheeks as Gina walked in.

"Hey, Ray-Ray. Good, you up. Daddy talking to that nigga Trigga about cleaning house. They took some niggas from the house to the middle of street and capped 'em. You better hope he let you stay here. He selling bitches to that big Magilla Gorilla, Rick Ross-looking mu'fuckin' pimp. You think Daddy bad? You ain't seen shit. You'd be dead by now, fuckin' with that silver-back, ape-looking nigga."

I couldn't say anything. I didn't have anything left to say, really.

"You hear me, Ray-Ray? Say something."

"I hear ya."

"You need to let me give you something to take the pain away again. You like the way that pill I gave you made you feel, right?"

I nodded.

After she'd got me awake, I was in so much pain, she gave me this off-white pill she called a molly. I took it. I would have taken anything to get rid of the pain.

"Don't hate me later for it, okay? But you my girl, and I gotta take care of you 'cuz none of these bitches took care me. I got fucked up a lot." Just as she pulled her braids back into a ponytail, a knock came at the door.

I got scared and started to cry. I was easily frightened now. I started backing away from the door. I didn't have any more fight left in me. I was sore, weak, and plain exhausted, so if they were coming for me, I was fucked in more ways than one.

"Who?" Gina leaned an ear against the door.

Whoever it was didn't respond. They just knocked another three times in a rhythm.

Gina started giggling and then opened the door.

"It's just Trigga. You safe, Ray-Ray," she said as she opened the door.

Trigga came walking in with three Happy Meals bags. She squealed like the kid she was at heart.

"Did you get me the little doll toys like I asked for, Trigga? Last time you didn't. Mess up my collection."

"Yeah, shit should be straight," his deep voice assured her.

I looked on, but for some reason, I didn't want him to look at me. I slowly pulled the comforter from the bed and covered myself. For the first time, I really looked at him. Short locks, tall, and stocky, he was built like he could run a football or track. Light honey-like eyes that looked like they had been lined with Kohl liner, and skin was brown with a red tint, like red clay. He had nice lips. Lips that looked like they could kiss my shame and pain away.

I wondered, if things had been different, if we could have met in a different time and place. He was fine, reminded me of a Prince Charming, if the Prince had been a killer. He was young too. I wondered how young, but couldn't really tell. All I knew was that he was a killer. Gina said I couldn't kill him, but I wondered if I could make him kill me.

When his eyes turned to look at me, I looked down at the shining hardwood floor. I pretended to find the lines in the hardwood interesting as Gina frantically searched through her Happy Meal bags. She was happy about her miniature dolls.

"Thank you, Trigga. Big Jake still here?"

"Yeah, my nigga in Dame office."

"You think he gon' come see me?"

I looked up in time to see Trigga smirk as he walked out the door. Gina giggled then started opening the plastic bag around her little dolls.

A few hours later, after Gina had dressed me in all red, I sat on her bed as she combed my hair.

"You gotta go in there and let Daddy know he can't give you away. Gotta give him some of that ripe pussy. Daddy loves new shit. And he loves new pussy. You know you still kinda lucky. He ain't fuck you yet. His dick kinda like super big, so it's gon' hurt 'cuz you ain't never had no dick. So like this molly gon' help you get in the groove of thangs. You yet wanna live, don'tcha?"

I just nodded. My head was airy. I didn't know if I wanted to live or not, but that pill she had given me just made me float away.

"Yeah, I want to live."

"And you want to stay here with me, right?"

I nodded again. "Yeah."

"Then listen to what I'm telling you. Just go in there and act like you wanna stay. Make Daddy feel good. I knows it's fucked up, but it's the only way you gon' stay, and it would get that bitch Sasha good. She think she run shit 'cuz Daddy say she his bottom bitch, but she been pissing him off a lot. So you squeeze in there and claim the throne. He down 'cuz now niggas turning on him, talking mad grimy 'bout him in the street. So what you gotta do, since yo' mama and daddy started this shit, is act like you wanna make it right."

She started humming as she brushed my hair some more.

I heard what she was saying, and although I was floating, my head in the clouds, I knew she was right. It was time I started to play it smart. If I wanted to get out of here alive, I had to start fighting with my head.

After she finished, she handed me another pill for later just in case this one wore off. "And drink some of that liquor he got, if you want to. That helps too. I know you wanna body these niggas, and you gon' get yo' chance 'cuz I'ma help you," she whispered then smiled wide.

I looked at her, and she nodded again with wide eyes.

"What?"

"I'ma help you I said, but first we gotta get you on good terms with the devil."

After she said that, she took my hand and rushed me out the door. My heels clacked the floor loudly as she led me down the long corridor over the extravagant banister, until we reached the left side of the house where Dame's quarters were located.

Niggas were looking up at me, making catcalls. A few said they couldn't wait to fuck me up like I did them. I stored that in the back of my head to always watch my back.

I looked at the large double doors that led to Dame's bedroom.

"He still talking shit wit' Trigga, but be in his room waiting on him. They been in the streets killing niggas. I mean, when Dame goes into the street to handle shit like that with Trigga, it's bad. I hate to say this, but yo' mama was a master ho, so you need to tap into some of that shit and save yo' ass."

Gina kissed my lips softly. She'd done that a lot over the last couple of days. She'd kissed and touched me. I hated to admit that I'd felt something when she did. I liked the way she kissed me. I didn't feel as if I wanted to die afterwards either, like I knew I was going to feel after Dame touched me.

"Now go," she said to me.

I was moving by rote. Something— maybe I was possessed— allowed me to push that door to his room open. I walked in and cringed, and my body started to shiver. Somebody must have cleaned my blood from his marble floor. His big California king-sized bed sat in the middle of the room against the wall. The thick solid-oak bed had four pillars with the initials DOA carved into them, as did the headboard.

Double stained glass doors led to an outside balcony, and there was another set of double doors that, I was sure, led to a closet. I could look straight ahead on my left and see the enormous bathroom. But what stood out the most was, his room was spotless. There was not even a strand of hair lying around.

I slowly walked across the room and sat on the bed. There was a small bookstand there. On top sat a bottle of brown liquor. I wondered if I should take a shot of whatever it was. I didn't know what else to think about other than what was about to happen to me. The effects of the pill kept me going in and out of sanity.

By the time Dame got to his room that night, I was asleep in his bed. He woke me up by slapping a hard hand across my already bruised and sore thighs. I was scared, so by habit I woke up swinging. He caught both my wrists and slung me to the floor. His bed sat really high up so that fall was a long way down for me. My hair slug around and covered my face as I groaned out and sat up.

Dame picked up a cigar and sat on a chair he had placed at the foot of the bed. "Why the fuck you in my bed?" he asked then crossed his leg, one ankle across his jean-clad thigh.

Somebody's blood was on his face, neck, chest, and shirt. And blood was on his shoes that were covered in a blue plastic thing. It looked like a shower cap for shoes. This nigga had just come from killing somebody. I wasn't about to become his next victim. So I put that urge, the need to kill that bitch nigga, to the side.

You gotta survive, Ray-Ray. Do what you gotta do to survive. My mama was in my head again. For a while I just sat where he had tossed me and looked up at him.

A gun lay in his lap, and on the side of him was a bloody machete.

My heart jumped to my throat. His eyes held no emotion. They told me that one wrong move and I was going to go missing. I didn't want to go missing. That made me wonder if the police were even looking for me. Had they found my parents yet? Dame was usually a suave man, always kept himself up, clean-shaven face, and his haircut was always fresh. But today he looked like a madman. His hazel eyes stayed locked on mine, as one hand played with the cigar and the other lay atop the gun on his lap.

Gina's voice played in my head. *"Show him you want to live."*

I slowly stood then walked over him. The red lace thigh-high dress I had on was really just a piece of fabric. The *V*-cut came all the way down past my navel. Breasts were about to pop out anyway, so I pulled the straps down to reveal them. Niggas like him didn't care about the bruises that decorated my body.

I kicked the little dress off and then stood in only the red thongs and six-inch heels. He didn't make a move. Didn't even look fazed. His eyes raked over my body without him moving his head. From top to bottom he looked at me.

"Turn around," he ordered.

I wanted to flinch but wasn't fool enough to do so at that point. I was still scared as fuck. Didn't know what the crazy nigga was about to do. My eyes closed, and I stopped breathing when I heard him move. The click I heard let me know that he had the gun cocked. He would have shot me had I done some crazy shit like before.

My breathing got even more uneven when I felt him stand directly behind me. He moved my long hair to the side and ran a hand over my shoulder then his nose alongside my neck.

I slyly raised my hand and popped the other pill, just so my nerves wouldn't betray me. I was prepared for whatever, as long as he just got the shit over with.

To my surprise, he turned and walked away. I saw him go to the bathroom, gun still in hand. That crazy part of me, the part that didn't give a fuck about living, told me to pick up the machete and go after him. But that part of me that wanted to see life outside of these walls told me not to be so stupid, he would shoot me before I even picked it up.

I sat there half-naked on his bed for another thirty minutes as he showered in the bathroom. When he called my name and ordered me into the bathroom, the pill had me walking on air. I walked in and found him standing in the shower. His back was to the closed glass doors, and I could see he had the letters DOA tatted on his back. That was what it felt like since I had walked into the house—dead on fuckin' arrival.

The shower was different than any I had ever seen. Instead of the water coming from a shower head, it came from the walls. I didn't wait for him to tell me to step into the shower, I just pulled my thong off and got in.

I had to admit that I stared at his body for a minute. I ain't ever seen a man naked before in person, not a grown man. I had seen it online though. And my bestie had showed me pictures of her boyfriend's dick on her phone. So I was a virgin in every sense of the word. My mama and my daddy, not wanting me to be like them, had told me to save myself for marriage.

Dame's body looked like it belonged on a poster in the gym. Every muscle was where it was supposed to be, with a few extra ones just because. My eyes traveled from his chest down to his abs and then widened when I saw his dick. Shit wasn't even hard, but I knew it wasn't gonna fit in me.

I didn't have time to think about that though because Dame snatched me to him and pushed my back into the wall. The spray of the water blinded me for a few seconds. His hand roughly touched between my legs, while the other one played with my titties.

I tilted my head when his lips touched my neck. I was confused. I didn't know what to feel. Couldn't tell if my body was reacting or not.

My mama whispered to me, *"I know you scared, Ray-Ray, but a nigga is most vulnerable when his dick getting hard. You can have a nigga like Dame in the palm of your hands with the right touch."*

I was rigid as I stood against the wall. There was a full-grown man touching me. I didn't know how old Dame was, but I knew he was too old to be fuckin' me.

Mama, I don't wanna do this, I said to her in my mind.

"I know, Ray-Ray, but you gotta. Believe me when I tell you, you safer in here than on the streets. For now, baby . . . for now just survive so later you can live."

I squeezed my eyes tighter and started to let my tears flow.

"Look at me, Diamond," she whispered to me.

I opened my eyes and saw her. I gasped then smiled when she waved and smiled at me with tears in her eyes. She stood there with her long curly jet-black hair flowing.

She was dressed in the same outfit she had been killed in. No bullet hole was in her head, and her eyes were full of life.

"I'm sorry, baby," she said as just as Dame lifted me around his waist. *"Ray and I wasn't thinking straight. All we wanted to do was score a quick lick and get you the fuck up outta here. We just thought we could trust niggas, and we trusted the wrong ones. We just wanted enough dough to get outta the country. We had some hid away, but Ray didn't think it was enough. We never wanted this shit for you. We wasn't the best, but we tried with all we knew. We tried."* She sobbed, reaching for my hand.

She was there, but so far away. I brought my hands around Dame's neck and tried to reach for her. I wished she could just take me away.

I swallowed hard when he lifted me and sat me on his dick. He was only maybe an inch inside of me, and it hurt like hell.

I knew he heard me crying, sobbing like the baby I was, telling him that it hurt, but that didn't stop him. He lifted me up and down over and over until he got as far into me as he could.

His moans, grunts, and groans were close to my ear. He went slow at first, and still I was barely able to stand it. So I tried using my hand to push at his hips.

Then he started pounding me against the wall. My nails dug into his shoulders as I grit my teeth, still staring at the ghostly outline of my mama, who was wiping her tears away and shaking her head, saying she was sorry over and over again.

Dame kept me locked up in the room with him for two days after that. He would leave before sun came up and then come back late, always damn-near drenched in blood. They said he was torturing somebody in the underworld. He made sure somebody brought me food all day. I didn't leave that room, and he made it clear that nobody was allowed in there.

Well, he let Gina come in, and he fucked both of us until he couldn't no more.

Dame's dick didn't seem to ever get soft. He stayed between my legs so much, my pussy lips were swollen and sore.

After the first couple times he fucked me, the shit ain't hurt no more, until the first time he did it from the back. When I tried to run away from him, he grabbed my shoulders and fucked me harder.

I was bleeding; it felt like my insides were about to fall out. My stomach started to hurt so badly that when he stopped, all I could do was ball up like a baby. I couldn't move for a few hours.

I wouldn't dare tell him to stop because it hurt, since he kept that damn gun and machete close to him always.

Gina put a molly in both my and her drinks. I was scared to take the pill and drink the liquor, but she told me to go ahead so I could just get through it.

Dame got off on watching Gina eat my pussy and watching her show me how to suck his dick.

I was pretty good at it, he told me. He also told me I couldn't suck another's dick or give another nigga pussy, saying my pussy belonged to him.

"That's good he told you that, Ray-Ray," Gina said to me as we showered together. "You ain't gotta worry about no random niggas fuckin' you. That means that bitch Sasha 'bout to be dead to him too. He ain't ever tell one of us no shit like that. He made us give up pussy from the door." She stood up and kissed my lips.

I was used to her kissing me now. I'd started to kiss her back. I got used to her touching me too and had started to do the same to her. Her body fascinated me just like mine fascinated her.

The water flowing around us, Gina giggled when she touched my titties like always.

Dame was in his room yelling on his phone for Trigga to cap some nigga from another block. Me and Gina got lost in our own world, until we heard him tearing up his room. That meant he was pissed.

Gina and I quickly got out of the shower, dried off, dressed, and then cleaned up after ourselves. That nigga flipped when shit was outta place. We both made sure to dress in red everything then rushed from the bathroom.

We came out to find him pacing the floor. He was back to old dapper Dame, dressed to the nines in a Brooks Brothers suit, expensive shoes on his feet. His hair and face were back to neat perfection. Only thing new was the cane in his hand.

He looked at Gina. "Get her dressed."

She asked no questions, just scurried out to go get whatever it was she was going to dress me in.

I made the mistake of asking, "Where're we going?"

"You think you got the right to ask me my business now?"

I shook my head quickly. "No. I'm sorry."

"You gon' see just how much if you get in my fuckin' business again. Here," he said, handing me a smartphone.

I took it and didn't ask what I was supposed to do with it.

"Any time that phone rings you need to answer it. Understand?"

I nodded. "Yeah."

"Excuse me?"

"Yes, Daddy."

"If I ever call that muthafucka and you don't answer, I'ma fuck you up." He walked over and lifted my chin, so I could look into his face.

Over the past few days, I'd often questioned how a man so beautiful could be so evil.

He stroked my cheek with his thumb. "Don't make me kill you, Diamond."

He called me by my real name, and for some reason, it angered me. *How dare he take the name my parents gave me and use it?*

"You belong to me now. Ask Gina about loyalty and what happens to bitches who forget who the fuck I am. Don't ever not answer that phone." He brought his plush soft lips down to mine.

I thought I would flinch, but I didn't.

Gina came back a few minutes later with my clothes, a red catsuit and spiked golden heels. She got me dressed so quickly, it was like I was never naked. She pulled my hair back into a high ponytail and glossed my lips.

Gina kept laughing. I didn't know why, until Dame walked me through the house. When I walked to the staircase to take his arm, the whole house was waiting at the end of the grand staircase. I could see that some old niggas were gone because there were a lot of new ones.

Pookie was still there, scowling at me. The stiches on the side of his face had to tell him I wasn't to be fucked with or taken lightly.

A few new and old girls were there too. The old ones looked as if they wanted to kill me. Especially Sasha. Her eyes were red with tears. From the bruises on her face, I figured she had fucked around and said the wrong shit to Dame again.

Dough Boy was there. His eyes were locked on my titties. He looked at me, smirked, and then licked his lips. Big Jake was standing at the door in a black getup that made him look like the bodyguard he was.

They all watched quietly as Dame walked down the marble grand staircase with me on his arms. For a minute I felt like a queen. Felt like nobody could touch me. Those same niggas and bitches that tried to get at me when I first got to the house looked as if they were scared to make eye contact with me now because I was on Dame's arms.

Then Trigga appeared from around the corner. He was in his usual attire, a black hoodie with sleeves pulled up, designer jeans, Tims on his feet, and brand new tee-shirt. This one had the death skulls on it.

I stared at those slave shackles or chains or whatever the fuck they were on his wrists again. I looked down at the floor quickly when we made eye contact. I never could read the look on his face, but I just didn't like him looking at me. Felt like he was looking through me, reading me, and I didn't like that shit.

Once Dame made it to the bottom of the stairs, he stopped, hooked the cane in the crease of his arms where my hand lay, and cleared his throat.

"As you can see, a lot of shit has changed around this muthafucka. More changes to come. Sometimes a nigga gotta lose his mind to gain clarity. Loyalty is a big deal to a nigga like me. I don't trust easily. Even the niggas I trust, I don't trust. Get me?"

Dame cast a glance at Dough Boy, who started to look uncomfortable, fidgeting and looking around the room at others.

Then he looked at Trigga. "Lotta y'all niggas need to learn to be quiet and watch like that nigga over there. The one y'all think slow because he don't talk much. My daddy always said, 'Be quick to listen and slow to speak.' That's a sign of a true OG. That's why Trigga rolling with me to this meeting of the bosses tonight. That nigga got my back whether he like me or not. He shows loyalty 'cuz he knows who putting that paper in his pocket. He knows who the fuck gon' kill for him just like he gon' kill for me."

I watched Dough Boy. He looked more uncomfortable now than he did before. Big Jake grunted as he stood at the door. Strangely enough, his eyes were on Dough Boy too.

"My nigga Big Jake gon' always ride for me too. There ain't another family out there that can take Big Jake's and Trigga's loyalty away from a nigga."

Dame removed his cane from his arm and told me to hold it before he stepped forward. Most of the women in the room flinched. A lot of the niggas were sweating.

Dame clapped his big hands twice then rubbed them together. "Trigga, Big Jake, Gina, Dough Boy make a move this way," he ordered.

Once they all moved, the room fell deadly silent. I was twitching because Trigga was standing right behind me. I don't know why that made the hair on the back of my neck stand up. It could have been because Gina said he had sliced Janky's and Slammer's throats.

"Now, I want all you niggas and bitches to look to the right of you," Dame said, and everyone did. "Now look to the left of you."

Everyone did that too.

"When you wake up in the morning, some of these muthafuckas won't be here."

Pookie was sweating like he had popped a molly.

As soon as Dame said that, the cooks started coming from the kitchen with so much food, it looked like a feast.

"Niggas and bitches enjoy your last meal on me." Dame laughed.

Dough Boy chuckled too, which made me turn to look at him. But what was most interesting was the way Trigga's eye twitched as he watched Dough Boy. I had a feeling something was about to go down at the bosses' meeting.

Trigga

Niggas were eating like it was the Olympics. Music thumped as Ace Hood spat about his Bugatti. Chicken, meatloaf, pork chops, greens, mashed potatoes, and other dishes filled the table. Dame had some bomb cooks, each one able to cook whatever he wanted—soul food, Chinese, French cuisine, whatever.

I stood next to Big Jake, behind Bossman, just watching. The cooks tried to feed us, but Big Jake and I were on the same wavelength, not trusting anything sitting on this table, not with the way Dame's mental had been changing. I'd learned in some books that, back in the medieval time, warlords/kings always had taste-testers, when people was running around poisoning others back then. Watching these fools at the table right now, there was no fuckin' way I'd touch anything from that table.

Dough Boy ol' hating ass yelled at me, "Ey, little nigga, Trig, you think you're the shit, huh? Here. Eat a fuckin' pork chop, man, You scared that shit is poisoned?" Nigga threw a pork chop at me.

People started laughing hard.

I stepped forward ready to put a knife in his throat, but Dame's low cough stopped me. I stepped back to where I was and crossed my arms over my chest, keeping my eyes on that fool. That nigga was on some other shit, and it looked like he was high as fuck too, forgetting Bossman was sitting at the front of the table drinking his Rémy.

"Naw, I'm good," I told him. "Had a king's meal beforehand, nigga."

Dame laughed hard at my comment. He leaned back and gestured with his hand for me to lean in to him. I kept my eyes locked on Dough Boy, just to fuck with him, nodding as Dame told me to go let our guests in.

Walking out, my eyes glanced over at Big Jake. He knew what I was about too but kept his face neutral. I noticed that he positioned himself closer to Gina, who sat on Dame's right with li'l shawty people in the house were calling Ray-Ray. I never understood why the fuck she got such a nigga name, but it was whatever.

She looked different than before, and I checked that she was playing the game. I knew the moment she stepped down the stairs in that red catsuit, which showed off a bare back and hips I never noticed she had before, with a set of tits that were sitting high and so swollen that my head almost tilted to the side, that her cherry was long gone. She walked like a woman who knew the world was hers, in a pair of gold stilettos that made her legs look like Bria Myles', and an ass to match. No lie, she walked differently and had this vibe around her that said she was Dame's property. She was kinda cute, I guess. I mean, yeah, I guess she was kinda sexy. Like Brittney Skye type of sexy.

I had heard Dame mutter to li'l shawty as they walked past me, "Do you value your eyes right now? Because I will rip each one from you."

I didn't know or care what that shit was about. Nigga was on some crazy shit sometimes. Not my business or problem.

Anyway, while I watched every female in the house hiss in jealousy, shawty kept her game on lock. Holding Dame's arm, her eyes shined brightly, but they were a little off. Why? 'Cuz in her eyes, I saw a killer ready to be born. Never a good thing with someone like her, because the broad was wild. If she wasn't schooled right, her bloodlust to get even might fuck up her world even more. Only reason I was taking note of that was because if she flipped, then she would mess up my money. So I stored that to memory and kept it buckin'.

I headed to the front of the mansion and came back with a team of guests. Additional chairs with gold plates had been sat out all around the table, in four points. Voices of various street kings sounded behind me.

Big Jake handed Dame a gold cigar, a signal to let him know that his guests had arrived.

Dame pushed back to stand, turn around, and hold his hands out. "Welcome, family. Have a seat and break bread with your good friend," he greeted with a wide smile.

Looking to the left and right of me, Armando, the Latin Kings' leader, stepped to Dame to shake his hand and took a cigar from him, as Gina stood in her bubblegum-pink catsuit, her two pigtails bubbly swinging around her body as she escorted him to his chair.

Next up was the Russian and Italian cartel leaders, Nicola and Valentio, who were led by Gina to their chairs. Following that, bosses from various Asian and East Indian mobs walked in. But what had the table quiet was the Nigerian Queens' leader Anika. Her bodyguards were mainly broads, but she also had some niggas she controlled. She was right there at the top with the LKs, Jamaican Kings, Dame, the Dragons, and the Italian cartel.

Speaking of the JKs, on Boss Anika's arm was their leader, Jamaican King Rasta J. Which was why the table got mad quiet.

Armando stood, walked up to Anika, and kissed her hand, a public show that the three were linking up.

Anika wore an all-black dress that was cut out on the side and held together by a gold braided rope on her hips.

And she sported gold bangles that went up her arms. Her curly thick natural hair sat up in a high bun and was sexy on her. As she slowly walked, I caught a glimpse of her plump ass and bare back that had tattoos on her chocolate skin that looked like something tribal. This chick—I couldn't even call her a bitch—she was bad, and if I thought I could, I would definitely hit.

Gina led the JK boss to his seat. Nigga came in with a Jamaican flag tucked in the handkerchief pocket of his all-black, silver-lined Marc Jacobs suit and a pair of black diamond shades. Only reason I knew that was because I was close enough to see nigga's tag. Some niggas got money and didn't know how to act like. Oh, well. I stayed in my lane watching everything.

Boss Anika's black-lined almond eyes drew my attention away when they locked on me. I wasn't stupid. Dame had told me to take care of her, so I did.

Standing tall, I took a bold move and rested my hand on the small of her back and led her to her chair, pulling it out to let her sit next to the JK boss. I stepped back and swore I saw her lick her plum-colored lips when she looked up at me before I went back to stand by Dame.

While I moved to position myself next to Dame, I saw Ray-Ray looking at Anika's attire. I could see she was impressed and wasn't able to hide that fact fast enough. She still had some learning to do. Gina was telling her on the low to chill with that, 'cuz I saw her pinch Ray-Ray's arms as she walked by to take her seat.

Shit was too funny to me. I so wanted to laugh, but I didn't have time for that shit. My attention was on the bosses in front of me.

I saw Sasha sitting next to Dough Boy. Her face was so red with hate, her eyes were dark like marbles. Shit kind of had me ready to put a bullet between those eyes because of the hatred steaming for her crazy ass. She stared hard at Ray-Ray; I knew it had to be on some female shit. She was officially no longer HBIC just that fast, which was also kinda funny to a nigga. If her pussy game was that good, then Ray-Ray coming in wouldn't have changed shit. But, yo, what can I say? Pussy was like that sometimes, especially if it was new, gushy, and tight.

"Thank you, Trigga." Dame stood again.

I gave a quick nod and muttered, "It's straight," before turning my gaze back on the table.

A smile almost crept over my face as I saw Dough Boy sitting up straight. Nigga was sweatin' bullets. I knew he had to be shitting himself. Sitting next to Armando, he didn't know what the fuck was going on. I just stood back enjoying this moment. Hated fuckin' lame-ass, unfaithful niggas.

Dame said, "Libation for all my good friends and associates." Then he said to the house cook, "Make sure their guards eat well too, Fredrick."

Dame rubbed his hands as staff poured into the room.

One of the bosses playfully asked, "Will you be lavishing us with your pretty treats? Especially that new ruby by your side?"

Out the corner of my eye, I saw Ray-Ray cringe, but she quickly played it off, taking a sip of water.

Dame growled low, "She's off-limits. It's good to have people around me, who say they got my back, got me covered, because business can't be done unless you know who you working with. Ain't that right, fam?" He paced back and forth with his glass of Rémy in his hand as he spoke.

Gina ordered a couple of girls to pour drinks for everyone at the table and light up gold cigars that lay across their plates. Each girl played their part by sitting on a boss's lap, stroking his chest.

For the women, Dame already knew their choices, so some had men lighting up their cigars, and others had women bending over and pressing their titties close to the female bosses' faces while lighting their cigars. Dame observed everything, as if he was in his mind moving chess pieces around.

None of the bosses said a thing, but they lifted their glasses to show support, some opting for water.

"Good. Because it's never a good look to have a man's reputation muddled in the streets, right? That's the utmost disrespect to a man and his work, and I wanted to address that with this dinner."

Dame paused to finish his drink. He sat the cup down and returned to his chair to steeple his hands and look over everyone. He sat like a man who was supreme ruler and the people around him were his subjects. His facial expression stayed calm, and no one could read his body language from what I could tell, except for the NQ's leader, who sat with a knowing smile on her face.

"I know you all are hearing rumors about me in the streets, that Dame and his crew are weak right now, not able to handle his territory anymore. Which has had some of you becoming bold enough to get disrespectful to me and mine. Some of you have even taken it upon yourselves to confront my crew behind my back."

Dame's voice had suddenly shifted in tone to become callous and cold. His elbow on the arm of his chair, he held his hand out for his cigar.

I watched Ray-Ray reach into Dame's jacket. She pulled out his cigar, prepped it, and put it between his fingers before lighting it.

The sound of someone sucking their teeth echoed in the room. I knew it had to be Sasha.

Bad move, I thought.

Dame twirled the cigar between his fingers, keeping his eyes on everyone before him. He took a deep hit of his cigar then added, "You must all know how that affects me deeply, how hurtful such disrespect can be toward the relationships we have going on here, not only with you all, but within my own house as well. Loyalty is everything, and I have been consistent in this for a very long time. Since I was just a kid running the streets, raised up by OGs in the hood, I have crossed the path of many of your old leaders, many of whom I've helped you all take down. Have I not?" Dame's eyes locked on Armando and several others around the table.

Armando cleared his throat and leaned forward, tenting his fingers. "*Mi amigo*, these things you have done, none of us here question your loyalty or our faith in you. So you are correct to state your voice in this."

Dame slammed his fist down and growled low, "Then why are my brothers and sisters not my keeper? Why do you sit in front of me and smile and play the game as if you and I do not have beef? You think I am so gone that a nigga is stupid now? Do you forget who the fuck I am?"

Every female and male boss at the table began to tense up the moment Dame's voice rose an octave, but it was when he laughed and sat back that their hair visibly stood on end.

I stood back signaling to a set of bodyguards that Big Jake had trained personally. Doors suddenly closed, and the room became thick with tension.

"Forgive me, forgive me. I meant no disrespect to raise my voice, although it seems some of you have given me nothing but disrespect. My own family turns on me and makes money trades with lords who say they are looking out for me and my betterment. Isn't that right, Dough Boy?"

Dough Boy's eyes grew large, and the moment he opened his mouth to speak, my bullet made contact with his shoulder. Each squeeze of my trigger had him slamming back in his chair with brute force.

I took my precious time in those kinds of kills. I lodged a bullet in his other shoulder and then walked up to him as he stared at me from his chair stunned. I said nothing as I stood behind his chair and gripped him by his throat, my gun pressed against his temple. He tried to move his hands, and I quickly pointed my gun to shoot at each hand.

I forced that nigga's head to look at Dame, who sat back with a cold grin on his face. My nails cut into Dough Boy's throat while I held his trachea.

Dame continued on, "See, this whole week has been nothing but me cleaning up my mistakes, some of those coming from my own house. People I held close to me thought they could play me and steal from me by fuckin' up a deal with one of my close lords. With that, I dropped them and gave Armando his deal by delivering him his pound of flesh to make these things even. But, no, that was not enough. Was it, *amigo*?" He glared at Armando.

Armando sat back saying nothing. It was clear he wasn't sure how to handle the situation, especially since his crew was passed out on the floor behind him from the food and drink they had consumed.

"*Sí*, that would be *correcto*, *amigo*. See, like you, I've been listening to the streets, beating truth from niggas and bitches who thought I wasn't shit, been watching as my crew turned their back on their boss. Watched as *you* approached my people, my team. But the major problem for me came when you fucked around and came at my right and left," Dame said, flipping his speech to Spanish, to fuck with dude's mental, I had to assume.

Bossman moved around the room, speaking with his hands, keeping his game going.

"The other problem was when my left forgot who it is that kept his mouth fed, kept his pockets stacked, kept his dick wet with bitches and even niggas, and who kept him laid up in a prime loft apartment with a Lexus. Yeah, he forgot who kept him laced up and had people in the streets calling him a boss. See, I don't do well when my dogs become bitches and start getting greedy at the mouth. That greed always eventually kills that dog. Ain't that right, Dough Boy?" Dame glanced at a shaking Dough Boy, who tried to talk, his mouth opening and closing like a dying fish.

Dame's eyes narrowed. "I told you multiple times that you don't twist loyalty."

With that, my gun slammed down against Dough Boy's temple. Then I tilted his head back to force his mouth open and slide my barrel in his mouth. A smile played across my lips, my eyes locked on him, and I hit that trigger, ending his life in a blink.

Dough Boy's teeth automatically bit down hard on my barrel, breaking each row of teeth while my gun kept going. Pulling it out quickly, I pointed it at Armando and stared him blank in the eyes.

"Then my loyalty gets fuckin' played when you come after my gun? *No bueno, mi amigo.* You overstepped your bounds the moment you came after Trigga. So what do you have to say to that, *amigo*?" Dame walked up to where I stood behind a dead Dough Boy's chair and pulled it out, snatched Dough Boy's bloody, slumped-over body, and threw it on the floor. Grabbing several cloth napkins, he laid them on the seat of the chair and sat down, as if he wasn't sitting over a dead body, and turned to face Armando.

Several people at the table gasped from me taking out Dough Boy, and at Dame's cold personality.

"Let me repeat myself, *hermano, mi amigo* from the streets, who I helped long ago. You turn your back on me now? Stab me in the back? How about you stab me while I look at you right now? What are you going to do?"

Armando sat back in his chair, his fingers against his temple. He sized Dame up and studied him before holding his hand out. "I say, *mi hermano*, my product stays yours. I will always keep my respect in your lane. No bullshit ever again. Peace, *amigo*."

Dame glanced at the hand and took it, and both men grasped forearms. Then Dame suddenly yanked Armando forward and slammed his fist into his face. The sound of bone cracking echoed around the table, and blood spilled on the chair and table before them.

Amusement had me focused on them and everyone else around the table. I saw Ray-Ray and Gina watching in awe, but quickly dropped their eyes to play submissive and docile.

Big Jake moved to grab the Latin Kings' leader by his shoulders, standing him up and wiping the blood from his face, while other bosses watched with raised eyebrows.

I noticed the Nigerian Queens' boss, Anika, still sat quietly sipping her water, watching the whole thing with a smile on her face.

Dame's voice quickly drew my attention while he stood again looking over the man who dared try him for his territory. "Now we are on even terms, *mi amigo*. Our deal is back on the table, unless someone is wishing to ante up."

Anika sat her glass down and cleared her throat. "We will cover whatever losses you had, and double that. You should not have any more problems with Armando. Isn't that right, love?"

The Nigerian Queens' leader's soft, accented voice flowed over everyone like a bitch gripping a nigga's dick, stroking it, and sucking it off. Every man at the table shifted in his seat, waiting for Armando's reply.

"*Sí*, no problems. We'll keep our original agreement and work in tandem with our Queen at the table." Armando stumbled back to hold his chair, pushing at Big Jake to step off him.

Dame smiled broadly and walked over to the Queen to take her hand and kiss her knuckles. At that same moment, the other bosses spoke up and added their own deals to the table, and Dame quickly let them know he would accept.

"Dough Boy, go get them contracts ready—Oh yes, I forgot that fast." Dame laughed.

Sasha spoke up, drawing attention her way. "Big Daddy, I can do that for you." The instant she felt all eyes on her, she gave a flirty laugh and smile, poking her breasts out to show she was worthy of all attention.

Dame raised an eyebrow and moved her way. His hands reached out to rub her shoulders, brushing her blonde hair to the side. His eyes blanked out a second, indicating that he had every intention of fuckin' her up later. He brushed his knuckles over the side of her neck. "Why don't you show my Diamond where I keep my contracts and you both bring them to me right now, baby? How about you go and do that?" he gently responded.

I knew at that moment she was all the way done, that it was on to the next one. In any other situation, she would be laid out on her ass, except that several of the bosses here were women. The Nigerian Queens' leader didn't play with women being hit in her presence, so Dame had to play his role carefully.

Sasha quickly stood, glared at Ray-Ray, and headed toward the closed doors.

I gazed at Dame, who was now flirting with Anika. Then I glanced toward Ray-Ray, who pushed away from the table, biting her ruby-colored plump lips, and hurried after Sasha.

As the door closed, I heard a scuffle and saw that Sasha had tripped Ray-Ray. Then Ray-Ray was pushing herself up to slap Sasha across her face with her nails. And the door closed after that. I felt like laughing my ass off.

Turning my attention back to my kill, I grinned wide, looking at Dough Boy's frozen expression.

Something within me was making my fingers itch, but it wasn't to squeeze a Glock, it was for playing with some pussy.

Ray-Ray

That bitch pushed me. If I wasn't afraid of what Dame would do, I would have mopped the floor with that ho. But a slap to show the bitch I wasn't afraid of her had to do for the time being. I bit down on my bottom lip, drew back, and slapped that bitch so hard, my nails drew blood. She stumbled then fell back on her big ass.

I rushed to stand over her with my fist balled. "You want that ass-whupping again, bitch," I fumed.

She sneered while looking up at me. "Don't get to thinking you hot shit since that nigga got you on his arm."

"Shut the fuck, stupid ho! You wanna walk around here mad at me for stupid shit. Maybe if you woulda kept your pussy game tight, you could still be the head bitch you think you are. I'm not about to get fucked up again for you and nobody else. Now, if you want Dame to come out here and ask what's taking so long, you do that shit, but I swear to God, if he puts his hands on me, I'm putting hands on you and I'ma snatch yo' ass baldhead this time, bitch."

I didn't know who the chick was speaking out of my mouth, but I knew I didn't want Dame putting his hand on me. I was already two teeth down. I'd fucked up enough as it was. Dame had caught me looking at Trigga a second too long and threatened to cut my eyes out. Then Gina pinched my arm to let me know I had done something else wrong. I was trying not to do anything else to cause Dame to go crazy on me again.

I backed up to let her up off the floor. She still looked at me like she wanted to buck or some shit, and deep down inside, I was wishing she would. I still remembered that ho had tried to cut me. I had a blade with her name on it.

She finally saw the insane look of fearlessness in my eyes and led me to the office Dame had downstairs. Only niggas I ever seen in his upstairs office was Trigga and Big Jake. Well, I saw Dough Boy once too, but that nigga dead now. Being in that room around all that power had me realizing that the situation I'd found myself in was real.

When Trigga popped Dough Boy without flinching and Dame watched on in silent rage like it was nothing, I knew life meant nothing to Dame. None of us meant a fuckin' thing to him. We were just living, breathing toy soldiers. That was it. I was going to fake this shit until I made it out of this shit.

I kept quiet as she walked ahead of me to get the contracts. I made mental note of what she had done, though, and I would make sure she paid for that shit.

"You better watch your back, bitch," Sasha stopped and said to me before we walked back into the dining hall.

My eyes roamed over the claw-like marks I had left on her face from the slap. I didn't like the look in that cold bitch's eyes. She didn't scare me, but my mama had warned me about chicks like her. This life was all she knew, and she had built herself up mentally to think that it would be all she would ever know.

I stared in her eyes and just imagined all the shit she'd had to see and go through. She was no longer a regular woman. She was what the streets had made her.

Once we walked back in the room, the bosses were all talking to one another, waiting for Dame to present them with their contractual agreements. Armando was looking at Dame from time to time like he wanted to murk him. He had to be pissed at getting punched in the face and not being able to retaliate in front of the other bosses. He never let on though.

As the night continued, bosses left one by one, in order of importance. Since Armando had tried some treachery shit, he was the first to leave. When the Jamaican boss left, Dame made Sasha go with him to make up for telling him I was off limits.

The last to leave was the boss of the Nigerian Queens, Anika. I was in love with the power she had. Those niggas in that room feared and respected her. Her guards were smart enough not to drink or eat anything offered to them. She was at the top of the food chain right after Dame.

I could tell that, after they saw Dame's bi-polar antics tonight, not one boss wanted to cross him. That nigga's mental was fragile, but I could see how taken he was with Anika. I didn't know why I felt some type of way about that, but I did.

After Dame dismissed the rest of the house, he left me and Gina sitting at the table with Trigga. He told him to watch us while Big Jake walked him and Anika out.

Gina giggled once we were all sitting alone. Dough Boy's dead body was still in the room with us. Trigga ordered that clean food be brought out. That surprised me. I didn't know he had that much power. I guess, since Dough Boy was dead, he was now second in command.

"Trigga," she sang out. "Better call the cleaners too, or else Daddy gone flip 'bout this blood on his floor."

He laughed low. That made me look at him. I hadn't ever seen him smile, much less laugh.

"You late." He smirked as he leaned back in his chair. "Already on that shit."

He was calm, considering he had just blown somebody's brains out. I wondered if it had been easy for him to kill my parents.

Before my mouth could catch up to my brain, I blurted out, "You killed my mama?"

The smirk immediately left his face. He sat up and glared at me.

Gina giggled again. "Oh, she thinks she's gonna kill you, Trigga," she said, pouring herself some of the champagne Dame was drinking.

When he looked at me, I didn't flinch. I squared my shoulder and held my head high as I sat in the chair to the right of where Dame had been posted.

"Yeah? You gon' kill a nigga, huh?" he taunted.

"I'ma get rid of every muthafucka—"

"You ain't smart enough," he said, cutting me off. "Too fuckin' wild, li'l shawty."

"Fuck you!"

"Don't fuck Dame's hoes."

He was cocky. Thought he was invincible because he could kill niggas without thought. It annoyed me. Thinking about my mama and my daddy made me more determined.

"I can kill you if I wanted."

He took the gun from his hip and slid it across the table to me. "Do it," was all he said, no fear in his eyes.

I couldn't tell if he was serious or not, and I didn't know what would happen to me if I killed him. I reached for the gun anyway. I picked it up and aimed it right at his head. It was heavier than I thought it would be. My hands started to shake with fear. I'd never held a gun in my hands before.

"You know how to shoot that shit?" He rocked his neck from side to side.

I could hear the bones crack as he did so.

While my mind was on the gun, Trigga had gotten up, moved around the table, taken the gun from me, and snatched a handful of my hair. My head was back, and he had the gun pressed against my left temple.

"You gon' kill a nigga, li'l shawty?" he asked. "With the safety still on this shit?"

Water rimmed my eyes as they darted to where Gina was.

"Leave her alone, Trigga," she mumbled.

I could tell she didn't know whether he was going to fuck me up or not.

My heart was racing because I didn't know what else to do or say. All I kept seeing was my mama's cold dead gaze as she lay lifeless with a bullet in her head. I kept hearing my daddy's hacking, his begging and pleading for my life.

I eyed a steak knife on the table and grabbed for it. Before my hand could wrap around the handle, Trigga had lifted me up from the chair by my hair, twisting my right arm behind my back. I couldn't catch my breath as he pressed my jaw against the wall.

"You too slow to kill me, li'l shawty."

His lips were close to my ear. I could feel his warm breath on my neck.

"And you think too much, show a nigga what you finna do before you do it."

The pressure he had on my arm hurt so bad, I thought he was going to break it.

"Trigga, stop," Gina whined.

I heard her push her chair back then felt when she tried to pull him off of me. I had already made up in my mind that, when he let me go, I was going to punch him in his shit.

After a few moments of Gina pulling and tugging on him, he let me go. I didn't know if I was pissed or just embarrassed at the smug look etched on his face.

"You okay, Ray-Ray?" Gina asked.

I nodded, but kept my eyes on the madman holding the gun idly by his side. He didn't take his eyes from mine as he lay the gun back on the table. He then pulled a knife from behind him and lay that on the table too.

"You stupid as fuck," he barked. "Gon' fuck around and get yo'self offed with all that blind rage and shit you got, li'l shawty."

"Yeah, I'm stupid, but you this nigga's henchman. He say jump, your faggot ass already know how high."

"Better a henchman than his come bucket."

My eyes darted to the knife he had laid on the table.

"Don't do it, li'l shawty. You ain't gon' like the outcome."

"Ray-Ray . . . Trigga . . . stop. Dame gone fuck all us up if he come in here now."

"Tell yo' bitch to stop it."

"Your mama a bitch," I retorted.

Gina stepped in between and then jerked me by my arm. "Ray-Ray, no!"

"I ain't nobody's bitch." I thought at that point I was pissed enough to try to stab him with his own knife, but Dame's laughter in the foyer gave me my sanity back. I straightened up real quick.

"Wrong, li'l shawty." Trigga strategically hid his weapons on him. "You that nigga's bitch."

My eyes narrowed, and teeth grinded. I wanted to say something smart in return, but didn't have it in me to speak out loud to another man with Dame so close.

"What's that shit you said about jumping and knowing how high again? I bet you know how low to go too, huh, li'l shawty?" he taunted, walking out of the room.

My eyes stayed trained on the back of his head the whole time. I wished like hell looks could kill because that muthafucka would have been dead.

"You better stop fuckin' with that nigga like that," Gina fussed. "I told you he was fuckin' sick in the head. You see how he killed Dough Boy? That boy don't care. And you don't say that shit about his mama, ever. I be hearing shit 'cuz niggas talk around me. His mama died in a fucked-up way."

"I don't care. He ain't gon' be calling me bitches and getting away with it."

"The longer you stay in this damn house, the more that's gonna start sounding like yo' name and shit. *Bitch, ho, slut, stupid, cunt, fuck toy, dicksucka*—and whatever the fuck else they feel like calling you—get used to it."

"That nigga don't scare me, Gina."

"It ain't about being scared of him. You betta get smart and listen to what I tell you. Trigga and Big Jake the only niggas in here that look out for me. They the only niggas that ain't tried to shove their dicks in every hole I own. The only ones that call me Gina, or Baby G, or doll face, or any sweet shit. Trigga ain't ever call me bitch. Big Jake ain't ever called me ho. You gotta form alliances where you can, Ray-Ray. You still think shit is game."

Since I had been in the house, I'd never heard Gina's voice so stern and commanding. Then I saw her wipe tears from her eyes and knew she was reliving all the shit that had happened to her in here. I guess she was trying to tell me it was better to have Trigga as my ally than my enemy. I didn't know, but I hugged her anyway. I didn't want to see her crying.

The next day the house was quiet. Dame was calm mostly. He had me sit in the office with him as he tried to get Trigga to help him figure out how to make up for the product and money they had lost behind what my parents had done. Part of me only felt as if he had me there to hurt me.

"Should have known that fuckin' bitch was up to something," Dame fussed, talking about my mama. "One thing you never do, Trigga, is trust a bitch sucking your dick and holding eye contact." He then laughed. "But then again, Shanna was the queen of sucking dick, so you can see how a nigga may have slipped up."

I swallowed and felt my throat closing with emotions. My eyes darted around the room and then to Trigga from time to time, but mostly stayed on Trigga.

The top right side of my upper lip twitched. I pictured myself picking up the golden letter-opener and stabbing Dame dead in his fuckin' throat.

Gina was out of the house. Dame had made her go back to Magic City to dance. She didn't put up a fuss or fight. She didn't say a lot to me, and when she kissed me, it was only a peck, not her usual tongue-down. I thought she was still mad at me.

"I wish I knew where her bitch-ass daddy hid the rest of my shit. That damn product came straight from mutha-fuckin' Vietnam and Colombia." Dame thumbed his nose.

I didn't think I would ever be used to him talking shit about my mama and daddy like that. One day he would pay for it.

I'd seen him test the product he was fussing about earlier. That shit had hit his brain instantly, mellowed him out enough to have him eating my pussy. He sprinkled some of that shit on my clit and had me bucking and jerking like crazy. I hate to admit it, but his lips and tongue on my pussy felt good. Damn good.

For the first time, I moaned out in pleasure with him. And for the first time he fucked me slow. I didn't know how to look at myself afterwards, since I enjoyed it.

"So whatchu gon' do 'bout it, boss?" Trigga asked him. "We done already searched they crib left to right, top to bottom."

"Searched all the spots they used to lay low in too?" Dame asked.

Trigga nodded. "Nothing."

"Damn."

Dame stood and then walked over to open the balcony doors that sat right behind his desk. Cool air breezed in and whisked through my hair. I hadn't been outside in so long, I started to feel like a caged animal. As soon as the doors opened, I wanted to run and jump over the balcony.

"I think them niggas had another person in on that hit, bossman. When I ran into them other two niggas jawing, they said something else a nigga wasn't able to hear."

I looked up at Trigga when he said that, and it finally dawned on me. Pookie was still alive because they didn't know he was in on it. I knew where the stash was hidden, but I wouldn't say anything just yet. Pookie was stupid. I knew he wouldn't have moved it. Judging by how silent that nigga had been, he was too scared to risk it. It was a good thing I had sliced his fuckin' face.

"If I find out another muthafucka was in on this shit, and I'ma fuckin' cut out his entrails and hang them around his parents' house to dry. Sick of niggas playing with my shit, my fuckin' emotions. You know how much fuckin' dough I done missed out on because of this shit?"

Before Trigga could respond, Big Jake pushed the door open. "Boss, you betta get downstairs. Sasha done cut one of the new bitches," he told Dame.

"I'm so sick of this bitch!" Dame roared as he picked up his cane and stormed from the office.

I halfway wanted to run down there just to see him fuck her up.

"It was Pookie," I said aloud when it was just me and Trigga in the room.

He regarded me slowly. "What, li'l shawty?"

"The other nigga in on the take . . . it was Pookie."

"And you telling me this why?"

"So you can tell Dame."

"Why you ain't telling 'im?"

"'Because he told me to stay the fuck out his business."

"How you know it was Pookie?"

"He was with my mama and my daddy the night they did it. Him, Janky, and Slammer, they was all in on it. Came in the house scared and nervous but was talking 'bout how they had just come up. It was duffle bags full of bricks wrapped in brown kind of duct tape. There was money too."

I could tell when I told him about the money I had his interest. Nobody had mentioned the money that Dame had been robbed of too.

"How long you been sitting on this shit, li'l shawty?"

"Since I got here."

Trigga stood and folded his arms across his wide chest. As usual he had a black hoodie on.

"So where is it?"

"The old trap house on Campbellton Road. The other half is at the house on Washington Road, at Janky and Slammer's grandma's house."

"So them niggas hid the shit in plain sight?"

"Guess so. That's where it's at though."

"You bet not be playing a nigga, li'l shawty. If I check this shit out, and you bullshitting—"

"I ain't bullshitting. It's there."

I guess I was feeling bad because Gina had told me some niggas raped his mama before killing her. I had too much pride to say sorry to the nigga, but I could pass him info. She'd also told me he was real young when his mama got killed. She even said she thought he had seen what happened to her when the niggas raped her. I hoped not. Nobody should have to see that shit.

"Why you kill people, Trigga?" I asked him. "Didn't you see your mama and daddy die? Why you kill people like you do?"

He didn't break a sweat. "Why you sucking Dame dick? Didn't you see your mama was your daddy's ho? Why you doing what you doing now? Why you ain't fighting and cutting niggas up no more?"

"So he kidnapped you and made you work for him too?"

"A nigga got debt just like you do, li'l shawty."

Sasha's screams rent the house. Her cries, begs, and pleas for Dame not to send her to the basement made my flesh crawl. I still shuddered to think about what would have happened to me if I had gone down there.

"Just don't see why you wanna work for a nigga that got the initials DOA carved in his bedposts, headboard, and back," I mumbled.

Trigga's face turned down in a frown.

"What you say? Say that shit again?"

It was almost like he was demanding it. He moved closer to me so quickly, I didn't have time to think. I thought he was bucking on me because I'd dissed Dame in his presence.

I leaned back in my chair as he glared down at me. "I ain't say nothing."

"Yeah, you did. What about DOA?"

"All I said was, he has it carved in his bedposts, headboard, and back," I stammered.

"Yeah."

Something had changed in his eyes. I could see it just like I could feel his mood change in the room.

Trigga

There was some shit I wasn't honest about at the start of all this bullshit and li'l shawty's words brought all of that to the surface. Rumors on the street were that I'd seen my parents get popped. As a kid I used to walk around and tell niggas that, when they got too nosy. That shit was lies. Some I told that they OD'd on some product. Others, I added that with the rape story of my moms before I got quiet altogether and silenced my story. No one was able to tell what my backstory was, and on some real shit, it was better that way. The more niggas knew about your business, the easier it was to get your weakness.

For me, the truth was in all the jawin' going on. My parents did get popped the way I told you. Thing was, I saw everything. I ain't just walked in on my mom getting ran through then helped her take those niggas down. No. I was locked in the house for the week they used my mom like their personal bitch. Watched as they tied and gagged her, beat her, made her open her legs by tying them apart, and they ran through her, flipping her to eat her out taking their dirty shirts to wipe her blood and their come away.

Yeah, I saw it all, except that last nigga, the one who got away. I couldn't get free to help my mom until she signaled me. Shit still was in a nigga's dreams every day. Every day I woke up thinking about that last nigga with the DOA tat on his back.

I stood in the middle of the hallway looking at nothing. A blank expression settled in my eyes, and for the first time in my life, in a long time, a nigga wasn't tracking shit. I heard, saw, felt, and smelled nothing.

Ray-Ray's voice finally broke through to my dome, when her hand reached out to shake me.

"Trigga! You straight tripping and acting like a stupid nigga now. Trigga! Wake up!" she screamed at me.

Had I been checkin' for her, like actually seeing her, I would have seen that she was staring at me confused, kinda pissed, not sure about why the fuck I was flipping out, and also trying to keep the other niggas from hearing me.

The sensation of her nails digging in my skin as she shook and gripped my arm had me turning around and snatching her by her throat. I lifted her so high in the air, her feet started dangling as she struggled and tried to kick me. Like, a nigga wasn't himself at all.

That nigga Dame was in my head laughing, over and over. All I saw was his fuckin' face in her, and I slammed her hard against the hall wall. Kept slamming her, until her screams cut through to me.

"You a lying-ass bitch! You lyin'!" I growled then yelled at her, not seeing nothing. I literally saw blackness. Darkness. She wasn't there. It was those niggas that used my mom like a fuck toy.

My fist smashed into the wall, causing pictures to fall. I squeezed Ray-Ray's throat.

She croaked out, "I can show you. I ain't lying. Let me go, Trigga, please!"

Her pleas sounded like my mom, and it fucked me up further. My mom had told me to stay hiding, and I did. *Damn! I fuckin' did.*

Ray-Ray continued clawing at my hands, cutting them to where they bled, but I didn't feel a damn thing. A nigga was all the way numb, but I heard her repeating that she could show me that she wasn't lying, so I let go of her throat.

The sound of her falling to the floor like a sack of potatoes had me finally seeing her for the first time. My locks swung around me as I shook my head, and I balled both of my fists and bowed my head in shame. I wanted to say sorry, but fuck! What could a nigga say about choking a shawty up like some scum-ass bitch?

So instead of saying, "My bad," my priority—no, my obsession—became seeing the proof of what she said. Anger had me heated, which made me point down the hall. "Show me," I commanded.

Ray-Ray's eyes darted nervously at my Glock, which I held in my hand. Yeah, if what she said was true, a nigga was damn sure going to use it.

She quickly took me to Dame's room, a place I never had stepped into. The moment I did, I wished I had never done so. Shit felt like my personal gateway to hell once I saw DOA carved in his headboard. Blood seemed to suddenly spill from each letter.

The sound of my pops being capped then the grunts and wet thrusts of the niggas digging my momma out echoed in my head. I heard her screams through her gagged mouth. She screamed in a way that said, "Stay hiding."

I remember seeing her on that bed looking at me with unshed tears. Tears she'd never let fall for these niggas, tears she only let slide down her battered face once she looked into my eyes.

In that moment, shit for me changed just that fast. I turned to walk out the room and zoned the fuck out. Everything was like a tunnel for me. I heard Ray-Ray running behind me and trying to stop me, but it wasn't working. She fell, being dragged by me as I walked on.

She screamed for Big Jake, who must have been coming up the steps. I didn't see him, and I didn't give a damn if I did. In that moment, homie or not, he could have gotten the taste of my fist in his mouth. I just needed to get out of this place, needed to find that nigga Dame.

Pushing through the hallway, it took Big Jake snatching me by my throat then wrapping his arm tight around it, locking me in a choke hold to keep me in place. My fist connected to his face, but he squeezed tighter, causing me to grind my teeth. A nigga was gone. I was ready to take my life and hand it to Dame, just to take his fuckin' ass out, and all I saw on rewind was that nigga over my momma, punching her, laughing his signature laugh, and flipping her to sit her pussy on his face, exposing the DOA tat on his back.

I swear to fuckin' God I was going to end him. His blood was mine. And all this time, like a stupid-ass nigga, I was working for my own enemy, getting close?

I struggled again against Big Jake. *Does this nigga know who the fuck I am? Is he playing me this whole time, making me work for him 'cuz the shit is funny? Yo, if his pops wasn't already dead, that nigga would get it too.*

I had learned in the streets that his pops had put a hit out on my pops, because some kid my pops had helped ended up in the pen then tried to take him out, using my pops' name as the reason for it. Nigga lied.

My pops worked the streets as an activist to stop all this bullshit in the streets, 'cuz he came from the same type of bullshit in Brooklyn. So Dame's punk-ass father was hating it. And he was even more upset that one of my pops' street kids had actually got in the pen and almost took him out. Yeah, now that nigga was eating dirt, and Dame was king of DOA. Bullshit!

The sound of doors closing and darkness surrounding me let me know Big Jake had taken us to our private spot in the house. He dragged me and yelled at Ray-Ray to turn on the lights. My mind flipped on rewind again. I needed to be let go right the fuck now.

"No, Trig, man, he's not here. He's with Anika, a'ight. Anika sent a car for him. That crazy bitch Sasha cut up some new trick, so she's sittin' in the basement now too." Big Jake tried to get me to chill the fuck out, but it wasn't working.

"A'ight, so let me go to find that muthafucka!"

"Bro, listen to me. It's not that time yet, trust me. Every nigga in this house gotta agenda, and now, Trig, a nigga I call my brother, my blood, you do too. You're smarter than this, homie," Big Jake's voice quietly muttered next to my ear.

I realized that I must have been shouting out everything I was thinking, and that shit had a nigga feeling crazy.

The sound of a door opening then locking, mixed with the click of heels and scent of sugar and bubble gum, let me know that Gina was in the room and back from shaking her pussy at Magic City. A part of me wanted to cap those niggas too for having her underage pussy up in there. Her soft gasp, then the jingle of her purse hitting the ground, seemed to fuck with me too.

"Big Jake, let Trigga go right now. You don't do that. That's not nice. Let him go."

Gina moved to tug on Big Jake's massive arm, but Ray-Ray pulled her back to stop her.

"Gina, chill. Trigga is on some other shit," Ray-Ray whispered.

I heard her tell Gina everything, and before I knew it, Gina was sobbing like a baby.

Every nigga had a sob story, and mine was blowing up in my face.

Big Jake's words came at me again as he tried to get me to stop bucking at him. No lie, I knew, somewhere in the back of my mind, that he was right. That just that fast, with the truth of everything, I almost lost my throne. Something Pops said never do. Not unless I want to.

The reality of that all settled in, and I stopped fighting. I lifted my hands in the air so that my guns would fall to the floor. Big Jake cautiously let me go and pushed down on my shoulders to sit me down.

Never in my life had I seen Big Jake look the way he did as he sat in front of me. His usually brown eyes were dark as sin. It almost looked as if the nigga wanted to cry while he sat back on his hunches.

That moment shook me up. I had never had another person care for me since my parents and Mama Lupe. Every person who cared for me had died, and I had stopped caring about them. Now Big Jake was sitting here looking like a nigga who had just lost the only thing that was keeping him grounded in the game, and I can't lie, a nigga felt like shit about it all.

My eyes darted left and right like a crazy nigga, trying to find a way to escape, even as my brain woke up, telling me to get back on my nigga shit. It literally slapped a nigga, telling me that I had one of baddest killas outside of me on my side, and not the nigga who called himself king of this house. I had the respect with true loyalty, and now I was punking out. I needed to get my shit in line.

"You don't want to do this shit, Trig, man, trust me . . . not yet. You remember everything you told me, homie? Remember how we talked about having plan B? About just getting by to get by? Listen, for real listen, bro, every nigga gotta agenda, remember I told you that? Just told you that again. Answer me." Big Jake shook my shoulders then pulled his own Glock on me, pressing it against my temple.

I licked my lips in that moment and nodded, rapidly responding, "Yeah, yeah, I remember, man. Blood bond, me and you. But you're going to have to put a bullet in my dome to stop me from killing that nigga."

Big Jake shook his head and kept his gaze on me. "Fuck that! I'm your guard, nigga. I'm not putting a fuckin' bullet in you, unless you try to get yourself killed, like you doing right now."

The only nigga in this house, outside of Gina, who could make me laugh, ran a hand down his face and stared at me like a pastor in a pulpit. I looked him in his knowing eyes.

Big Jake said, "Listen, you will, my nigga. We all get shots at the motherfucka. Even me. Listen, God makes shit happen in a way we never understand. Yours was to get next to Dame, so was mine."

Big Jake put his Glock away then pulled out his cross, a necklace he told me his grandmother had given him the day he learned he was going to be drafted in the NFL. He held it tight in his hands and kissed it. "Remember I told you I got shot in the streets, kept me from going to the NFL? Well, Dame was that nigga that ordered it. He wanted me to be his bodyguard, told me to fuck that NFL shit, that I'd make more money working and protect him than I did in the game. I told him naw. He came after my grandma then me. Now I'm here. Every nigga got an agenda. He thought I didn't know he did that shit, but yeah, I did. I made him think I didn't. Big Jake, Dame's pit bull, loyal bodyguard, and protector was my role. But, on some real truth, fuck that shit! Every nigga gotta agenda, even me. ENGA tatted on my arm for life."

What he told me blew my mind. He'd never told me that part of his story, and I never questioned his truth, just rode with it and felt like I could trust the nigga. *Damn.* I dropped my head and covered my hand over my face. Shit was crazy, too fuckin' crazy, but I was not about to let that Dame nigga break me down.

No tears, no bitch-ass weakness, none of that. A nigga didn't care anymore. Big Jake was right. I needed to get back on my plan, and I needed to follow his own game.

I looked up at the brotha that always held me down when I thought I couldn't trust not one damn nigga in the street and I sat still. "A'ight. Back to the game."

Pushing my hoodie out my face, I looked around at everyone who surrounded me. Everyone one there wanted Dame dead, and now I was part of that shit.

I glanced at Ray-Ray and remembered what I did. "I didn't shoot your people, shawty, and my bad for how I just did you. Y'all don't have to worry about shit from me. I'm back to me, doing the same shit I started to do. Now my game has just changed." I pushed up from the chair Big Jake sat me in, and we both gave each other dap.

Gina then said, "So we gon' kill that nigga, right? Piss on his grave and he ain't even in that shit? 'Cuz I got my story too. See, Baby G was never wanted. Was called a mistake baby. So ma momma put me out at sixteen 'cuz she only had me just to try and keep my daddy. So, 'cuz all we did was fight, the streets was ma home. Then Ray-Ray's momma found me and brought me to Dame. That sour cabbage patch-pussy bitch Sasha then played her game and got me sent to the basement. But Big Jake helped me before that, didn't ya?"

Gina gave the sweetest smile. She looked like a normal eighteen-year-old who wasn't fucked with badly, one who looked in love, while she looked at Big Jake.

"Then Dame came down there and watched wit' Sasha as they piped me. So, ahuh, I got my agenda too. You all we got, Trigga. You are. You and Big Jake the only ones that protect me, brought me pretty things, Happy Meals, made me feel safe in this chaos. Don't let him turn you like me, Trig. Please don't. Can we please take him out? Please?"

The love, concern, and loyalty in her voice had a nigga feeling stupid for how I acted before. I had nothing I could say for real outside what I did. All these tears from her was fuckin' with me. I could see Ray-Ray still looking confused and unsure about everything that was going on, which in that moment brought me back to reality.

"No more tears, baby doll. I got you always, like I told you day one. You remind me of who my baby sister coulda been, like before all that shit you went through. Know that. I always got you." I watched her blush then smile before sitting down on a table next to Ray-Ray.

Quietly exhaling, I cracked my neck and then lowered my voice. A nigga was back in the game. I knew the house had ears, so everything we did from then on out had to continue to be done in code. Me and Big Jake quickly taught Ray-Ray our code. We had to school her. She now was part of this fam, because of what she had shared with me. Now a nigga could be down with her crazy ass, but she needed to learn how to be smarter about shit.

Big Jake and I quickly shared what our plans had been from the start of working with Dame. We'd never intended to stay with this crazy-ass nigga. It had always been to get money then leave.

Big Jake's additional plan was to step out of the way of a bullet one day that would be aiming for Dame, and now I was in on that part. That nigga was going to get his, and everyone quietly talking was aiming to doing it.

I let them know that Dame was working on getting some new pure shit from another cartel set overseas, the Vietnamese and French.

"Nigga is scraping to get his money back, thanks to how li'l shawty's parents played him. Now we need to get those stashes and money that they hid, and we need to teach li'l shawty how to throw bones, a'ight. I feel like I'm some scheming-ass nigga right now, so we need to go back upstairs and do our shit."

Everyone stood watching me. Big Jake gave me dap. I reached out and tugged on Gina's braids then she turned to touch the side of Big Jake's face. Ray-Ray was standing looking down at the floor, holding her arm, before Gina tugged on her, pulling her away.

I quickly reached out to grab Ray-Ray, turning her around to look down in her big eyes. "Thank you for sharing. Like I said, my bad. And what's your real name?"

A nigga felt real lame once Ray-Ray looked up at me and tried to get some attitude in her, sucking her teeth.

"Why? What's yours?"

See, I ain't neva been about some chick trying to game me, so I wasn't about to let Ray-Ray punk my ass. I was still Trigga, regardless of all this extra-sappy violin shit, so I gripped her arm and lightly shook her, pulling her closer to me.

"Look, chill with all that bullshit, a'ight. If you want to survive, you come in this family with your agenda on the table, a'ight. When alone, we all talk to each other on some real nigga shit. Big Jake is Jackson Hawkes, Baby G, is Gina Lewis, me, my name is dangerous, mama, because of who my people were, so only Jake knows. So I'm just asking. Your momma treated me right, and I had nothing but respect for her. That's why I help you. So if you're with us, then you got a family for life, one that will hold you down and take down whoever the fuck you need, 'cuz your enemies are ours. So with that, li'l shawty, what's your name?"

Something in the way Ray-Ray looked up at me had a nigga hearing my mom's words again. *"A jaguar can never be made pussy, and jaguar is always a queen."* Just her closeness alone had a nigga feeling funny, but at the same time, I could tell she still was on some bullshit, so I let go of her hand and walked way, annoyed with her kiddy-ass games.

While my back was still to her, I shook out my locks and ran both hands down my face as I heard her quietly say, "Diamond. And one day you're going to tell me your name, nigga. I'm down for this family because I ain't got anyone like y'all, been hurt in this game like y'all, so yeah whoever your enemies are mine, too. E.N.G.A. And because you liked my mama. Thanks for helping me. And my bad too; now we even."

A smirk flashed across my face as something about this moment had me thinking about Kendrick Lemar's "Poetic Justice."

The sound of my cell thumping Geto Boy's "Trigga Happy Nigga" let me know Dame was sending me on another hit. I put my hoodie on my head then slid my hands in my pockets before turning around to look Diamond in her pretty doe eyes. "Pookie will get his next, and then we'll work from there, a'ight?"

Diamond stood watching for the longest while my cell kept ringing. My dick slowly left its imprint in my jeans when she licked her lips, giving me a sexy smirk.

She stepped up close, where her feet were in front of mine, then whispered, "A'ight."

I hit answer on my smartphone then lifted it to my ear. Dame barked out some more orders. Dame had fucked with the wrong ones in the trap. His time was definitely about to be up. Game was back on, and his goods were now about to be ours.

Episode Two:
Every Nigga Gotta Agenda

"Feign disorder, and crush him."
—SUN TZU

Ray-Ray

Shit was moving fast, almost too fast. Trigga had a plan. I didn't know what that plan was, but I knew it involved us taking out Dame and getting the hell out of the game. I hadn't seen the outside of Dame's mansion since I had been brought into the house. At times I found myself hating my parents for stealing from the nigga and then having me inherit their debt. I knew that before Dame would allow me to leave, he would kill me first. Once a nigga like Dame had control over your life, it was no longer yours and would never be again.

"So, how we gon' get rid of Dame, Trigga?" Gina asked as we all stood around that room.

Trigga had just found out that Dame had been one of the masterminds behind murdering his parents and raping his mother. The raw, uncut killer instinct he possessed showed in the way that nigga's upper lip kept twitching.

"We ain't really got time to be jawing, Baby G. We gotta get out of this room before niggas start to notice we all missing. You know how they talk in this joint."

"We don't even have a plan," I said. "How we supposed to take a nigga like Dame out without one?"

Trigga looked at me. I could tell he was still frustrated and annoyed. He ain't look like he wanted to be answering no twenty-one questions.

"Look, first thing first, li'l shawty, we all gotta play a part in this shit for us to get out of here alive. I ain't trying to wait months or weeks to get shit popping. A nigga want out. My mental ain't right, right now."

"And some of us may not make it out alive," Big Jake said, almost cutting Trigga off.

"Don't say that, Jackson," Gina's baby-soft voice said. It was so light you almost didn't hear it.

She walked over and wrapped her arms around Big Jake's waist. To be honest, it looked like a gnat trying to hug a big-ass bull. I could tell she was in love. I wondered just how the hell she could find love with all that had happened to her. And how could Big Jake love her, knowing what Dame did to her and what he made her do? It made me wonder if a man would ever love me if he knew what I let Dame do to me every chance he got.

But I couldn't focus on that because what Big Jake had said rang true to me. By the time all of this would be over, there was a possibility that one or none of us wouldn't make it out of there. I just felt that shit in my heart. It could have been fear, simple fear, but I felt it.

"Yo, he's right, li'l shawty." Trigga looked from Gina back to me. "You gotta be smart now. No wild shit. Play ya cards and keep ya eyes and ears open. You hear me?"

I nodded. I kept my eyes on Trigga, just like he kept his eyes on me. Something silent passed between us in that moment. I had to wonder, when all this shit was over, would he even still want to be around me. Probably not. He would probably go on to bigger and better things. I didn't know when or if I could return to school. I was only sixteen with nowhere to go. Shit, I didn't even have no family to run to. I would be alone when all was said and done.

Maybe I could go live with my best friend Dominique and her parents, I thought. Yeah, that would be what I would do once everything was over.

"Come on, Big Jake, bro, we got to get the fuck up outta here." Trigga turned to look back at me. "Play ya cards right, li'l shawty. Remember the codes to look for," was all he said before him and Big Jake disappeared again to do Dame's bidding.

For the next two hours, until Dame got back home, me and Gina talked in codes. I had to make sure I could read them and understand them at any given moment. All of the stories told, from Big Jake's to Trigga's to Gina's, mirrored mine. All I knew was that the end was soon. I prayed to God that I'd live long enough to see it and enjoy the day when Dame would no longer rule my life.

I didn't see how Gina had been able to survive this long. I was ready to give up, and it had only been two weeks, maybe three. Shit, I couldn't tell anymore. The days had started to run into one other. I couldn't imagine being attached to that nigga for two years.

"Dame an evil nigga, baby. It ain't gon' get no better."

I looked up and saw my mama standing by the window of Dame's room. The sun was shining, I could tell. She was still in the same clothes she had been killed in. Sometimes I wondered if she was just a figment of my imagination. I couldn't tell, because it felt like I was living a constant nightmare.

"It has to, Mama. It has to."

"Naw, baby. That nigga gon' kill you before he see you walk free of 'im. Always do whatcha gotta do to survive, Ray-Ray. Always."

"What the fuck you and Gina in here bumping yo' gums about?" Dame asked as soon as he walked into his bedroom, jarring me from my thoughts.

That told me he had been watching us. She and I had been silent for at least thirty minutes before he'd walked in.

I'd been so caught up in what was going on with Trigga when he had choked me up, I had forgotten about the cameras all over the house. I was hoping he didn't see or hear anything.

"Nothing," I answered a little too quickly.

His hazel eyes cut over at me, and his lips were turned up like something in the room stunk. "Get the fuck off my bed!" he ordered. "And why the fuck y'all shoes all over my shit, bitch?"

My right eye twitched when he called me a bitch, and I knew he saw it, from the way his frown turned into a semi-smirk. The look on his face dared me to do or say anything he didn't like.

Gina quickly jumped up and grabbed our shoes.

"Drop them!" he ordered her.

She did without hesitation. The nervousness with which she darted her eyes between me and Dame unsettled me.

"Diamond, get the fuck up and clean my shit!" he barked.

This nigga is on one, I thought.

Gina and I exchanged quick glances as I got up and began to clean like he demanded.

"You a deaf-mute or some shit now, ho? You don't hear me talking to you?"

"I do. I'm up cleaning like you asked me," I responded with just a little too much attitude in my voice.

Before I could even roll my eyes, like I had planned to, he snatched me up by the back of my hair just as I was kneeling to pick up the shoes. I didn't even know what I was being snatched up for, but that was how it was with a nigga like Dame. At any given moment he would beat your ass, and you had no idea why.

My eyes found Gina again. She was standing, wringing her hands and chewing on her bottom lip as she watched on. The fear in her eyes was real.

"Keep talking to me like you stupid," he told me through gritted teeth. He had my feet damn near dangling off the floor, one hand trying to snatch me bald, the other hand around my throat.

My eyes started to water, and that healthy fear I had of him covered me. "I didn't say nothing, Dame."

"You still talking now, ho? And call me by my name again."

"Daddy, I—"

"Shut the fuck up! Let another muthafucka tell me you was eyeing them, like you don't know I own every muthafuckin' thing about you, and I'ma fuck you up to the point nobody gonna recognize yo' ass but me. What the fuck was you staring at Anika so hard for? Huh? You know how much money you just cost me, bitch?"

This nigga was getting at me for some shit that I'd done the night before. I really couldn't think, because his big hand was like a vise-grip around my neck.

"She didn't know, Daddy," Gina said, her light voice shaky.

Her reward was a quick backhand that sent her stumbling across the room. Her body crashed into the table against the wall before she hit the floor hard.

I closed my eyes, but he made me open them with another vise-like grip around my neck.

"You bitches getting outta hand, costing me fuckin' money. And a nigga already about two million short because of the dumb shit your ho-ass parents pulled off." As he talked he jerked my neck and backed me up until I had fallen back on the bed. "Don't you ever in your muthafuckin' life look at another muthafucka, male or female! You understand me?"

I thought the nigga was about to kill me. The back of my head felt like it was being shoved through the mattress, and my eyeballs were about to pop out. My head started to swim, and my chest started to burn because I couldn't breathe. I couldn't answer him, couldn't even nod.

The vein in the center of Dame's head looked like it was about to explode. I was so focused on trying to breathe as my hands gripped at his wrist, I didn't even realize he had pushed my dress up around my waist and snatched my underwear off. When I realized what was about to happen, my mind screamed no over and over again.

Yeah, I had let the nigga fuck me as many times as he wanted. I ain't have a choice. But I didn't ever want to experience what it felt like to be raped. I didn't want to know what it felt like to have my pussy violently taken.

I guess that was what had me reaching and trying to swing to fight back. His hand only left my neck after he had used his muscled thighs to force my legs open. I swung blindly. My open palms caught his face as I clawed his eyes and screamed, trying to get away from him.

That nigga looked like he was possessed. The more I fought him, the more he seemed to be turned on by it. He got control of my swinging fists after a while and used one hand to hold my hands over my head.

My screams rent the air. "Nooooooo!"

But no matter how I screamed, "No!" and "Stop!" what I feared most happened. When he shoved his dick inside of me, it was more painful than when he had taken my virginity. His dick felt like it was coated in sandpaper, like he was shoving a Cadillac where a ten-speed bike should go. I could feel my pussy ripping because Dame was like an animal on top of me. There was no moisture, no wetness to ease the pain, but only raw digging inside of me that had my pussy on fire and feeling like it was being shaved with a sharp blade cutting into my skin.

When he grunted loudly and then laughed as his hand pushed down in my face hard, I knew he was trying to kill me. His teeth found my titties and nipples, and I swear to

God he was trying to bite them off. The more I struggled, the harder and faster he pushed in and out of me, and the harder he bit down on my titty.

Dame sat back on his haunches and took control of my hips as he jackknifed me. Once again, it felt like my womb was about to fall out. I cried out loud, praying for some kind of reprieve, but none came. He didn't even seem to care that I was punching and clawing at his face.

He growled out like a rabid animal, and his hands found my throat again, like he was trying to choke me to death while raping me. From time to time he would slap me in my face for good measure.

It didn't matter; I was still trying to fight him off. It made little difference because he was too big and too strong. Then he grabbed a pillow and held it down over my face.

I guess Big Jake was right—Some of us weren't going to make it out alive.

It became harder and harder for me to breathe, and my chest was on fire. The dizziness took over, and after a while, so did blackness. The more consciousness I lost, the harder he used his dick to stab me. He did it harder, faster, deeper, and rougher each stroke, until he shot his demonic seed inside of me.

As he released his nut, he pushed the pillow down harder over my face. My arms went limp beside me, and finally I stopped struggling against him. He moved the pillow only then and gazed down at me. I could barely see him.

"Next time, I'm going to kill you and wear your eyeballs crystalized around my neck to remember you by," he told me, his voice calm, cool, and collected like he hadn't just raped me.

He got off the bed humming the song, "I Only Have Eyes for You."

This couldn't be real, I found myself thinking. *It couldn't be.* He didn't have to rape me, since he'd been fuckin' me against my will and doing to my body what he wanted anyway.

Gina's sobs in the corner of the room reminded me that it was real. What had just happened was my reality and would be until either he or I was dead.

Trigga

Master Sun Tzu said in so many words, in order to survive the art of war, you gotta fake the game and support the other cat's arrogance. He also said, in the game of warfare, it was all based on deception and that opportunities grew as they were seized.

Learning that nigga Dame who was my boss, the man I devoted my skill set to, was the same who birthed me into this game of vengeance had a nigga feeling played like a muthafucka.

The power in the anger I felt had me leaving his spot to go get inked up, so that I wouldn't take that nigga out right then and there. It was each word of power and wisdom Sun Tzu said that was freshly inked on my body. I'd gone against my own rule of never getting inked, just to keep my mind at ease. Coded verses ran down my forearms and on the right side of my neck. Those words kept me cool in my plotting and reminded me of the foul shit that nigga had committed against me.

I was chilling listening to *The Art of War* while glancing at my inner arm to get encouragement not to barrel three bullets into that nigga's skull and slice his throat as he fell on his knees. See, that was my dreams and soon to be his fuckin' nightmare. The screams of every broad he ever hurt with his power echoed in my mind, the screams my moms never let out.

My pops schooled me on how to shoot and clean every gun you could think of, when to shoot, and why. At that time it wasn't 'cuz of hurt feelings. Naw, he taught me how to heal and take responsibility for what I put into this world, this game. My responsibility was to break Dame and end him all in the same moment. Those words repeated in my dreams.

Cold Glock. No pity. No shame. Just his blood coating my hands and my pops' as the Trap lost all power and the streets went black. I always woke up then. My chest was always heavy with that empty feeling that Dame was still breathing and that he was now my master. The shackles I got inked on my wrist were, no doubt, real.

Swift as the wind. Quiet as the forest. Conquer like the fire. Steady as the mountain.

Sun Tzu's words and that of the master Malcolm X always kept me grounded, and if it wasn't for Big Jake, I knew I wouldn't be here to handle my mission in life. To return the favor of what was done unto me and mine.

The block was busy as usual. Homeless cats slowly walked by looking for spots to chill or asking for whatever they could. Niggas and broads lost to the needle, bottle, dust, or all of the above and more stumbled by thirsty as fuck. My name popped off on some of their mouths, but they knew not to even come at me as I sat outside the house of one of Dame's PBs (product bitches). PBs were chicks who stashed small amounts of product and sold it under the guise of different businesses.

Minx's home was a salon with a barbershop in the back. I sat on the front of her porch only because her A/C was broken; otherwise, I never let myself sit out open to be shot or fucked up.

Ma's thighs were thick and amber, cushy-soft. Ask me how I know. 'Cuz I sat right there between them while her fingers played in my locks. My red Jordans rested on each step next to my glass of ice water. My dark jeans matching my black hooded leather jacket set off my checkered red button-up, which concealed my Glock. Minx had said she liked my style. I ignored her but appreciated the compliment.

I actually kinda dug her only because when she worked on my locks, braiding them back like she was doing now, she would sing, and her thighs always smelled like vanilla. Never understood why Dame didn't bring her into the house, but it was probably because she had a foul mouth and liked to fight a lot, which was annoying as fuck.

Made my mind think back to Dame's spot, where Ray-Ray (aka Diamond) was still housed. If this was supposed to be her life for now, stuck with that nigga Dame until I popped him or someone else did, then my hope was that she took what we schooled her on and worked it to get like Minx quickly for her safety.

Minx had a decent setup. She looked to be twenty-one or a little bit older. Tits sat high, ass round and lush. I know she had a clean pussy. Seen Dame hit it once or twice. But I didn't know for myself. Sometimes broads had to snatch up what they could to survive, just like niggas, and maybe Minx was like that and maybe Diamond would get like that too.

Diamond had hit me with a lot of questions about the plan. On some real shit, I didn't have time to tell her, and a nigga kinda didn't want to tell her shit, just in case Dame got to her and did some more crazy shit to her to make her talk. I knew she was a part of this team, so I needed to tell her something, just wasn't sure how much and when.

Now with that nigga being my target, my old plan was ready to go down. I just had to fit it around Jake, Gina, and now Diamond. Having worked for Dame for so long, growing up in the ranks, shit almost felt like destiny that

I got set up right where I was. My Glock ready to rest against that nigga's head, shit kinda had me smiling. The sound of my cell blazing "Trigga Happy Nigga" cut through my audiobook and thoughts. Right away, I knew it was that nigga Dame. He had been deep into working on something new with the Nigerian queen and Jamaican Kings.

Dame had been mad silent on any new moves for us all on the block and in the main house. With his right hand freshly murked by me, it was up to that nigga Pookie and me to handle business, which made my finger itch like crazy. Working with niggas you didn't trust really wasn't that hard when you knew you planned on taking the muthafuckas out real soon.

Anyway, Dame was back to handling house business. Since I was new to the role of being his right, I was learning some shit I had no idea about. And the fact that he was telling me to hit him up ASAP meant I had some more shit to learn.

As I headed out, Minx hit me with the ducats she made from her dealings and a fiyah plate of food for Dame and me—baked mac and cheese, ox tail, greens, and some soft bread. I quickly let her know I was on my bike and wasn't the fuckin' delivery, so she kissed my cheek, took the food, and gave it to one of her homegirls to bring to the house later.

Getting back to Dame's place didn't take long. I had my bike only because I was close to Dame's and wasn't trying to draw attention. I always flipped my routine, just in case. Feel me?

Dropping my hood, I dug my hands in my jean pockets and headed through the house to his office. One hard knock on the door let him know it was me. The sound of talking on the monitors greeted me while I walked through, closing the door behind me.

"Don't even sit, nigga," Dame coolly ordered. He stood at his full height, back facing me, dressed like a Miami don. Nigga had on all white, from the leather Italian shoes he sported, to his dress pants, on up to his open button-down shirt. Dude was on some extra shit, for real.

The desire to paint the walls and his clothes with his blood almost made my eyes roll into the back of my skull, but I kept my cool, sucking my teeth and curling my mouth, showing my teeth. Not sitting at the moment was good with me.

I walked forward then stood wide-legged, holding the straps of the backpack I sported. Glancing quickly to check my surroundings, because you never knew what might be up with a crazy nigga like Dame, I calmly pulled out his money for the day from my bag. I slapped down each stack neatly on his desk and put my all-black leather backpack neatly on the floor. It was then, as I sat the bag down, that I saw the frozen image of Diamond and me in the hallway on the screen.

Through all the fuckin' drama, I had forgotten he had eyes everywhere. I knew I had to think fast and remember to give props to Big Jake on how he handled me, because all the shit I spat out was not heard. Heading into Dame's room wasn't even shown, which was a close call. But I knew that nigga was pissed, the way he scoped the cameras, but I was slightly amused. Naw, I was most definitely deeply amused at the moment.

Dame turned to me, his high-yellow complexion tinted red in anger, his nostrils flared like a dragon from a cartoon.

"Tell me what the fuck you doing yakkin' up with my Diamond?" he growled. His eyes were the color of soot, and he was spitting fire. "And you tell me that shit in a way that doesn't have me cutting your nuts off so fast."

Like on some real shit, that nigga growled like a fuckin' dog, sounding like DMX or some shit. This lame-ass nigga was crazy.

Anyone who knew me well, and that was no one, would have known I was ready to fuck with that pussy-nigga's mental, but because I had to keep this front up, a nigga had to keep playing like I was down for this punk, even though I wanted to murk that cat.

"Was word on the street 'bout ya stolen stash that was hidden. Found out that ya shawty may know more than she was letting on, so I had word sent to her to question her for you since you was strengthening ya house with the Nigerian queen, bossman. That was it, and that was all." I shrugged.

It amazed me how fast I was able to twist this shit around and cover all of us in the process. The plan was to take the stash for ourselves and pin that shit on others, but things changed, and this nigga Dame was looking mad suspect.

Not only was dude looking mad suspect, but the nigga looked like he had been fucked up by a cat. Shit made me laugh on the low. Nigga was sporting several slashes across his face, and across his eye and eyebrow.

Quickly doing a once-over, I noticed that it looked like something tried to bite that nigga's neck, and I heard my mom's words in my mind, *A queen is a jaguar, and a jaguar can never be made pussy. Damn, Diamond!* That muthafucka deserved what he was sporting and more.

"I found out some shit that had me pissed off about who you keep 'round you, bossman. Shit was not a good look, not at all. I learned that ya nigga Pookie was linked up with ya diamond, Ray-Ray's parents. Shawty told me that she had just remembered that she heard him in the house. You weren't here to tell, so I got lucky and was able to find out for you.

"Ya diamond is devoted to you just like all ya dolls are now. You got her right where you need and wanted, bossman. Because she wanted to show you her loyalty by telling you what she had heard from Pookie's lips about the location of the stash. That's what you see"—I pointed at the screen of Big Jake holding me back, stepping closer to his large, dark oak desk, not even fazed by the way his soulless eyes tried to dissect me.

"I was 'bout to take that nigga out. Then I knew I had to question your property to see what she knew, so I didn't murk that nigga." I paused to lick my lips, rubbing my fisted hands in front of me. I played my role, making sure to lace my words with hints of shielded fear, when in reality I felt nothing.

"I got ya coins back, bossman, all of it, and checked the safe houses out, since I had to wait, bossman. Pookie needs to be handled. Nigga's grimy as fuck. Everything else is icing."

Now the waiting game was on. It was like some *Jeopardy* bullshit in the flesh.

I could oftentimes read Dame's moves. If he was about to kill you, his light eyes would go dark, but not before they lightened. If he was gonna play you, his middle finger would start tapping either on his thigh or on whatever was near his finger. If his lips turned into a quick scowl and his eyebrows dropped, you knew to duck and ride the fuck out.

Right now his face was blank. There was nothing to read, which meant the nigga was thinking. I knew even that could be a trick because if he leaned right, just even by an inch, shit was about to drop off.

He moved to the left then leaned back. I watched him in caution but not fear.

"Everythang is icing. You must not be scared of me, nigga, huh?" he asked, his voice dangerously low. He had a flash of a crazy look in his eyes for whatever reason. Like nigga was on some shit, paranoid, hearing-dead-people type of crazy. Shit was getting real.

I said nothing. Knew not to even respond.

"Naw, I see ya are, sweat on ya brow. Boo, nigga! Boo!" Dame's voice rumbled. He swiftly shifted then jerked forward, bucking at me. Laughter spilled from his contorted face while he clapped both hands together. That nigga was cracking himself up, as if he knew something I didn't.

Man. I almost busted that nigga in his fuckin' throat. My jaw ticked in annoyance, hidden by my hood. I rolled my shoulders to keep cool and played the game. Inside though, a nigga was battling with himself. I wanted to bash that nigga's head. All I did was step back and not flinch at that monkey muthafucka.

"You da the only loyal-ass nigga to my name, and that's how it should be. You question her, but you already know, you touch what's mine again and it's ya life. Understood?"

I knew to answer then. "It ain't even something to question me about, bossman. I don't want your world. Know what I mean? Don't want ya jewels or dolls. I'm here to be ya gun and protect your kingdom. You never gotta worry 'bout me ever touchin' what's yours. My word is bond. This is why I went through the right ranks to get to her, Big Jake then Gina. Niggas like Pookie seemed to want more than they can handle. Might be time to give him what he can't swallow, if you trust me, bossman."

Dame moved around his office, noticing the stacks that lay on his desk as if checking for them for the first time. He picked up and fanned through each one.

"Now this is what I trust—my ducats. Any man who brings me my dollars and does not undercut me earns my respect, and you . . . are my prized property, Trigga. Took you from the gutter, polished you into my weapon, watched you bring me mad stacks and keep my shit in

line as my eyes, sometimes seeing more than I do. Never
was my intention to bring you into my world as my right
hand so soon, nigga, but shit happens. You talk about not
wanting what's mine. Nigga, well, I'm grooming you to
get your own kingdom, this one, once I move on to bigger,
better thangs. So don't disappoint me, Trigga. Don't.
Because it ain't shit to kill what I most prize."

Listening to him was like listening to bees fuckin' in the
wind. I couldn't care two shits about his dramatic bullshit
and rites of passage. Blood was what I wanted, and if
being patient and accepting what I didn't want was my
means of getting his blood, then I'd be 'bout that life. So I
nodded in respect and relaxed my stance.

I quietly responded, "Yeah, bossman, my loyalty is
yours, Dame."

The harsh slap of a couple of stacks against my chest
then raining down at my feet caught my attention. This
muthafucka really didn't understand who the fuck he
created, but I let him have it. Wasn't shit else I could do.
Feel me?

The sound of Dame's office chair squeaking let me
know he was sitting at his desk. I casually dropped down
into a crouch and picked up the cash he threw at me.

"Claim your pay, and let me sit and think on what to
do about that bitch, Pookie. Don't snap his life so quickly;
he may be useful to the game. As my right, you need to
protect not just me now but this house and what's in it.
That means the dolls and my diamond. Like I said, that
doesn't mean you can touch my diamond, nigga. Sear
that shit in your skull. The dolls you can do what the fuck
you want, as usual, but Ray-Ray is mine. Understood?"

My head tilted in a nod while my mind worked the
game. Promise, the cat was jealous as fuck. All he could
talk about was me touching Diamond. Part of me liked
that I shook his foundation, but I knew that nigga. His

type of crazy was wrapped around his image. I knew that whatever he was thinking was going to have Diamond in danger. Wasn't shit I could tell him. He had it already set in his brain, so I listened as he set down my new rules as his co-regent.

"As my right, the prince of this house, you need to keep a fresh crib so you moving up. Big Jake will give you the keys to your new spot, and you can stop riding around on that busted bike. I'll get you a better one, plus another new whip. A'ight, your pay is up more than before, and you still my gun, so you doing double time.

"Some major players are coming in soon. I'll have to school you, so you can negotiate and know how to talk to these cats. A'ight, get out my shit. I'll hit you up again later. Welcome to the inner circle, nigga."

Bitterness settled in my throat the moment my eyes settled on my boss. I saw me taking the Japanese sword he had on the wall behind him and using it to slide through the middle of his throat, working through bone and shimmying it upward to slide through his skull. The game had changed and what I was envisioning was proof that I had watched too much *Ghost Dog* and *Kill Bill* on DVD.

The sound of Dame snapping his fingers while reading a notepad drew my attention.

"Yo, before you go. One of those playas I'm working with are some Russians. Look up krokodil and school yourself on that shit. We might have our hands on that product and will distribute it soon. A'ight, bounce."

"A'ight, I got you, bossman." Stepping back, I pounded my fist against my heart then walked out, closing the door behind me.

The sound of him rewinding through the videos let me know he may have said one thing about me, but his growing obsession over Ray-Ray was showing me his weakness and mistrust of me.

Wasn't shit a nigga could do. Pussy always controls the game, once it gets introduced to a leading dick, and most times, that was when that playa starts decaying.

I headed down the hallway from Dame's office. The urge to glance at the letters DOA over Dame's headboard pushed at my mental. I needed to see if I wasn't tripping. I knew I wasn't. Had taken a picture then deleted that shit once he had come back. It was just fucked up how karma could be.

Right now, I was karma's weapon not Dame's. That nigga's approaching death marking me as his reaper was one of two things that kept me going; the other, touching his property.

I rubbed my hands together as I passed some of the house dolls. Sasha's scheming ass was at Magic City, so I didn't have to watch her and make sure she ain't try to put her hands on Gina or other new girls in the house. Sour pussy was evil pussy. It was fucked up how twisted Sasha was becoming. Usually I didn't give two shits what she did, but since Diamond was top bitch, everyone was feeling Sasha's wrath.

"Heeeey, Trigga."

Feminine echoes around me had me tilting my head up and down. I gave my "waddups" back and moved through the house. Some chicks asked me to bring them back things. I had no issue with these broads, many of whom were around my age or a little older. I'd slow my roll just to make a list of what they wanted and often didn't have time to get on their free days. Or I'd make a note of some product they wanted, which had me going in my pocket.

Cell in my hand doing a quick 'Net search, the name krokodil was nothing new to me, but the fact Dame was asking about it was interesting. Word on the street was, it was a new drug making the rounds overseas. It was called triple K over here and used by kids in the burbs or trailer parks because it was easy to make. Shit was supposed to be so powerful that it ate people from the inside out, turning their skin into sores or scales and shit. I never understood why bitches and niggas would take literal poison. My motto was, if you just wanted to die, then walk in the street and let that shit be done.

The fact that Dame was about to pump this into our neighborhood was bothering me. Heroin addicts would grab anything for a cheap high, and if he brought this poison to the people on a massive scale, many would die quickly and painfully.

Turning the corner, I counted off the cameras visible to everyone. While I was in Dame's office, as he spoke, I had memorized every camera angle displaying on the screens. One of the many perks of Dame trusting me somewhat and his mixture of crazy was that he slipped up sometimes, and this was one. I now knew where every camera was positioned, and with Big Jake being security, I knew he could tell me where the others were. It now made sense why Big Jake had moved me in the house. Certain shit was angled off on the video, where Dame couldn't tell what the fuck was going on.

So, the game was on, and I had orders to play out. Pookie was now on blast, and Dame was letting me in. Bodies were gonna drop real soon, and my only aim was to make sure that Dame was one of them.

E.N.G.A.

Ray-Ray

The next day I woke up with a mission. I got up before Dame and headed out to his weight room to work out. I had to get my mind off being forced to give up my body and then have to lay in the bed beside him. I was so sick and disgusted, I found myself getting up in the middle of the night to vomit.

Trigga was in the house, but truth be told, I was scared to look for him or ask about him. As pissed the hell off as I was, I ain't want to die. Not unless I took Dame with me. That was my mission—In the next twenty-four hours I was going to start shaking up the house to take it down from the inside out. I just didn't know that Dame had been planning a shakedown too.

"You okay, Gina?" I asked her.

"Yup. I'ma be all right," she said as she smiled and looked up at me. "You know why?"

"Why?"

"'Cuz I'ma have Big Jake's baby."

"What?" I jumped up and rushed to her.

I had been sitting on Dame's bed. We had just come from downstairs getting our hair done because Dame demanded it. A chick named Minx came in with her crew and hooked all of us up. Gina said Dame always did that for them because he had to keep his elite bitches, his main product, looking good and ready to sell at any moment.

"Dame think I threw up because he was fuckin' me in my ass, but I took that shit 'cuz I ain't want my baby to get hurt."

I hung my head when she said that. As usual Dame was on some other shit. It seemed like he wanted to make sure our day was fucked up just because he could. He had roughhoused Gina just like he had done me. Only, with Gina he forced her to take his dick up her ass and threatened to kill her if she screamed. I knew sometimes Gina was a little off in the head, so I figured it was so easy for her to act as if what he had done didn't bother her.

"You're pregnant?" I asked in a whisper, just to be sure.

She nodded then held a finger up to her lips, telling me to be quiet. Then she mouthed the word *camera* to me.

She nodded with a bright smile. "Big Jake say he wanted a son before he leaves this earth. I'ma try to give 'im one. Hope it's a boy like he want. He don't know though. Wanna surprise him on his birthday."

I didn't want to kill her happy mood, but I had to ask, "But, Gina, how do you know it's Jake's baby?"

She looked at me and blinked slowly a few times. "It has to be, Ray-Ray. It just has to be." She answered like it would kill her to find out she wasn't carrying Jake's baby.

As bad as she wanted it to be Jake's, there was a big chance that it wasn't. I knew it, and I knew she knew it. Although I didn't know if what she was telling me was a good thing, the fact that a baby growing in her belly was keeping her sane was enough for me to go along with her happiness.

"When is it?"

"What?"

"His birthday?"

"In two days."

I was just about to say something else when movement at the door caught my attention. I knew it wasn't Dame because he would have simply just come into his room and started to whup our asses. I rushed to the door and looked down the hall to see Sasha walking away. I didn't know if she had been eavesdropping or what. I called her name, but she kept walking like she didn't even hear me. *Bitch.*

Although I wanted to choke that ho, I couldn't pretend like I wasn't scared that she had heard me and Gina. My worried looked turned into stone-cold hate when I saw her stop and speak to Pookie as he came up the stairs. If I could have killed the nigga in that moment, I would have.

Pookie caught me looking at him then nodded his head in my direction. Sasha turned around then rolled her eyes and kept walking. I wanted to go and "accidentally" push that bitch down the stairs.

I turned back to Gina and closed the door. "You think she heard us?" I asked Gina.

She shook her head. "Naw, if she had, she would be running to tell Dame now."

"Whatcha gon' do if he finds out?"

She shrugged and ran a hand through her freshly permed hair, since she had taken her braids down. "I don't know. Just gotta make sure he don't. 'Cuz if he do, he gon' make me get rid of it, like he did with Sasha and a few other girls. He say he ain't in the business of housing pregnant pussy."

After that, me and Gina didn't speak out loud about what she had told me. We couldn't risk Dame finding out, but I knew as soon as Big Jake found out he was having a baby it would be game time in overdrive. Thinking back, I wish to God I'd kept the memory of Gina's smiling face close to my heart, that I'd hugged and kissed her one last time.

"We need to get to Decatur," Dame said to Trigga as they walked into his bedroom. "Got a couple niggas, some cops, high officials we need to holler at."

I had been laying on the bed but quickly jumped up. I wasn't fool enough to glance in Trigga's direction. It would have been nice to make eye contact, but I valued my eyesight. It was no question that Dame would try to gouge my eyes out just as he had threatened. I was crazy at times, but not stupid.

Trigga and Big Jake had been the only two people Dame would talk to about the new shipment he had coming in. Still, I was confused about why he had brought them to his bedroom. He had never done that before. He walked right to the open double doors of the balcony and took a seat in one of the white cushioned lounge chairs. Gina had left to go do her shift at the club. I was excited to know that she and Jake had found a way to still love each other through the madness of their lives.

"When we need to go do that, bossman?" Trigga asked.

"Now. We need to get a move on because my shit comes in by the end of the week." Dame grabbed a silver-plated gun from underneath the chair and slipped it into the holster he had on. He always had a weapon somewhere.

As always that nigga was decked out like he worked in a corporate office. He had on grey dress pants and a thick black tee shirt that hugged his muscles. He kept that cane near him, and I couldn't help but wonder why.

Trigga said, "So we just gon' forget about the other shit?"

"What other shit?"

"I told you about Pookie and that lame shit he pulled."

My head jerked in the direction of Trigga's voice. He stood at the door of the balcony, his arms folded across his wide chest. The black hoodie he had on looked like it was on backwards, but it wasn't. It looked that way because of the skull on the hood that zipped up to hide half of his face.

He had told Dame about Pookie? I mean, at first I had expected him to when I'd first told him that it was Pookie who had pulled that lick with my mama and daddy, but after we had all talked, I thought we were going to take the money and stash for ourselves. I was confused.

My eyes darted to Big Jake, who was standing with a scowl on his face that said something else was on his mind.

"Naw, nigga. We just got other shit to worry about right now. You check on that shit we talked about?"

Although Dame was talking to Trigga, when I turned my gaze back to him, his eyes were locked on me. He snapped his fingers, and I knew what that meant.

I walked over to him expecting him to tell me to sit down beside him, but what he did next told why he had brought Trigga to his room to talk. He pulled his dick out and laid it on his thigh like it was nothing.

Dame snapped, "Do I have to remind you how much a nigga hate to wait for his afternoon dick-sucking?"

I shook my head and barely whispered, "No, Daddy."

I knew if I had hesitated or said the wrong thing, I risked being thrown over the damn balcony or worse. I wished like hell I'd had some of those white pills Gina had given me before. Or, better yet, that I could have just folded or misted into thin air. To have Big Jake and Trigga stand there and watch me suck this nigga's dick was a crippling embarrassment.

I got down on my knees, and Dame grabbed his dick, then the back of my head, then shoved it into my mouth. He pushed my head so far down, I thought I was going to choke. My throat was burning, eyes watered, and my nose felt like it was stopped up. The fact that I knew he had ass-fucked Gina raw earlier messed with me.

"Breathe, Ray-Ray," my mama said. *"Just close your eyes, relax, and breathe. I'ma tell you some weird shit, but it's gon' work and make that nigga come quick."*

I could feel her kneeling next to me. I never thought I'd have my mama telling me how to suck a dick.

"Ball your right fist with your thumb on the inside, and it will make your gags go off. You won't have none. So no matter how this nigga shove his dick in your mouth, you won't choke on that shit," she explained.

Just so I could stop gagging, and with the hope that he would come quick, I did what my mama said. So while he sat there talking with Big Jake and Trigga about what he needed them to do, I was stuck sucking his dick like my life was dependent on it, and to be honest, it did.

Trigga

This nigga was on one. Couple of things had my mind on rotation as I stood in Dame's room. One, DOA seemed to stand out like flashing lights for me, and two, Big Jake and me were standing watching this nigga get his cock handled while barking out orders to us 'bout what we needed to get ready once we went up to Decatur.

Spit on flesh—the sound of Diamond's mouth workin' her suction like a pro—was all we heard after a while standing there. I wondered what the fuck was Dame's problem. A chuckle escaped from me, making me shake my head.

I knew what was wrong with him. Nigga was basic and on some territorial bullshit. Whateva, man. No doubt, watchin' Diamond had my dick interested, but since she was on her knees like a ho because of Dame, the image of her like that kept my shit limp, which worked in my favor.

Dame glared at me. "Fuck you laughin' at, nigga? Something I said was comical relief?" He sat wide-legged, trying to act like his wasn't ready to slob at the mouth as Diamond worked him up. His hand clenched his cane, and his light eyes were already dark.

By the way he was breathing, that nigga was two seconds away from a nut, which was lame, because she had just started. Or it was just that good.

"Naw, bossman, something I was thinkin'," I quickly explained, so as not to deal with some dramatic bitch-assness from him, "do we need to get on ya level, bossman, and get us some nice threads? Just was laughin' at myself thinking about that shit. Never wore a suit before but was thinkin', since I'm ya right now and Big Jake ya guard, we gotta represent you with the movers and shakers. Just thought that was funny. Feel me? Us in suits. You pull that off. Me, Big Jake? Naw, I don't know, bossman." I would have rubbed my jaw, but the way my hoodie was set up, my face was partially covered with the image of a skull, so I crossed my arms over my chest, just watching.

I tried to get Big Jake to play in on the act, but something was off with the nigga. Earlier, when he came to get me after Dame told us to basically come watch him get a nut, dude seemed quietly distant, as if I had did some shit to him. Now, dude was standing like a gargoyle, cold and deathly, like he was known to be in the streets as Dame's guard. I wasn't feeling that shit 'cuz it was directed at me. Before now, even as we played the game, we always made sure to have some secret cues, which Dame couldn't pick up on, that we were cool. But now even that wasn't there. Nigga was ice-cold, eyes blank. Shit wasn't cool at all. Something had happened.

"A'ight. Bounce. Hit up some spots to get a suit. You two got like four hours. You late, that's ya ass," as Dame said that, nigga came all in Diamond's mouth. He grunted then pulled back and let that shit rain on her face.

If I thought he wasn't trying to fuck with both of us, the moment he locked eyes on me then held Diamond by the back of her neck to press his dick against her face, I knew he was on some challenge shit. *This nigga!* So, I did like I always did with crazy niggas like him. I crossed my arms and let out a rare laugh then walked out. Nigga shit, I swear. New pussy makes even the most loyal nigga dumb.

Big Jake followed me. I really wanted to find out what the fuck was up with homie. One thing about this game, if your crew wasn't in the same head as you, then it could fuck up the whole rotation.

Because the house always had some snitching bitches in it, male and female, I waited until we got outside and got into the black-on-black Escalade that was Big Jake's responsibility. I got in the whip, and we rode off. I wanted to see just how long this nigga would hit me with some bitch-ass silence shit. So once, we made it out of the Trap and hit up the spot Dame told us to get our suits at, I got out then waited for Big Jake to round the car. That was when I walked right at his side, looking straight ahead as I spoke low.

"Nigga, fuck is wrong with you, huh?"

Big Jake said nothing, just kept walking.

Wasn't shit I could do about it, so I got quiet with him, thinking. Until that nigga snatched me by my throat and pushed me down the side of the building, slamming me into a brick wall. All I saw was stars for a moment as I smelled the sour odor of trash behind us. The familiar feel of steel against my temple had me feeling like a betrayed nigga, and anger had my fingers itching. I quickly drew the gun I had hidden in the sleeve of my hoodie and pressed it against Jake's side as I stared death in the eyes.

Jaw clenched, my nostrils flared, and my eyes narrowed. "I ain't even scared to die, but before I go, two things—Fuck is up with you? And you going with me, nigga."

Jake's huge fist found my face, stunning me. *Did this nigga just hit me? Is he really about to go there with me?* I mean, yeah, he had me up by my throat, but fuck his life, yo! He really was placing hands on me; all loyalty was off at that moment, so I swung back, connecting to his jaw.

As we scrapped in the middle of the alley, the sounds of our grunts then the sound of the safeties coming off our guns echoed around us. Because he had hit me, I was able to break free. I stood facing Jake's giant ass. Blood spilled down his face, and I swore I saw tears mixed in. He pulled out his cross and kissed it, the one his grandmother had given him, and I knew some shit was up.

A cool breeze stung my face. My hood fell back, and some of my locks had loosened to cover my face and stuck to the sweat and blood that covered me. Nigga still wasn't talking, but just by his actions, I knew it had to be about his grandmother. That was when the pieces started forming.

"Yo! I didn't take your gram out, man! I wouldn't stand there in your face acting like I did. Nigga, think, bro! I'm ya boy!" I hissed out, pissed all the way off, slamming my free hand against my chest. *Who the fuck got to him? And why?*

"I trusted you, fam, helped you out when you had no fuckin' body."

I shook my head in confusion. I wasn't down for this shit. That was one thing that bothered me—fuckin' with my reputation, especially when I knew it was lies.

"Yo, I ain't did nothing to you, Jackson! I wasn't even Dame's gun when your grams was taken out. I ain't do that shit! That ain't my MO ever!"

Jake's huge solid chest rose up and down as he tried to catch his breath. His large hands fisted even as he held his gun out my way. Dude looked like a wounded Doberman, red eyes and flaring nostrils. I could tell he didn't want to do this, to take me down, which helped me not write this fucka off and pump a bullet right into his skull. He was my fam in this war, and I had to hold him down like he did me. It just was hard right now 'cuz nigga looked possessed or high.

Jake spat, "Naw! Fuck dat shit, yuh heard! I heard Dame talking about that shit to some of the new niggas coming through, said it all, and said they needed to get like you 'cuz that was ya first kill for him."

My first kill for Dame was never some old lady. That was one thing I'd never done, killed women, elders, or kids, and I never will, unless they like Dame. Dame was a lying muthafucka and trying to start some shit. More like, get me killed. His own fuckin' gun? Can you believe that shit? Or was he trying to get Big Jake killed? What the fuck? Yo, nigga was bound for hell for real.

"Jake, man, we don't have time for this bullshit. You need to think, homie. On my word, that's not my M.O. Never slung bullets at my elders, women, or kids, homie. Never. And my first kill for Dame was not your gram, it was some punk-ass nigga who stole some product from one of the houses. I never done you wrong, except to fuck your face up just now, bro. Think on that shit. I wouldn't have trusted you or brought you into my real home, nigga! Or lace you up with that auto shop! I ain't like that, man. That wasn't me!" I holstered my gun to show I was being about truth, holding my hands up and out. All I could do was wait while Jake studied me, trying to see if I was telling the truth.

See, the difference between Jake and me in this killing game was, if it was me in his shoes, how my mind work, nigga woulda been dead as he was talking his truth. But, that was me, and this was Jake. We had history and a code of respect.

Jake's hand quickly came up to wipe the sweat, blood, and tears from his face. He shifted back and forth then holstered his gun. Both of his hands came up to cradle the back of his low-cropped head as he looked down at his feet in pain. I never realized until then how much he looked like David Banner until now.

"That was my heart. Raised me as a baby, Trigga. On my word, how he laid that shit out, it sounded like what you told me, man, made it sound like you were the lying one. I . . ." He looked up at me and then punched the wall.

Broken brick crumbled around where his meaty fist made contact, and I kept my distance.

"Look, man, something is going on, a'ight. That nigga runnin' his mouth with lies, bro. I need you back on the team, or I can put a bullet in you right now. Feel me? You held me down when I had no one, so get that shit together. E.N.G.A., nigga! That even means Dame! He got some shit planned, and he's pissed because he thinks I want Ray-Ray. So he's acting stupid, which is dangerous. Don't let that nigga run game, bro. Don't do that. You know our plan, so stick to it. On my word, I'll find out who he ordered to take out your grams, and I'll help you take that nigga out if he's still alive. But don't make me take my own bro out, a'ight. Don't, man."

For the first time in a long time, I realized I cared about someone outside of my parents. He really was like a brother to me.

Jake's eyes locked on me, his shoulders slumped. I studied him while he walked up and held his hand out in peace.

"I always believe God don't put too much on anyone that they can't take," he said. "You would have taken me out, but like you said, bro, I would have taken you out too. Blood brothers for life, man. My bad for dropping trust."

The voice of a preacher was back in my homie. When he spoke like that, I knew he was a'ight and could be trusted. So I took his hand, and we both bumped shoulders then stepped back. I pulled some of my loose locks back and fixed my jacket.

Jake did the same, fixing his clothes and rubbing his jaw. We checked our watches to see how much time we had then quickly went inside the shop, leaving that bullshit behind us in the alley.

Rich folks moved around, getting help from different workers, broads, and dudes who kept walking past us, ignoring us. We stood at the entryway for like a good five minutes before they looked at us with fear in their eyes.

My pops always told me that a man reflects who he is in how he dresses before even opening his mouth. This can be used for good or to fuck with people's mental. With me and Big Jake, right now, we were fuckin' with people's heads, and it was just what it was. How we lived was how we dressed, and ain't shit we could do about it, except for the coin Dame gave us. Before anyone could call the cops or feel threatened, Jake spat out Dame's name, and everyone in the shop changed up their look and started helping us out.

Jake glanced my way as if still having a hard time shaking that we almost lost our lives due to Dame's bullshit. As some redhead chick who looked kind of nice took my numbers, he came over and gave me dap one more time while my arms were stretched out.

I let a smile spread across my face and nodded. "I was just where you were, homie, and you helped me. So it's icing. We good for life, if you really mean it, bro."

"You know I do, bro. Anyway, you right, punk. This suit shit is extra," Jake joked, moving back to where a dark-haired chick ran her fingers over the inside of his legs to get his numbers again.

"We can provide you both with some nice vests. We'll put the jackets on the side and keep you two professional, handsome as you two are, and flashy," the redhead said, glancing her blue eyes up at me as she kneeled before me.

I could tell she was trying to flirt now, but I wasn't into it. Once a person ignored me just once, then I pretty much was not into noticing that person ever again. Wasn't nothing the broad could do for me but finish my outfit.

"Yeah, vests would work. Leave all flash to bossman; that's his style," I said, looking at my reflection.

Had to say, what they had me trying on was kinda dope on me, if I wanted that business look. I sported black slacks with a red shirt. Then the redhead fitted a vest on me.

I picked up my cell to look at Youtube to see how to wear a tie. I wasn't really about putting a tie on. Shit reminded me of nooses, but for the look of this fit and not to hear bossman's yapping mouth, I let the redhead put one on me. I worked the knot in a way that didn't make me feel like I was choking. I never had my pops here to show me how to do these things, which made this all bittersweet for me just that fast.

Dame took that from me, but it was cool. Payback was coming. I remembered watching my mom pick my pop's outfits. Remembered how he seemed to love how she dressed him and worked his ties or ironed his suits. It was something private about it. And fuck if I didn't know the right word, but it looked like they were fuckin' without actually fuckin' when she dressed him, and it made me proud as a kid. I wanted that.

My mind went to Diamond. I wondered what it would be like to have her do those things for me. Wondered how sexy she would look if I could watch her pick out a fit that matched me now, some type of dress that hugged her curves and made her dark cinnamon skin glow.

"Hey, Trigg, you look like a college kid, man. Good look," Jake joked, breaking me out of my thoughts.

Laughing, I rubbed where my beard only covered my chin. I had to agree, I looked good. "Fuck you, nigga! You look like one too. Nah, wait . . . ya look like one of those frat dudes from *Stomp the Yard.* "

Big Jake gave a booming laugh. I noticed how both chicks turned red like a hot dog at how we spoke to each other, and that made me laugh harder.

"Yeah, we'll take this and check out some shoes. We need this stuff now; we only got an hour left," I quickly said, rolling up the sleeves of my shirt around my biceps. I checked my form again.

The redhead kept unbuttoning and buttoning my shirt to see my abs. Shit was funny to me.

We picked up some black Italian shoes with bottoms that we could run in, that went with what we wore. Then we paid the owner, who was, to my surprise, an elder brother. When he spoke, he sounded like Idris Elba in Prometheus, kinda looked like him too. He gave us his cards, shook our hands, and then showed us out. We left out of the suit place in our new threads, looking caked-up, with new shades, giving us that icing. Big Jake had on all black with a red Rolex. The muscles in his arms were so tight when he crossed them, I thought his shirt was going to split.

The moment we texted Dame, he blew up our cells, telling us to sit outside of the house so we could head to Decatur. After pulling up, we both got out, cuts on our faces and all. We already had come up with a fallback if Dame asked what went down. I was about to remind him, just in case, when I heard him growl low in his throat.

"Remember to chill," I muttered to him. "We got this."

Jake gave a nod, putting on his shades, and I did the same.

Dame came out talking loud and shit, flapping his gums like the bitch he was, while speaking with Pookie, his arm draped over that lame's shoulders as if they were homies. Shit made my abs clench and my fingers itch.

I saw Diamond slowly walking behind Dame. She wore a dress that definitely would match me well. Her fit was a red and black short bandage-like dress that stopped at the middle of her thighs to show her legs. Only then I'd realized how thick, long, and pretty they were. Her big doe eyes were shooting blades into Pookie's skull. It was obvious that if she had any hidden blades on her, she would have cut that nigga up like scissors.

The sun covered us all in its light, making me shift just a little. The way I was standing, it appeared as if I was watching Dame, but really, I was watching her. Her ink-black hair was up like usual, big diamond studs in each ear, and her lips were like rubies.

Gina walked at her side in a similar dress, but it was candy pink. Her long hair curled around her face, falling down the side of her shoulder, framing her face, which caught my attention.

My eyes narrowed the closer Gina got. I realized why Big Jake had growled. Her caked-on makeup couldn't cover all of the bruises that showed on her baby face and neck. Dame had fucked baby girl up. Had hurt her good. It was visible by the way she was walking too.

I knew that killing that nigga might be too good. The act of torture was now added to the list of murking that nigga. What kept iggin' me was the fact that she was even there. It had me wondering what was up, because now it seemed that Gina was his extra doll now too.

"Hey, this nigga Pookie is that shit," Dame said. "He got my stacks high. Trigga, Big Jake, all you niggas of the house, pay attention. This is a nigga who just got my product in some new hands. Got-*who did you say*?"

Pookie stuck his chest out like he was king. He had on a bright Halloween yellow made-by-Steve Harvey-looking suit. His hair was braided back in two pigtails and gripped the front of his jacket as if airing it out. That nigga had to be roasting.

A coon-ass smile spread across his lying smashed-pumpkin face, he said, "I got a cousin in Cali who is hitting me up. I might, I mean I got him interested in our product and will ship it out to L.A."

You had to be stupid to believe the words coming out this nigga's mouth. Strike one, that I knew he was lying wasn't even the obvious "might" that slipped from his mouth. It was how that nigga stuttered, the way his eyes shifted like a rat. Left and right. And how red in the face he got, as if he was holding his breath praying that we believed him.

Dame's loco ass just cheesed along, gassing him up. "Hey, it's big thangs in your future, Pookie. We got something big about to pop off, and you just helped me look even better. We need to ride out, and you coming. Going to introduce you to a new world, nigga. This is only the beginning."

Pulling up in front of us, a black limo hit that brake. Big Jake went into bodyguard mode and covered Dame while he got in, then Diamond and Gina. As Diamond and Gina slid into the limo, I got a nice view of ass, tits, and thighs, perks of working for this devil nigga.

Diamond sported some flashy shades, which I was good on. I could feel her watching me but in a way that Dame couldn't tell. If she didn't have those shades, I knew without a doubt that Dame woulda fucked her up. The longer I was around her, the more I knew if I got the chance to get her alone, I'd eat her pussy till she couldn't stand anymore.

I knew that, no matter how much my dick wanted to get into her wetness, I couldn't, because a smart nigga was a blind nigga. Dumb, crazy niggas could quickly tell when their pussy had stepped up into new dick, and Dame was a crazy nigga. And because my dick was bigger than his, he'd definitely know if I had made Diamond's walls mine.

"Ey Ey! Bossman got the best ass in the Trap. Must respect!" Pookie's loud ass grinned at me. His voice lowered when he reached out to dap me and my own hands were still in my pockets. "'Bout to step up, nigga. Step right into where you at. Ha!"

I ain't say shit. I just stepped back, slammed the door before his foot could get all the way into the car, and turned my back to the limo smiling when I heard that nigga's baby-soft cry.

Heading to the Escalade with Big Jake, we all trailed the limo heading to Decatur, while me and Big Jake spoke in code, making plans, and back on track as brothers in bond. Wasn't nothing breaking us but death; that was our code.

E.N.G.A. was back on track. Now I had to keep Big Jake calm because not only did he have to figure out Dame's lies, he was also worried about Gina. Dame was beating her ass too much for our taste, so we agreed that it might be time to try to change some shit up.

Ray-Ray

"Hey, Ray-Ray, Gina."

Both me and Gina looked up at Sasha, shocked to see her speaking to us. Me and Gina had been sitting on the patio that sat off Dame's room, waiting on him to come back. Gina was telling me she had talked to Big Jake, and that he and Trigga had got into a fight. I ain't know what about because I didn't get a chance to ask.

The night before, Dame had taken us with him to some meeting in the middle of no fuckin' where. Politicians, clergy members, members of law enforcement and the like, all crooks, sat there in that big warehouse with him plotting on how to get his product into the United States and how to make sure it flooded the streets of the *A*. Niggas were grimy, and by niggas, I meant the police too. I knew anybody associated with his ass was a menace and wasn't protecting anything but their pockets.

I had seen shit like that in movies, but I ain't ever witnessed no shit like that. They brought in these two white bitches that looked like Jessica Rabbit and made them try some knew shit that started with a *K*. One of those bitches started bleeding from her eyes, and the other completely passed the fuck out then woke up like a fuckin' zombie. Bitch started scratching her own skin off but was begging for another hit.

When Dame asked Trigga to spit knowledge about that shit they gave them two girls, I got angry at him. Why he know all that shit about that stuff? Was he gon' be pushing that shit to folks too? So he was gon' be one of them niggas posted in the trap all day now? Then how the fuck was he gon' find time to kill the nigga and get us the fuck up outta this place?

For real though, I was really feeling some type of way because of what he saw me do yesterday. I already knew that Trigga wouldn't want shit to do with me after seeing the way I sucked Dame off. I could just cut that fantasy of me and him being together out of my head. No way, with the way Dame nutted all in my mouth and on my face, would Trigga see me as more than the ho Dame had made me. I was just wondering if he understood that if I didn't do it Dame probably would have done some weird shit to me.

Like when he called Sasha in the room that morning and made me sit my pussy on her face. He told Sasha that her pussy had never been as good as mine. Then he made me grind on her face while he sat in his chair and played with his dick. I was half-scared that bitch would bite my shit or do something to hurt, but she was so happy to be back in the nigga's good graces, she did whatever he told her to.

"What, Sasha?" Gina asked with attitude, bringing me back to reality.

We knew that bitch was full of shit and wasn't trusting the fake-ass smile plastered across her face. She stood with her arms folded across her nonexistent titties in a lace bra and coochie-cutters.

"Don't get no nasty attitude, bitch," she told Gina.

I wanted to bop that ho right in her face.

"Daddy the one told me to come out and tell you to prep Ray-Ray for her first night at the club."

I was skeptical. I looked at Gina then back at Sasha. "Dame gon' let me leave the house without him?" I asked.

Sasha nodded. "Yup. He said hurry up too because he want her to be trained and ready for amateur night too."

I looked back at Gina, who was looking at Sasha like she stunk.

Gina said, "Don't be playing. You sure he said it? I'ma call 'im and see myself."

"Bitch, you call Daddy phone while he doing business and he gon' bus' yo' shit, ho. Keep fuckin' 'round, acting like you don't know who the fuck Dame is, callin' him for stupid shit when I jus' told yo' ass what he said."

Gina jumped up. "You best watch ya fuckin' mouth, talking to me like you crazy, sour-cunt bitch."

Sasha dropped her hands and stepped to Gina like she was about to buck. If she had put her hands on Gina, I was gon' slang her old-looking ass over the balcony on everything I loved.

"You better get this bitch ready to go before Daddy get here, or you gon' be back in the basement with pipes up yo' pussy."

I knew that was a sore spot for Gina. I shoved Sasha so hard, she fell back into the double doors. "Don't be talking slick outta your mouth, like we won't get in your ass," I snapped. I was expecting that bitch to jump up and swing, but she didn't.

She got up, but all she did was push her fake blond hair out her face and give a smirk. "Daddy ain't gon' be in that club, bitch. I'll catch you slipping. And when I do, it's your ass." Then she turned and walked out of the room.

"You gotta watch dis bitch, Diamond. Something up wit' this ho. Something ain't right, Ray-Ray."

I ignored my mama's voice only because Gina had sat down crying. She kept mumbling over and over that she had to get her baby out of here.

"We will," I told her as I kneeled down in front of her.

"Shhhh. Don't talk about it here. We can't talk here. Cameras, all around fuckin' cameras," she quickly said then jumped up.

She took my hand and pulled me into the room. She went into the other walk-in closet and came out with a pair of hip-hugger jeans, a red tank that showed my belly, and some six-inch heels that were boots that came up my thighs.

"Hurry, get dressed," she said quickly. "If we leave early you can go with me somewhere. Don't ask where 'til we leave here."

"You sure about this, Gina? That bitch could be playing us."

Gina stood like she was really thinking on what I had said. "Even if she is, we still need to go somewhere. I gotta check on something. We can just say that bitch came in here and told us. She on the cameras."

I nodded and started to get dressed. I had to admit I was kinda excited to be leaving that house again. I started thinking about ways I could escape. But there was something in the pit of my stomach telling me that something was off. I could still hear my mama in my head too.

Even as we got dressed and left the house, she kept telling me that something was going on. I ignored her because I just wanted to get out of the house again. In my mind I kept thinking that me and Trigga could maybe run away with Big Jake and Gina, and that they could have their baby without having that nigga Dame breathing over them. I started to daydream about what it would be like to wake up and have no crazy nigga trying to fuck me in every hole I owned, to just be free. I started to miss my mama and my daddy again.

I was real happy until I saw Pookie waiting at the car that was s'posed to be driving us to the club. He was in baggy black sweats, fresh white Air Force Ones, and a fresh white tee. The nigga's face reminded me of the bottle my daddy used to drink gin out of. He called it bumpy-face gin. His braids had been freshly done, but it didn't do nothing for the shit that was his face.

"Hurry that fine ass up," he said to me, showing all thirty-two of his dingy teeth.

That nigga really thought he was something, since Dame had told him he was getting promoted.

"Don't say nothing to 'im, Ray-Ray. Just get in the car," Gina whispered to me. "You got yo' phone? Gotta have yo' phone 'cuz if that nigga call it and you don't answer, I don't want—"

Pookie barked, "Bitch, stop yapping yo' fuckin' gums and git in the car, ho!"

Gina didn't say nothing. She just got in the car. I knew Gina was normally quiet, but since she'd found out she was pregnant, she had been taking a lot more shit than normal. I guess she really was trying to protect her baby.

I took her lead and kept quiet too, but I made sure I had my phone on me like she said. I didn't know what Pookie had on him and didn't want to be the reason Gina got blanked out on because of my mouth.

Once we got in, Pookie closed the door and walked around the red Navigator to get in. He drove us for about a good twenty minutes before saying anything to us.

"So, you 'bout to be popping that pussy at The City, huh?" he asked, looking through the rearview mirror at me. Then, just like that, his smile turned into a sneer. "I still owe you for this fuckin' gash on my face, ho, and watch I get what's mine. I'ma getcha, ho, when you least expect a nigga to. Keep that shit in da back of ya skull, bitch."

"You better leave her alone before I tell Trigga about dem lies you helped spread 'bout him killing Big Jake's grandma," Gina finally said. "We both know it was you helping to tell them lies, nigga. Trigga gon' blow the back of your head off, and we gon' see if you can think wit' yo' front."

"Fuck that pussy-nigga! When I'm at Dame right hand and shit, I'ma off that nigga too, just like I helped with that bitch's daddy and her ho mama. Ho, bitch-nigga don't scare me. Retarded muthafucka. Fuckin' deaf-mute nigga."

It was then without a doubt I knew that nigga was as stupid as he looked. I wanted to jump from that backseat and punch that nigga in his shit, but Gina grabbed my hand and squeezed it.

"Bet you won't say that shit to Trigga's face," she told him.

"Ey, yo, shut up, bitch, before I smack you in ya shit. Retarded bitch. Ey, you and that nigga Trigga should hook up and make some more retarded babies." He laughed like a hyena, like he had said the funniest shit ever. "Imagine two retarded muthafuckas fuckin'. One of y'all quiet, and the other one talking to her gotdamn self."

Gina spat back, "Y'all niggas talk big shit but be scared as fuck of Trigga. Scared that nigga gon' body you niggas like he do. Mad 'cuz Dame brought him on and he outranked all you niggas off the bat."

Pookie stopped the truck. Then he turned around and smacked Gina so hard, her head almost broke the window. He growled at her, "Say something else to me, bitch, and I'ma fuck you up!"

I hit him in the back of his head over and over as hard as I could before he elbowed me in my eye. I fell back against the tan leather seat, and he went to work on my face, smacking me over and over, until Gina cried out for him to stop. She threw herself over my body and started kicking him for dear life.

The slaps he delivered against my face stung like hell. My face was burning like it had been set on fire.

"Stupid-ass bitches!" Pookie said after he stopped.

Then he smacked both of us one last time before he moved back to the driver's seat of the truck and started driving again.

I was wishing like hell I'd had a blade or something. I would have killed that nigga right then. My eyes were watering, and it felt like he had smacked blood from my nose.

Gina cradled my head against her chest and told me everything was going to be okay.

Then just like that she started humming and laughing.

I knew the song she was humming. "Say Hello to the Bad Guy" by Jay Z was my daddy's favorite shit, so I would know it anywhere.

She started shaking her head and spitting the lyrics out like she was in the studio with that nigga Jigga when he was making it. She kept getting louder and louder.

I had to admit she was scaring me with the way she was acting.

So imagine how scared Pookie was when she jumped up and grabbed his neck, a blade in her hand.

As she sliced down the other side of his face, the truck swerved wildly in and out of traffic. Horns blaring hurt my ears. I didn't have on a seat belt, so the movements threw me all over the back of the truck.

She kept cutting through gritted teeth, and that bitch-nigga was yelping and screaming, just like when I cut his ass.

He finally swerved the truck to a stop.

Gina flew back into the seat because of how hard he hit on the brakes. She quickly pushed the door open to the back of the truck, grabbed my hand, and pulled me out.

We could still hear Pookie yelling bloody fuckin' murder. But Gina had me by my wrist, and we were running like our lives depended on it, especially when we heard gunshots ring out after us.

Me and Gina didn't stop running until we got to 17th Street in front of a doctor's office. There was blood all over the front of her shirt, and people had stopped to look at us strange.

"Come on, go in here with me," she said as she pulled me inside of the doctor's office.

My heart was beating, pounding hard against my chest. I'd just been shot at. Part of me was afraid I had a hole in me and just didn't know it.

People screamed out when we walked in because Gina was covered in blood. There was a black woman in scrubs standing by the big welcome window. When she turned, I saw the immediate resemblance to Gina.

Is that her mother?

Gina didn't stop until we got up to the woman. "Mama, you gotta help me," she spat out.

The woman looked like she had just seen a ghost. Her entire face drained of color, and she was as black as me and Gina. "Y-you can't come in here," the woman stuttered.

"Mama, you gotta help me, or I'ma tell all these damn people that you put me out on the gotdamn street and now I gotta sell my pussy to survive."

Gina said that so loud, I wished I could have gone somewhere to hide. The gasps that came through the place were so loud, all her mother could do was snatch her by her arm and pull us down the hall, past all the gawking nurses and onlookers and into a private exam room.

Gina's mama slammed the door and locked it then turned to get in Gina's face. "What in hell do you want? Is it money?" She took one look at my face and then shoved tissue in my hand, like just looking at the blood coming from my nose disgusted her.

"Yeah, money. And I need you to check on my baby."

Her mama's eyes widened. "What? A baby? I knew it. I knew you were going to get fuckin' knocked up."

"Well, whatchu expect when you throw me out, Mama? Huh? I'm selling pussy for a pimp, and I'm knocked up. You gon' give me some money and check on my baby?"

"Oh my fuckin' God. How much, Gina? How much to make you fuckin' go away?" The woman looked at me once again then grimaced like I was a bum or something.

I kept trying to stop the blood with the tissue she gave me.

"Fifty *G*s."

"What the fuck?" the woman aggressively whispered.

"You got it, Dr. Lewis. We both know you do."

"I don't have that kind of money just lying around."

"Write me a check and check on my baby, and I'll be gone, Mama. You won't see me no more. No, better yet, transfer me some money to this account."

Gina handed the woman a piece of paper and she looked like she was about to have a heart attack. She snatched the paper from Gina's hand and stormed from the exam room and came back a few minutes later with a check.

"I put the fuckin' money there, and here's some more in a check form. Don't ever come back here, Gina."

Gina took it and shoved it in her bra before taking her pants and underwear off to get on the table.

Sure enough, Gina was pregnant. She squeezed my hand then clapped. We talked about baby names and how she was gon' tell Big Jake he was going to be a daddy.

All the while my heart was beating a mile a minute because I was still scared shitless after what had happened with Pookie.

For the first time I heard my daddy's voice. *"Shit 'bout to get really real, baby girl. That nigga coming for you. You got Jenkins' blood. I ain't here to protect you, but you better not let no nigga take yo' life without fighting for it."*

I looked around hoping I could see him, but I didn't. Only heard him as if he was sitting right beside me. I didn't want to seem crazy, so I didn't answer him back like I normally did for my mama.

Gina's mama told her she was about twelve to thirteen weeks along. When Gina heard the baby's heartbeat she started to cry.

Her mama still looked like she was repulsed. "Do you even know who the fuckin' daddy is?"

I knew she had just heard us talking about Big Jake so she had to have been skeptical that Gina really knew who her baby daddy was.

"Naw. But I don't know who my daddy is either. So we both hoes, Mama."

Her mama didn't say anything for a long time. She just looked like she wanted Gina to get as far away from her as she could.

I didn't know what to think. To think her mama was a doctor and would put her own daughter out confused me. I mean, you expected to hear shit like that from chicks who mama was fulla shit or those who were in the street themselves, but not a damn doctor. And she thought she was so much better than me and Gina. I could tell because of the way she kept her nose turned up when she looked at me.

My train of thought was broken when Gina's phone rang out. I knew it was Dame, the way her eyes widened and the way she hopped on the table.

"Come on, Ray-Ray. We gotta go."

She pulled on her clothes quick, and we hightailed it out of the back of her mama's office.

"Don't ever come back here, Gina," her mama yelled behind us.

"I won't, bitch," Gina mumbled under her breath.

The door slammed behind us, and we started speed-walking down a side street until we got back to the main one. It wasn't that hot out, but my nerves had me sweating.

Gina's phone kept ringing nonstop. I knew if Dame was calling her, then my phone was next.

I reached in my back pocket, and my heart dropped. "My phone is gone," I said in a panic.

"What?"

"My phone is gone. It must have fallen out when we ran from Pookie."

"Oh shit. Oh shit. Oh shit. Daddy got trackers on these phones. You know, those GPS shits?" She beat the side of her head as she walked around in a circle. "Come on. We gotta find a way to the safe house."

"Safe house?"

"Trigga and Big Jake got a place that nobody know about. If we can get to there, we safe, but that nigga got eyes everywhere and—"

Before the words could leave her mouth, a big black Hummer pulled up to the side of the street where we were walking.

The back door opened. I was wishing it was Trigga and Big Jake in there with Dame, but it wasn't. It was just Dame, Pookie, and another nigga from the house name Blackout. Another nigga I had cut up when I first got there, and the same one that was in the room with Sasha when I first got to the house. They called him Blackout because that nigga was so black he looked like a shadow or oil spot.

Blackout was driving, and Pookie was sitting in the back holding a bloody shirt over his face. Blackout hopped out the truck and threw both me and Gina in the back. She landed on the floor next to Dame's feet.

Dame kicked her so hard in the face, her scream got stuck in her throat. I didn't even have to look at Dame's face to know what was about to happen. I didn't even get a chance to think about what was going to happen. He punched me straight in my face as soon as my body hit the seat.

Everything went black.

When I woke up, it was to Gina's screams and pleas for Dame not to hit her no more. I moaned out as I opened my eyes.

"Ahhhhhhhhhhhhhhhhhhhhhhh! I'm sorry. I wasn't trying to run, I swear," Gina cried out.

My vision was blurry, but I could still make that we weren't in any room in the actual house. Every nigga and bitch on Dame's team was surrounding him and Gina who was on her knees in the middle of a cold concrete floor, the same floor I was on.

"Bitch, you must be outta your muthafuckin' mind to leave this muthafucka without me telling you."

"I didn't. I thought you told Sasha—"

"Don't put my name in it, bitch!" Sasha's voice rang out. "I ain't got shit to do with it."

I wanted to reach out and touch that bitch, but Dame had grabbed a handful of my hair and was dragging me to the middle of the floor where Gina was. I didn't even have time to realize I was finally in the underworld, the fuckin' basement.

"So you just gon' not answer the muthafuckin' phone I gave you?"

I looked up into the eyes of a fuckin' madman.

He had his belt wrapped around his fist, his face twisted like he had a deformity. He punched me in my stomach, and blood and bile flew out of my mouth. "You trying to run from me, my diamond? Huh?"

I shook my head, answering as quickly as I could. I knew he was going to hit me again. "No," I screamed out.

But that didn't help. He just kicked me this time then snatched me up by my hair and threw me face first into the concrete wall.

I staggered, tried to get on my feet, and the back of his hand caught my face, sending me crashing to the floor again.

"I wasn't trying to run," I managed to get out. I didn't think I could be understood, because pools of blood dropped from my mouth and my lips were heavy like they had cement injected in them.

My jaw, once again, felt like it had come unhinged. Dame was a big swolle nigga. No way he should have been beating my ass, punching me in my face, as big as his hands were.

"Oh, and, Daddy, this bitch down there is pregnant," Sasha told.

"Pregnant? You pregnant, bitch?" he asked, leaning over Gina. "How the fuck you gon' make my money with a baby in you? You gon' get rid of that shit."

"No," Gina whined low.

I knew that was a mistake as soon as the words left her mouth.

"What the fuck you say to me?"

"No. I'm not getting rid of my baby."

I was semiconscious on the floor, but I could see when Dame walked over and kicked Gina in her ribs. When she fell over, he brought his big foot down as hard as he could into her stomach.

"You ain't gotta get rid of it, bitch," he ranted, kicking her again. "I will."

Tears fell from my eyes for her, not my own pain, but because she had just heard her baby's heartbeat. Judging by the bloodcurdling scream she let out, I knew Big Jake would never know he was so close to being a daddy.

Dame kept beating and stomping her. I knew he was going to kill her. When his steel-toe boot connected with her face and her head snapped back, I found strength from somewhere and got up.

As fast as I could, I threw my body over hers, which seemed to piss him off further. He unrolled the thick leather belt from his hand and started to beat both of us with it. I would have given anything just to hear Gina scream, just one scream, to let me know she was still alive, but I got nothing. All I heard was my own screams, and all I saw was the faces of niggas and bitches sneering and laughing.

I saw that bitch Sasha standing with folded arms next to Pookie, and I knew in that moment, me and Gina had been set up.

The leather belt landed across my naked body. I was sure my body was looking like Jesus looked when they beat him before putting him on that cross.

I still didn't move from Gina's body. Even as I tried to hold my hand up to keep the hits from getting to me, I kept her covered as much as I could.

Mama, if I die in here today I'll be glad. I can't keep doing this, Mama! Why you and Daddy do this? Leave me here like this? Too much pain and hurt. Can't do this.

Even as I talked to my mama, I couldn't help but wonder where Trigga and Big Jake were. They were noticeably absent, and after so many kicks, hits, and punches, so was I.

Trigga

"Hand me that stash."

"Which one, bro?" Jake said, moving quickly behind me.

"Nigga, any of them, man! Move fast, an' secure that bitch's mouth."

Jake tossed me the stash then bent down to send his fist forward, cracking teeth, then snatched it back before tying the mouthpiece. "I did. Damn. You know I'm just the guard. This shit is your thang, punk."

"Yeah, yeah, man." I laughed then squeezed my trigga. *Pow-Pow!*

Me and Big Jake moved around a group of trees, clearing up our footsteps and lacing the land with bags of dust, lime, and other products.

Trick-ass bitches think they gon' run game on me, set up members of my newfound fam. Naw, shit ain't 'bout to go down like that.

See, everything was on point a couple of hours ago after getting orders from Dame. Jake and I was out, running errands, making sure bossman's networks were giving us the right units of drugs to bring back to the house.

We left that spot, heading to several PBs houses, when both our cells went off. Since Jake was driving, I clicked on the message, which was sent by one of "my eyes" in the house. And the shit I saw moved up the plan. Shit was popping off in the underworld. The image looked like this was some World Star shit. All I heard was niggas and bitches *oo-ing* and *aahing*, shouting out various *damns* and whatnot.

As the camera turned, I saw that nigga Blackout flashing nothing but his whites as he gassed up Dame, who was kicking Gina and Diamond like they wasn't human. Everything in me got mad quiet and shit. I was heated. Like I was no longer in the car, nothing but that image was playing. I memorized everything, and everyone.

Sasha's clown face was grinning, her hand on her hip, as she stood next to Pookie. Nothing but her pink, flabby peeling lips whispered in his ear before she shouted out that Gina was knocked up.

My mouth straight up dropped when she said that shit. Gina was breedin'? I listened while that broad Sasha then shouted out some shit that Diamond was sneaking out, tryin'a runaway and shit. That's when Blackout and Pookie threw my name in there, saying they see me talkin' to Gina and Ray-Ray all the time. On hearing that, Dame kicked the fuck outta Gina.

"Fuck, nah!" I shouted.

His foot landed into her stomach as he stomped her. It was like I could feel each blow.

Gina's and Ray-Ray's screams filled the car and had a nigga's jaw clenched tight. The screen shook as my eyes tried to get a better angle than it zoomed in. With one final blow that I saw Dame give to Diamond then Gina's head, my cell cracked in my hand then flew into the dashboard, almost breaking.

I yelled for Jake to pull over but wasn't nothing to tell him to do, because he already was pulled over looking at his cell, gripping the steering wheel of his car.

Jake yelled, "We got set the fuck up! They set our fam up, Trig! That's what the fuck this is about!"

My head shook. I slowly pushed my hoodie back in disbelief, listening and watching until the end. My eyes ended the message with more intel about what was going on, telling us that they had heard Sasha lie to Diamond and Gina to get them out the house. They had also heard that Gina had sliced up Pookie's face then ran off to some doctor, where they got caught. All this shit was sloppy and messy as fuck. Now they were in the underworld. Wasn't shit I could do to save them from "the seven punishments," which was already going down as we watched. I was ready to place my blade against each nigga's throat.

Jake's growling yell took me back to the car and outta my mind. "Gina's having a baby, man? And that motherfucka got my girl down there tryin'a kill her and it!"

The fact that the car was moving again made me realize Jake was ready to kill.

I reached over and swerved the car over on the side of the road to get him to stop before we both got killed. "Pump them brakes, nigga! Chill the fuck out. I need to think, homie. You know we can't run up in there. Our plan would be all the way done. Feel me? Naw, we gonna get them bitches back.

"See, Sasha thinks no one knows about her weakness, but I got her fuckin' ass. And Pookie?" I let out a harsh laugh as I rubbed my hands together. "I got that nigga and Blackout too. See, you don't fuck wit' what ya think ya know about. I let my hand be shown too much. Time to close that shit up and play this shit all the way forward. Feel me?"

Jake stared at me confused, hurt, and all the way pissed off. I could tell all he wanted to do was to get back to Gina, and I could feel him on that shit. I wanted to get back to them too. Wanted to take all them fuckas out and snatch up Diamond and Gina. Everything had to happen in due time, and now this shit was being sped up.

"What the fuck we 'bout to do, man? What we gonna do? Ain't shit we can do. Dame crazy, man. We ain't making it out this shit without some of us falling an', I ain't about to let Gina be that one."

On some real shit, I played all the angles out in my head, and everything Jake was saying was true. See, I had my plan too, not just the group shit. Dame had not only fucked up once, but he'd just fucked up for a second time. Shit, the fact that everyone was at Dame's taking pieces of Gina's and Diamond's flesh didn't feel like some accident, not with us out here running simple-shit errands. That nigga Dame had specifically sent me and Big Jake on this errand run after he got a phone call that had to be from one of them niggas.

Nah. Felt like we were being played and manipulated. I dug in my jacket and pulled out my pop's and mom's journals. I only carried them on simple assignments when I know I'm going straight back to my crib. I memorized every line in each book. Shit was second nature to me now, so I knew what page to fall on. Licking my lips, a name stuck out for me, one I had been hearing on the streets as a small kid and could never get to—Phenom.

"Chill and listen. That nigga is done. He's in his last hours. Check it. You eva hear 'bout the invisible street king? A nigga known for having mad Glocks and any kind of weapon you want. Nigga can make senators run game for him?" I asked, while looking at the words my pops wrote.

Son, our demand for community control flows naturally from the science of our life. It teaches that we are the Supreme Being in person and the sole controllers of our own destiny. If we know this, work for the community, we get to peace, because in the absence of peace is chaos or confusion, and in the absence of confusion is order. The streets are nothing but chaos, and you will be that order. Remember these teachings. Find Phenom. He will give you your inheritance.

"Yeah, man, dude is like a legend, got hands across the nation, they say. Phenom. What about him?" Jake stepped close to me.

It was like my pops knew his time was coming. Closing my parents' books, I put them back in my jacket and glanced at Jake. "We 'bout to meet that nigga in the flesh. I got a way to get to him. We make a statement to that bitch Sasha, bring chaos. Then I go get us our way out."

"A'ight, bro. Whatever we gotta do to turn that nigga and his bitches into fertilizer," Jake growled.

Game time was on. Everything I did so far had a reason to it. If the unit Dame was linked up to came for us, best believe, I could work out something. The LKs wanted me on their side, as did the Jamaicans and Nigerians. It was always a way out in something, so I guess it was good that what Jake was telling me ran through my head. 'Cuz a nigga had to get at this plan and wasn't about to let some fear shit mess up Jake's mental. We all were getting out of here some way, or we would become the masters and controllers of the overall game.

"Check it. Dame just got us in the game with big leaders. This is what we do. We got cards, so we make sure those big bosses want us. Feel me? The politicians, the old money, we make sure they want us, and we use them like they will use us. That's our fallback until we can hide, but right now, since that ratchet, Beyoncé wannabe, loose-pussy-lip bitch Sasha wanna set some bitches up, with Pookie and Blackout helping, yeah, I got some shit for them."

I pulled out a black notebook that I had strapped to the inside of my hoodie. I also only carried it when I was out on duty. Then I'd hid that shit in a way that even those niggas who watched me never saw. Thumbing my nose, I flipped through it.

Jake's emotions were getting to me. It had my mind working, sifting through the plan like a game, and it fueled me. I lived for the type of shit Dame, Pookie, Sasha, and Blackout was pulling. Gave me lessons and made me stay tight on my shit. Which was why I needed to calm my homie down, or else the plan would crumbled. And then

I'd have to go back to plan B, C, and D—me and my Glock taking out Dame by myself.

"What we doing, bro?" Jake asked, the veins in his forehead visible.

"Look, I need you to chill—Take out your gun and load it then unload it. This ol' cat in the streets taught me that, to calm me down when I used to blow up and shit. Do that and listen. Bodies 'bout to drop. Sasha got money and product stashed she stole from Dame herself. She also got a nigga who she meets with in the streets to sell for her. She's mad close to him; I never used to know why, but I do now."

I brought up pictures on my cell to show Jake who I was speaking on. "Nigga is her brother, and he's foul as fuck. We get to him, take him out, drop Pookie's prints, then we go to Pookie's. The more on him, the more pain he can get. Feel me? And you know Pookie got stash, so we lace it with Sasha's shit. And then we snatch up that nigga's cousin. He's not even from L.A. Bullets to his head, Sasha's prints. All of that, and we leave Dame a nice note—DOA. Let him see that these bitches been playing him up the middle. Then we link Blackout to all of it too. Feel me?"

Jake sat back in his seat flexing his gun. He loaded it then took the bullets out, and repeated the process. He slammed his head against the headrest. "A'ight, but we doing something to Blackout's peeps too. He has some cousins in the street who are goons too. Take them out."

"You know it. Hide this shit, and let's get this going. Everything we do gotta work where Dame can't get the math of how long we been gone. Bet?"

Jake started the car and pulled off with a grunt. "Bet."

Riding through the A, we hit up all of Dame's PBs to make our time look good. Stashing our ride, one of Dame's PBs was a chick Jake and I used to help, so she covered us and didn't ask any questions. She always trusted in what we did, so we knew we could trust her with this cover. She also hated all them niggas in Dame's house, including Dame, so it was all good.

Yamamoto Tsunetomo's *The Book of the Samurai* said some shit like, "if a man was mad strict, then the people he commanded would be untrustworthy, and if he over-trusted them, then they would become uncontrollable." Dame had been all of that, which was why his house was falling.

We went through the plan as fast as we could. Both Jake and I had items that belonged to our enemy, so we used what we could, lacing Pookie's and Blackout's place, then snatching some of their people. House to house we went. We'd tie up some niggas, made them grip Glocks then take out people, repeating the process over and over while we rode through the *A* in Pookie's brother's ride, dropping bodies left and right.

I stood over bitches recording some of what we did, just to save it for Sasha, Pookie, and Blackout. Our masks covered our faces, as well as our hoodies, but I didn't give a fuck if they knew who we were, since they were dead to me anyway. Shit was sublime for me, and from the look on Jake's face, shit was just as good for him too. Everything we did, we did for Gina and Diamond, and to fix the plan.

When it came to Sasha's place, shit got a little hard. We circled the abandoned two-level house. I circled the back, taking the porch stairs, and landing in the main bedroom. Jake went through the basement. Place smelled like ass, pussy, shit, and piss. Everywhere I stepped, fresh or dead roaches crunched under my kicks.

A four-poled bed was in front of me. Dirty sheets with come spots lay crumbled over the huge mattress, dried condom wrappers lay on the bed and the floor, and clothes were everywhere. Damn sure didn't know how the fuck anyone but someone homeless or on that shit could

live in here. Which made a perfect hideout spot. Sasha
had learned a lot being Dame's bitch, but now she was
about to learn what it was like to be mine.

Jake appeared down the hall ahead of me, in the
kitchen. He gave me a signal, telling me the place was
empty, then we wrapped around downstairs. We moved
quietly, listening, until we heard that nigga blasting his
music and yelling about some video game. Loud stomps
from his feet made the ceiling above us rumble.

I quietly climbed the stairs. Trash was everywhere,
graffiti on the wall. Just for the fuck of it, I picked some
trash up and threw it to get that fool's attention, but his
TV was so loud, he didn't hear shit.

I rounded the corner and saw Big Jake watching from
the corner of the room. His mask covered him up, making
him look like a monster in darkness, and his gloved hands
held his silver Glock.

I walked to the side and kicked a chair down. "'S up,
nigga? Damn. You ain't 'bout shit if you ain't hear me and
my partna." I laughed.

Sasha's brother sat up fast on the couch. His brown eyes
locked on me. He shook his head. Nigga looked just like a
male twin of Sasha, 'cept nigga was huge like a wrestler.
He had locks like me, but they were matted, looking like
stuffed red and brown caterpillars. His sagging jeans were
dusty as fuck, and his shoes were off his feet. The sound of
him cracking his knuckles made me grin, ready for battle.
Was I scared? Naw. Did I worry I couldn't take him down?
Fuck, no. I loved challenges. This nigga was about to be a
fun kill.

"I know you. You that special-ed, mute, bubba-gump
nigga, Trigga. I got some shit for you," he barked out.
Gold flashed from his crooked teeth.

Nigga sounded like he smoked too many blunts and
swallowed acid. His voice was both scratchy and deep. It
annoyed me.

"Am I, nigga? If I am, think on why I would be hitting your fucked-up place? Smells like your sister's cunt for real, son. Ya needa handle all that." I laughed, fanning flies that flew by.

"Man, fuck you! You played my sista," he roared out.

I pointed my gun at the sloppy nigga in front of me. He was nothing but stank, rolled up in fat, and hot air with white eyes.

"Naw, she let herself get played—played in the ass, mouth, cunt, throat, armpit, probably her eye and ear too. I don't know, nigga, but your sister is foul, just like you, and like you 'bout to be. I'm going to have fun letting my gun make her my bitch. Feel me?"

"Yo, fuck yo' life, nigga!" Sasha's brother spat, charging at me.

I laughed and then shrugged. Guess I wasn't gonna get any fun out of him anyway, so I stayed where I was, watching him spit while he spoke, his saggy titties slapping through his stained beater as he rushed me. Shit was kinda funny to me. All I heard was *Slap, slap, slap.* Made me think of some thick pussy riding me. It kinda made me want to fuck for a moment.

My boot kicked out a table to push him back, and it took Big Jake to body-drop that nigga, just to hold him down. Nigga was built like a tank, but Big Jake was stronger.

Jake yelled out, "*Attenshhhunnnn*, you bonecrusher-ass nigga!"

Several rounds of emptying our Glocks took out that nigga. We left him right where he fell in the middle of the living room, surrounded by roaches and dog shit, and that was the end of Sasha's blood.

While we marked Sasha's place up for show, you know, just in case shit didn't pan out the way a nigga planned, we snatched up two of that nigga's goons who were also Sasha's cousins and dropped them in the back of the trunk of our ride.

Darkness from the sky was our friend. The streets seemed to be mad quiet for some reason, but it didn't bother me none. Matter of fact, it worked to our advantage, moving around like we were, as we headed to the drop-off spot with these bodies. Time seemed to tick off, but the way we moved quickly and professionally, everything fit in right on time.

Now we stood in the forest of Georgia. Blackout's cousins and their rides were behind us, and Pookie's cousin's ride parked opposite of it. Three niggas sat on their knees, bound and whining, their faces bloody.

Jake walked behind the lame-ass niggas to untie them. He moved smoothly but quickly. As he pointed his gun, a bullet from its barrel followed with him, leaving bodies to fall on each other like dominoes. We didn't have time to make this perfect, but we did have time to make it look like each nigga squeezed their own triggers at each other, so no *CSI* shit could pop off. That was our only moment of concern, to make it look good and not fake.

I buried each body, adding lime over each hole in the ground. Had to leave a couple niggas alive back around the block, just to make it look good too.

We had kicked in doors yelling Dame's name, along with me calling Jake Pookie, or him calling me Blackout.

Sweat soaked into my mask, and the muscles in my arms tightened with each shuffle then positioning of the bodies.

While we worked, our cells popped off, even my cracked cell phone.

"'Wassup, bossman. Yeah, we handled your business and 'bout to chill and eat, thinking about Laylah's. Got you some extra ducats, and no doubt we'll get those plantains you dig. A'ight." Jake ended his call and looked at me.

"Nigga's eyes itching?" I asked.

Jake gave off a harsh laugh then emptied his gun. "Yeah. Hate that nigga."

I switched out my gloves, walking back and forth, as I spoke. "Me too, man, trust that. Check it. These niggas are dust. I need you to be my eyes and take me to the Nigerian queen's messengers. Been checking her for some time now. I know, without a doubt, she fucks with Phenom, so I know if she sees that I want to talk to her she'll do it. So let's get back. All of this is set right, looks like turf shit. We can ride out and fix the GPS, a'ight."

Jake gave a slight nod while taking off his mask. "I got you, man. We'll do that then I'll circle this shit around to Laylah's restaurant to make sure we look legit in our shit. "

"Right, man, you on that same page then. Let's be about it. Yo, good look to pick Laylah's, since it's in Castleberry Hills near the NQ's crib," I said, giving him dap.

We headed to drop the cars at a scrap yard, switching them out. Trackers were on everything Dame gave us. But because Jake knew about cars, Dame's eyes, and how to fix it, I now lay on my back under our car fixing the GPS and tracking systems. We had to cover our track while staying on time.

"A'ight, Trig. Let's get your message sent and be out. I need to get to Gina. If I lose her, if she loses that baby, you know that's gonna break Gina, man, and I'm not down for that. She ain't deserve this fuckin' life. If her momma had been good to her, she'd be okay now," Jake said, pacing back and forth.

My hands worked fast, twisting on the GPS. As the familiar beep went off, I sighed, looking at nothing but the bottom of our ride.

"Yeah, I know, bro. A lot of stuff would have been different, but check it, you wouldn't have met her then."

Jake's grunt then the loud ding of his foot kicking the bumper of our ride had me quickly sliding back out from under it.

"Whoa! Watch that shit, man. I'm just saying, wasn't no beef there."

Jake fisted his big hands as he spoke to me. "I know. Look, let's just go. Not feeling talking about what coulda been, you know."

He was right. The "what coulda beens" always made shit harder.

"A'ight. And we'll get some way for you to get alone with Gina. Bet?" I looked at Jake's shoulders drop before he ran a hand over his waves.

"Yeah, bet. You our leader. I trust that, man, even to the grave." Jake walked up to me and gave me dap again.

Jake's time with Gina was his heaven, so I knew he was down when he gave a smile.

We hopped back into the Escalade and then made it to Laylah's, where I was able to send a message to the NQ on the low through Laylah herself. She owed me one from something I did for her. It was good to have resources that hated the same people we did and who actually respected us for what we did because, had we not learned about that nigga Dame, everything we did would be tricky.

Everything was in motion. I was the chaos that would bring the peace. My name wasn't Trigga without a reason, and the house of Dame was about to fall by my hand.

Ray-Ray

When I woke up, Dame was sitting in a chair at the foot of his bed. There was a bloody machete to his right and he held his gun in his left. I cursed God for not letting this nigga kill me while I was in that basement.

"Why you make me do this to you, Diamond?" Dame asked me, his voice deep and calm, his posture relaxed.

I tried to open my mouth, but my jaw felt like it had been wired shut. I knew it was swollen, and the pain I felt was almost unbearable.

"Why you make me put you in the basement? Huh?"

As my vision became clearer, I could see he was covered in blood. I swore I saw meat hanging off the blade of the machete, like he had just slaughtered an animal.

My mind immediately went to Gina. *Oh God, Gina.* I closed my eyes and groaned out. Tears burned as they fell down my face. *Lord, why?*

A knock at Dame's door interruptd my thoughts.

"Enter," he said.

Fallon and Guss, two other niggas who ran drugs for Dame, came in and tossed Gina's almost lifeless body at Dame's feet. She was bleeding badly, but I thanked God she was alive, although barely.

After they left out, Dame kicked Gina away from him like she was nothing more than trash. Cuts and gashes decorated her naked body and face. From the way she was whimpering, I knew what had happened to her again in the underworld.

"You know you're my diamond, right?" Dame said to me. "You made me leave you in that fuckin' basement so other niggas could fuck you, and then I had to dismember the niggas who touched you. You make me fuckin' crazy, Diamond. This is your fault." His voice rose and then cracked like he was emotional.

I could tell from the ache between my legs what had happened to me, but I didn't want to think about it. I couldn't take my eyes off Gina. I didn't know what day it was or how long I had been unconscious, but I knew my body ached in places that it shouldn't have. So I could only imagine what Gina's body felt like. I was no doctor, but I knew she needed to get to a hospital. I was quite sure she had lost her baby because blood was still pouring from between her legs.

When Dame stood up, my eyes darted back and forth between him and Gina. I just wanted him to leave me alone. Wanted to be left by myself so I could check on Gina. Just wanted to not be where I was.

Anger instead of fear took over my senses. I was done. Sasha was officially a target. All I could think about was picking up something to smash that bitch's face in. I had to wonder if Big Jake or Trigga had heard about what happened, but knowing how gums in the house flapped, I was sure they had.

Another knock came to the door just as Dame had stood and walked over to the bed where I was. The machete was in his hand, and he looked like he was high, with his glossy eyes. I knew that look. It was the one he always had after playing in his own pure product.

"What?" he barked out at the door so loud, it made me jerk in surprise.

"Boss, Trigga and Big Jake pulling up to the gate fast, like some niggas after them or something," Guss reported.

"Fuck you telling me for, nigga?"

"'Cuz word on the street is that some shit popped off with a turf war with our house and—"

"The fuck?" Dame shouted out, just as a loud crash and bang could be heard all around the house.

I could hear feet running and niggas screaming up the stairs that Trigga and Jake had just crashed through the front gates of Dame's crib.

"Get the guns," Dame ordered as he rushed out of the room with Guss.

I could hear girls screaming and running.

"Get the fuck in your rooms!" Dame commanded, smacking one of the girls in the back of her head as she ran down the hall.

Once he was gone, I slowly dragged my body from the high bed, falling on the floor hard. I crawled past Gina and kicked the door closed. It would lock on its own with a push of the button on the wireless remote. I crawled against the cold marble floor until I got to Gina. My girl was bad, messed up to the point that she was missing teeth. Instead of crying tears, she was crying blood, and just by touching her, I could tell she was feverish.

"I'm so sorry, Gina," I whispered as I held her head in my lap.

I hadn't known the girl for long, but I swore I loved her. When I didn't have anybody else, I had her. She took care of me like she had known me all her life. Her eyes fluttered like she was trying to open them, but she couldn't. They were swollen shut.

I pushed the matted, bloody hair from her face and rocked her in my arms. "Please don't die on me, Gina. Please. I ain't got nobody else, really. Please don't die."

I mumbled that through my tears, but all Gina could do was try to squeeze my hands. I watched in utter defeat, knowing I couldn't do anything to save her, so I just rocked her while complete chaos surrounded us. I didn't know what was going on. As I gazed down at Gina, her lips moved, like she was trying to say something.

"I can't understand you," I whispered to her as I leaned down.

She tried to speak, but all she could do was cough, swallow, cough again, then spit up blood. I saw my daddy and mama all over again. She kept moving her lips like a fish.

"Water? You want water?" I asked her.

She nodded very slowly. Then she winced and closed her eyes tight.

I grabbed the golden pillow from Dame's chair and placed it underneath her head. Yeah, it hurt me like fuck to move, but if she wanted water, I was going to get it. It gave me hope that she would live. As fast as I could, I moved from the floor and grabbed one of the glasses Dame used to drink his bourbon and tried to walk fast to the bathroom. I turned on the cold water and made the mistake of looking at myself in the mirror.

My jaw looked like I was holding a golf ball in my right cheek. Eyes purple and bruised, it looked like some of my hair had been snatched out by the root. My lips were also cut, and skin was missing from my forehead from when Dame had slung me hair first into the concrete wall.

I looked away from my image. If I didn't get out of this life, it would kill my youth, just as it had stolen my innocence. I filled the glass with water and walked out, only to come to an abrupt stop. Gina had sat up. Well, she was sitting back on her knees. I knew she was looking at me because of the semi-smile she was trying to give me.

For a moment my heart swelled. She would live. There was hope.

She whispered, "Th-they killed m-my baby"—She swallowed slowly then moved her hands to her lap—"killed him . . . her..."

She was naked, and one of her breasts had been sliced open. Tears rolled down my face.

"Gina . . ."

"But . . . they won't . . . kill me." She tried to smile again.

Just like before, I felt hope. I closed my eyes with a small smile.

"Tell Ja-Jackson I l-love him," she muttered, making me open my eyes.

What I saw stopped my heart. There was a blade in her hand. She held that hand to her neck and sliced her throat from ear to ear.

A deafening scream leapt from my lungs as blood spewed from her neck, the glass crashed to the floor, and her body fell backwards. I kept screaming as I rushed to her side. My body shook like I had the chills.

I dropped to my knees, trying to stop the blood from spilling with my hands. I belted out, "Ahhh, God! Gina, no!" I was so terrified and out of my mind with grief, I didn't even hear Dame rushing into the room with Trigga and Big Jake in tow.

"What the fuck?" Dame shouted as he looked around. It didn't take him long to figure out what had happened. "Get this bitch up off my floor and call the fuckin' cleaners." He grabbed me and pulled me from the room kicking and screaming.

I didn't know where he was taking me. To be honest, I didn't care. I'd just seen the only friend I had in the house slice her own throat. Gina was gone. Yeah, she had cut her own throat, taken her life, but I blamed Sasha. I blamed Dame. I blamed Pookie.

I caught a glimpse of Big Jake falling to his knees like a sack of potatoes next to Gina's lifeless body, his face contorted. I knew his pain was real because he didn't care who saw him cradle Gina like a baby in his arms as tears rolled down his handsome face. Gina had tamed the giant, brought out the beauty in the beast.

Trigga's hand on Big Jake's shoulder seemed to anchor him in his grief. Dame didn't see it because he was too busy threatening my life as he dragged me into another room.

Four hours later, the house was quiet. Dame's room had been cleaned to perfection. The gates to his mansion had been fixcd. After he dragged me to his other room, he held a gun to my head and told me that if I screamed again he was going to bury me next to Gina. So I could only grieve through silent tears. After that, he showered when word was brought to him from the Nigerian queen's messengers that a meeting was being called.

The whole house sat around the dinner table as every street king and queen once again sat around Dame. Tension was thick.

Trigga's lip kept twitching. Big Jake was here, but his mind appeared to be somewhere else, his face emotionless. Sasha sat at my right side by Dame dressed in Gina's favorite color, bubblegum pink. That bitch was trying to be funny.

I walked down the stairs in all red—red spandex shorts that showcased my ass, matching sports bra, and red Jordans—my hair brushed back into a ponytail. Did the best I could with it, worked through the pain. The bang covered the big scar on my forehead. My jaw was still swollen, but I could talk a little better.

Dame's eyes were burning another hole in the side of my head because I wasn't supposed to show my face. He had told me to stay in the room, because he didn't want the Nigerian Queens, especially Anika, to see my face. Fuck him. I wanted like hell for him to say something to me that I didn't like. The whole room got quiet when I limped in.

**

See, while I was up in the room, Dame had tried to lock me in, but my daddy came to talk to me. Dame had left out some coke.

"Sniff some of that shit, and it will take the pain away, baby girl," my daddy said. *"Yeah, it's fucked up for me to tell you this, but you gon' need it. You wanna beat a ho ass, don't you?"*

I looked up slowly as I sat in the center of Dame's bed trembling with anger and fear, my daddy standing right there in his usual getup—fresh white Jordans, designer jeans, and a designer button-down. There was no bullet holes in him.

I nodded.

"Then line that shit up and take it to the head," he said.

"I don't really know how, Daddy."

"Bullshit, baby. You a Jenkins. We know all about doing muthafuckin' drugs, you feel me? Grab that blade right there."

I did as he said.

"Now pour a little bit of that shit on that mirror."

I grabbed that mirror that Dame always used and sat it on the table in front of the bed.

"Now use that blade to line you up about four lines, roll up that dollar bill right there, and take that shit to the head."

I did just like my daddy said. Sniffed all four lines through the rolled-up dollar bill then dropped my head back to sniff back the snot that was trying to fall down. I felt when my daddy sat on the bed next to me.

"That's right, baby girl. To the dome. Lay back and let that shit settle in for a bit. Once it do, you ain't gon' feel shit. Then you take yo' ass down there and handle yo' business."

I nodded and did exactly as he'd directed, and sure enough, I didn't feel shit.

***

That's why I was sitting next to Dame, staring Anika right in her eyes as she gazed at me. I couldn't tell what that look was in her eyes, but as usual, she kept a knowing smile on her face. Still, I couldn't shake that feeling that something else was going on that she wasn't telling. I knew she was cool with Dame, so if she wanted to start some shit, she could get it too.

My head slowly turned to Pookie, and I smiled hard, a cheesy one. That nigga was going to die tonight.

I sniffed loudly and then took a big gulp of water. The shit fell down the sides of my mouth. I was geeked like a muthafucka.

I said to Dame out of the blue, "You know this bitch stealing from you, Daddy?"

Dame tilted his head and leaned forward. "Say what now?"

"This ho stealing yo' shit and selling it in the street."

Sasha's eyes bugged out like someone was choking the life from her.

Dame chuckled as he leaned over and whispered in my ear, "You know I'm going to fuckin' kill you when they leave, right?"

"So," I said out loud. "That's why they lied on me and Gina. Heard her and Pookie talking about it on the stairs. So I tried to play it off like I didn't. That's why she lied and told me and Gina you said for us to leave the house. Tried to get us killed so we couldn't tell."

Sasha jumped up and yelled, "You lying-ass bitch!" and smacked me in my face.

Yeah, I was lying. Trigga had left me a code where only I would see it in Gina's old room. He laid a doll on the bed with blonde hair with a piece of peppermint candy in a small Ziploc bag. It looked like crack rock. That blonde hair meant Sasha, since she was the only one in the house

with it. That candy? I took it to mean that she was selling
Dame's shit, or it had something to do with some kind of
product. I could have been wrong, but it was too late to
turn back now.

That bitch had done exactly what I had wanted her to
do. I jumped up from that chair like I was super bitch.
The first thing I did was grab that big ho by her hair and
tossed her ass across the room. I felt none of that pain I
was in earlier. Higher than a fuckin' kite, head floating
like I was on a cloud, I was going to whup that trick. I
could hear chairs being pushed back from tables.

"Now this is entertainment," a male voice with a
Russian-sounding accent said.

"Yo, Dame, which one of dem hoes is yo' bottom bitch,
my man?" someone else asked him as my fist connected
to Sasha's face over and over again.

She reached up and clawed my face, but I didn't feel
that shit. I stomped her in the face as she went down to
the floor.

Just to put on a good show so Dame wouldn't be the
wiser, I screamed out, "You stole my daddy shit, bitch.
Fuckin' up my daddy money, ho!"

"Ahh," the Russian said again. "I take it the one laying
the smackdown is the bottom, er, *beech*."

Niggas cracked up.

I could see Timberlands coming my way. I knew that
was Trigga, so I tried to beat that ho as much as I could
before he pulled me away.

"Naw, Trigga," Dame growled low. "Let her handle that
shit."

I knew he only allowed me to go to town on that bitch
because he couldn't do it with Anika in the house. I was
beating Sasha so bad, I didn't even realize when she
had stopped swinging back. I'd torn her dress off her
and kicked her in her pussy before I realized she wasn't

defending herself anymore. She lay in the middle of the room in a pool full of her own blood. Just like Gina.

"Bitch!" I screamed out and gave a running punt kick to her face. I wanted to finish that ho right then and there. I picked up the heaviest vase in the room, well, the vase closest to me, straddled her while standing up, and was set to bring it down on her face, but Dame told Trigga to grab me.

"Naw, don't kill that bitch yet. That ho gon' make me my money back," Dame fumed. "Drag that bitch downstairs," he told another soldier.

We all knew downstairs meant the basement.

When Trigga snatched me back, the vase crash landed on the floor, while Sasha lay moaning on the floor.

Forgetting I was still in the presence of a madman, I lay my head back against Trigga's chest and laughed. I was sure that by then everyone in the room knew "Scotty" was calling me. Some of the men in the room offered Dame cash just to take me with them for the evening,

"What the young one says is true." Anika scowled at Dame, whose face was contorted in anger. "Your product is being distributed watered down on the south side. Bodies were dropped. A turf war has been set off, and it's looking like niggas from your house started it."

Dame thundered. "Hey, I don't know shit about no turf war!" The vein in his forehead was protruding again, and his hazel eyes had darkened.

"Watch that tone when you're talking to me, Damien," Anika hissed. "I'm not one of your girls."

The Russian, who looked like that big pale mofo from the *Rocky* movies quirked a brow and smirked. "She is beautiful in her sass," he said, talking about Anika.

"Your shit has been sloppy for a while now, and until you get your house in order, I'll be staying my distance." Anika rose from the table, snapping her fingers, and all her guards fell in line behind her.

Armando, the Latin King, rose to his feet. "I know I've been pretty silent, but my allegiance has always been with Anika. If she's keeping her distance, so am I."

There was a smirk on Armando's face that told Dame that he knew something that Dame didn't know. He buttoned his double-breasted black suit jacket and signaled his guards to follow him out.

The Jamaican King rose to his feet next. "Yuh already know way me stand, brudda. If Anika goes, so do I."

It looked like the king's house was crumbling, and this time he was going down with it.

Trigga

Diamond had wilded out and got on some real ratchet shit. Was sexy as fuck. I watched as she took Sasha's head and slammed that shit down on the floor. Smirked when she stomped that broad in the ground. In my mind, I was laughing my ass off and wished she had finished that bitch off, but then I remembered it was too soon to end her torture.

Diamond was slumped against my chest, eyes rolling and shit. Shawty was sniffing, almost sweatin', so I knew she musta gotten into some dust. What had me tripping though was how Dame was watching us. Nigga was cutting me with his eyes. I almost gave a wide smile at that nigga. I had what was his in my arms, and she felt good too. But my mind was on some other shit.

One, I had noticed through the dinner how Anika spoke. Shit was, like, in codes, codes like I'd learned from my pops. I realized she got my message, and had one for me too. Dope. My network with her was down. Also, when Armando walked by, I noticed how he gave me a signal of allegiance. That tripped me out too. Another one on my side. This shit was falling into my lap like clockwork, all of it going down without Dame noticing a thing. Why? Because nigga was stuck on pussy. Young pussy.

Now, on to number two, Gina had taken her life. The blood everywhere, how she went out, played over in my head. It was as if I was seeing how my mom got killed by that nigga Dame. Sasha needed to pay, Dame needed to pay, Pookie, Blackout, everyone that helped that nigga Dame end Gina's life needed to die, and I was happy to be the one to do it.

Diamond needed to be handled, because Sasha needed to have a private conversation with a nigga. I turned to the side to give Diamond to Big Jake. Pookie and Blackout walked up to me to try to get to Sasha, but I pushed past them niggas.

"We got that bitch, Trigga dog," Blackout said to me.

Feeling how Dame watched me, I kneeled down to snatch Sasha by the back of her neck then dragged her body behind me like a rag doll. Bitch didn't deserve to be picked the fuck up. "Naw, ya don't. Y'all need to get at them niggas that was chasing at Jake and me. Find out who started the turf war behind bossman's back. Defend the house. Feel me?"

Nigga got in my face like he was going to step to me, so I did him a solid and punched him right in his face. I watched him stumble back before sending my Tims right into his muthafuckin' chest, while pulling on Sasha's hair.

Blackout pushed back, trying to punch me, but he was clumsy with it. So I was able to slowly walk back, laughing.

Dame slammed his cane on the floor. "Go handle that shit, Pookie and Blackout!" he yelled. Then he called behind me, "Ey, yo, fuck you going, Trigga?"

Everyone in the house had cleared out. Dame had gotten played again. Nigga was about to bring hell and fuck up everyone in his way, like the bitch-ass nigga he was.

The vein in my temple began to throb. "Taking this broad to the basement, like you asked, bossman."

"Nah, nigga, you assumed that shit." Dame started to go in.

Keeping my voice level and calm, I quickly stopped his shit at the pass. "Bossman, looks like the rest of the bosses are trying to get your attention. Let me do my job for you and take care of this disloyal bitch."

Malice glinted in his eyes. He looked like he didn't know what the fuck to do in the moment. His house was falling, and he was sitting stupid. Nigga definitely wasn't a true boss; I could see that shit now.

So as he sat on the side of the table thinking on how to grow fuckin' apples, or whatever the fuck that nigga had going on in his dome, I yanked on Sasha and walked off on him. I ain't have time for his split-personality bullshit. I was on a time frame, which included fuckin' this bitch up more.

As I headed down into the basement, I heard a whistle down in the hallway. I knew no one was around, and where the whistle came from, which was familiar to me, no cameras were there. So I twisted Sasha's hair in my hand and slammed her face hard into a wall and dropped her where she lay. Her soft whimper let me know that bitch was still out.

Moving quickly, I dropped down to one knee and looked into the darkness. The person I called my eyes stood there holding a card. I reached into my pocket and pulled out a piece of candy in exchange for the card.

"What she say?" I asked.

The soft voice of my eyes happily grabbed the candy and gave me a smile. "She said tha world is yours, and ta hurry up, she's mad bored with his life."

A slow smile spread across my face. I stood then looked down. "You need to disappear and go chill with her. She'll keep you safe, Ghost, until I get to you, a'ight."

"A'ight. Trigga?" Ghost's soft voice asked.

"Yeah, baby girl?" I kneeled down to look into her big doe eyes.

See, for about as long as I been in the house, Ghost had been there. She was one of the lost kids like me, but mad younger, around eight or nine years old. Her mom hid her well in the house from Dame, his own daughter, by dressing her up like a boy. Me and Gina had promised always to watch her once her mom died, and she became my eyes. I'd also schooled her on my pops' and moms' teachings.

"I miss Gina. Fuck that nigga up. I don't care that he ma daddy. You ma real daddy. So fuck him up. Thank you fa the candy," Ghost said, reaching out to hug my leg, before disappearing through her secret ways.

I rolled my shoulders then popped my knuckles as I walked to Sasha, yanking her up. "You know I will, baby girl, on my word."

Sasha started waking up the moment her body rolled down the stairs. Yeah, I just tossed that bitch down like the trash she was.

The smell of blood still scented the basement even though it was clean. A glance far into the darkness of the basement made me smile.

I yanked hard then picked Sasha up and laid her on the table. See, the table was known as the lunchroom 'cuz this was where bitches and niggas lay as they got ran in. So, for now, Sasha looked like she needed to be put on the lunchroom.

"Uggg! Hey! What? Trigga? Get ya gimp-ass hands off me! Get off me! Where am I? The fuck you doing?" Sasha screeched, fighting me.

She kicked her legs, hitting my chest, but I just kept on tightening the leather straps at her arms. Each time she kicked or swung, I tightened the bonds some more, until I looked her in the face then punched her dead in the mouth, sending several of her teeth sliding into her mouth, choking her up with her blood before she spat at me.

"See, you fucked up, Sasha, so now it's me and you." I pulled my mask down and pushed my hoodie back.

This broad really thought she was about some shit, like she wasn't going to get hers from what she had done to everyone in the house. I chuckled deeply then playfully slapped each side of her cheeks before snatching some of the blonde extensions in her hair by the root.

"OW! Get off me! I ain't did shit to you, nigga. Oh, you mad now 'cuz of that bitch Ray-Ray. Wait till I tell him you fuckin' her. You ain't shit, Trigga!" she yelled, bucking at me.

I had to laugh again. This broad really thought she was a dime. Did she not see where the fuck she was at? "Bitch, do you realize where you at? The basement. Your time is mine, ho." I stepped back and reached into my hoodie for my cell phone while she was bucking and screaming. I scrolled through it, shaking my head and laughing. The light from my cell covered me as I searched through my files looking for that special video I had made.

"Fuck you, Trigga! You ain't been shit since you came in here. You think 'cuz you Dame's right you got power. Just like I always have, I'll survive the basement, and when I'm done with you, nigga, you gonna be mute fa real. With a dick in ya asshole too! Now what?"

See, now, when a broad turns into a bitch, I usually couldn't give two shits. But this bitch right here wasn't a woman. Which was why I punched that bitch in her pussy then landed another against her face.

I leaned down to show her my cell. "Shut the fuck up and watch," I cooly said, my hand gripping her throat. My lips parted into a smile the moment her eyes widened at her brother's then cousin's deaths.

"You set me up!" she screamed. She tried to move but couldn't.

Her screams and attempts to buck at me made me laugh aloud. I hit delete on the video then pulled out my gun and pressed it against her temple.

"Naw, you set your own self up, and now me and you 'bout to play, Sasha." Leaning over her, I slammed her head back hard on the table, grabbed a leather strap, and then covered her mouth with it.

Behind me were tools of torture Dame liked to use. His machete was gone, but a jagged rusted iron rod drew my attention. I reached for it, flipped it through my hands then traced it over her body, cutting into her skin.

"You don't fuck with me and not expect to get some loving back. So, rock-a-bye baby, you got an appointment with Trigga."

My eyes stared into her shocked and now scared gaze, and her pleas quickly spilled out.

I reached behind me to turn the lights out, leaving only the flickering florescent pool table light to turn on as her screams then gargling sound of blood caught in her throat filled the basement.

Several hours later, I sat in my car in the parking lot looking at the note the Nigerian queen had given me. I had to laugh. I saw my real name written on the back of the same card I had just gotten the day before from the suit shop Dame had sent Big Jake and me to. On it was my name with a cell number then on the other side was the name Phenom. The nigga I'd wanted to see.

Getting out of Dame's wasn't hard at all. I let him know that I was going into the streets to find out about the turf shit and explained that Jake and me had been running from some niggas who'd been gunning for us because of it.

Of course, the nigga didn't care. He was busy trying to save face with some of the bosses, so he let me go. I checked on Big Jake who stood outside of the bedroom

Diamond was in and gave him our code that I was about to finalize this shit. I knew he was broken. The way he looked at me, I knew he wasn't even really there, but he was going to manage to hold me down even though he'd lost Gina. I respected him for that.

So, for her, I moved fast. I hit the numbers on my disposable cell and waited.

"That didn't take long, *K*. Are you at the location, sweetie?"

The syrupy, sexy voice of the Nigerian queen straight up purred at me and had a nigga sitting up straight. Naw, it wasn't for the fact that her voice could make a nigga's dick hard, but this broad knew my real name. I didn't know what to say for a minute.

"*K*, we do not have time for this. Answer me, or I'm done here."

Ultimatums didn't work for me, but tonight for my fam, I'd handle it. "Ah, yeah, I'm here. How you know my name?"

Her soft giggle had me clutching my cell. Shit wasn't cute anymore and was pissing me all the way off.

"You'll find out shortly. I just wished to tell you that my house will protect you, honey, especially after tonight. You bring me that negro's head once you are done, yes?"

I blinked for a couple of moments. I could hear the smile in her voice as if she knew more than me. That tripped me out too. "A'ight, so what's really real?"

"You'll find that out soon, I said. Now are you bringing me that prize, yes or no?" she asked again with a soft, sexy command.

"No doubt. But what you get from it?"

I listened to her laugh again, pausing to whisper something to someone in the background before talking to me. "Just for you, you get to know what no one knows. I get to see that negro's head on my mantel and smile at the muthafucka who dare to put his hands on my blood. See, Diamond is my niece, and I do not take kindly to what the fuck he did to my sister and my niece—my blood."

She stopped talking for a minute, and I heard doors closing in the background.

Then she spoke up again, saying, "Her mother and I fell out. But had I known what she had planned, I would have helped her. And had I known that bitch Damien had taken my niece, things would have been very different. Therefore, you see an eye for an eye, sweetie, plain as day, and a favor out of many long overdue to you. Now go around the back and handle your business, Trigga. We'll be in touch."

Like that, she hung up on me, and I sat back, mind blown. Don't trust anyone was what I grew up on, and now I saw that the people I didn't trust knew more shit about me than I thought. Wasn't jigging on how much she knew about me, that she knew my name, so I definitely was going to check back on that shit, once the dust cleared.

Getting out of my ride, I kept my face down and walked to the back of the store. The lot was empty, the building empty, but the storage door was open. Part of me wished I had gone with my first mind and had Jake here, but fuck it, if a nigga was 'bout to die, then that's what it was gonna be.

I stepped in quietly and walked through, following the open doors. I smelled cigars and heard the sound of a lighter. All around me were suits, clothes, shoes, and mirrors, nothing else. The hair on my arms stood, which had me turning around again with my gun ready.

The sound of a British accent came at my right side. "I knew when you walked in that you were my blood. Look just like your pops."

I turned to point my gun that way, noticing that Idris Elba-looking cat sitting with both feet up on a desk, smoking his cigar. He was dressed in black slacks, white shirt, and black vest. Around his neck was a loose tie, and a gun lay right next to him.

"Fuck you know about that, sir?" I asked, narrowing my eyes.

I watched the man shift forward and study me. I couldn't remember his name for shit. He had the eyes of an OG, like he knew everything. Then it hit me—*this is Phenom*. No way. Couldn't be. Not some British cat. Fuck outta here.

"Because that nigga was my fam," he said, "and you are my nephew and blood. Been looking for you for years. Call me Phenom."

His accent quickly disappeared into a Brooklyn swag. Nigga sounded just like my pops through and through. No fuckin' way! I kept my gun leveled on me because shit felt like games being played.

"Yeah, the fuck right! This some game? Get me, Phenom," I urged, keeping my back to the mirrors as I watched him.

"My nigga, let's cut all this shit at the pass. You been lookin' for me, and I've been lookin' for you. I promised your pops back on the block that we'd always look out for each other. Fam first. Nigga was just like you. He was Battle, and I was Phenom. Came to the *A* to follow my sister to school. Me, I went overseas."

He paused to watch me. "So you comin' to me for what, nephew? Guns? Because I can give you that and then some, as your right. Put the shit away because, like on some real shit, I could have taken you out in the parking lot. That trigga shit ya got from me and ya pops, so chill and speak. Chaos is order, and order is chaos—this is the way of the street."

Phenom kicked a chair my way and then leaned back watching me, rubbing his goatee.

I was on some other shit at what he just spat. Code from my pops. No one knew that shit but him. This nigga's name was all through ma pops' and moms' words, telling me to trust this dude. The code next to it, and now this dude is in the flesh. The legend of the streets? Damn. I had a fuckin' uncle? Blood? Blood that had been looking for me? Blood that was one of the baddest niggas in the game? Yo, shit was dope. I woulda stood there longer just pondering that shit, but a nigga really didn't have time. Who knew what the fuck that nigga Dame was back at the house doing to Diamond?

I took a seat and hit the man with what I needed and what was going down. "Check it then." I dropped my hood back and rested my arm on the back of my chair, keeping my eye on this cat who called himself my uncle.

Yeah, he knew the code, but I been on the streets for a long time without this dude, so it was going to take more than him spitting out my background for me to trust him all the way. But he could for damn sure help a nigga, since he was willing.

"Ya already know then that I'm that nigga Dame's hand. So, shit, this nigga is going crazy. Like seeing dead people and talking to shadows and shit. Nigga been fuckin' up his money, fuckin' out the house, some of us are done. I got names of who need protection, and I got names of people I plan on popping. You can have that shit and do me honor, and I'll do our family honor. Been following my lessons through that knowledge Pops and Moms gave me in their books."

Phenom snuffed out his cigar, nodding. "Street code books. Your pops Battle and I created that back on the block, using the words we picked up from our teachers on the street. Feel me? Anyway, a'ight. So what you need?"

We dropped into deep discussion, formulating plans. He let me know what areas would hold me down, and what areas that will come for me and my fam once Dame goes down. I had thought some gangs would come after us once we ended Dame, but Phenom quickly schooled me on that. Dame's hand was never as strong as he thought.

I schooled him on some of the things I went through, talked to him about Big Jake then told him about Gina. Talking about Gina made him bow his head as if he knew her, and that move alone let me know how much he had been watching me. The rest of what I told him, he already knew, except for what I needed.

"How you know this shit? And who is that Nigerian queen to you?" I had to ask.

Phenom had me walking through his shop, taking me underground to his offices after I had told him what I needed. We walked by some of his crew. Some faces I knew from the block, some from other boss lords.

"I know what I know because I've been looking for you since our fam was taken out. Got word overseas about what went down, pulled up my old contacts, started my business back up, and then came to the A. I set this up as a cover while I looked for you, but I lost you in the system so I stayed around waiting and taking out DOA, and leaving the rest for you.

"Anika is my woman. She does her, and I do me, but that's mine. That's why she's down for you, and 'cuz she respects ya work and that you and your new fam been protecting her niece."

"Damn! Really?"

I glanced and saw some major senators and people who worked for the mayor of ATL on monitors.

Phenom continued guiding me through his spot, stopping to hand me a bag. "No doubt, nephew. Remember national consciousness?" He turned to look my way.

I nodded, and we both spat out at the same time, "Consciousness is awareness that we are all one, no matter where we are, and we must work and struggle as one to liberate ourselves from the domination of the outside world and bring in a universal government of love, peace, and happiness for all."

Phenom smiled wide, showing his dimples. I was mind blown. Dude was dope.

"Now listen. What ya asked for is in there, passports, accounts, and money. I got ya tickets, but I switched the location. I got people around the world, know what I mean? And now they are yours. Sending you and your fam to London, then to Nigeria, once you finish your shit. We'll stay in contact, and from there, you got a choice. Your pops didn't want this shit for you. I didn't either, but we fall into the game however we can. It's up to you on how you make it work for you through legit means or not. I promised ya mom, after ya sister was gunned down, that I'd protect you, and I will even in the grave. And I promised ya pops that I'd school you. You've done the rest. I only got a little to help you with in schooling you, but we'll talk about that later when I meet you overseas. You got power, nephew. Do what you gotta do."

My uncle's words hit me with clarity. It hurt to think about my fam, but for them, I lived to get this vengeance. See, this was for my baby sister Assata, who was gunned down by DOA members trying to take out my pops as she played in the park. She was only five. This was for my mom and pops after they finally got their hands on them, and for me. Now this was also for my uncle. Power was bond. I slung the black bag he gave me over my shoulder then gave my uncle daps.

"That nigga don't know shit about being a boss. He's just a nigglet playing with his toys. Be about that life and return what he has put out into our community," Phenom schooled.

I gave a nod, looking around my uncle's underground operation. "That nigga is chaos, and I'm the order. Thanks, fam."

Walking out into the night, I pushed back my locks then pulled my hoodie over my head and got back in my car. Dropping off what I was just gifted to the safe house was the next stop, and then killing that nigga Dame was the endgame. Nigga was about to be that motto he called himself living—DOA—and I had Diamond, who he called his property, to get at.

Ray-Ray

"Big Jake, was that Pookie you were just talking to?"

I stuck my head outside of Dame's bedroom door. I was hot and sweating, so I was naked as fuck. But I didn't care. At this point, all the caring I had in my heart had left when I saw Gina take that blade across her neck. Anytime I closed my eyes, I saw her body falling backwards as blood spurted from her neck like a geyser.

Big Jake looked at me wide-eyed then turned away at the sight of my underage naked goodness. I walked up to him as he sat slumped over in the chair by the door.

"Ray-Ray, you need to go back in the room," he said.

"Nope. Was that Pookie?"

He nodded. "Yeah, that was that pussy-nigga."

"I'll be back."

He grabbed my arm and stood. His big ass towered over me like a brick wall. "Wait a minute, shawty. Where you going?"

"To handle something. Trust me, it won't take long."

His dark chocolate eyes watched me like he wasn't sure that I should have been going anywhere alone. And, to be honest, I probably did look frail and weak. If I hadn't been high out of my mind, I probably would have felt it too. But the only thing I felt was vindictive, murderous even. Something fragile in me snapped when Gina died. I may have even lost my grip on reality. I'd been through so much in such a short time that I ain't even think I was sane.

"A'ight, you got five minutes. After that, I'm coming to get you."

I didn't say anything, just took off running in the direction I'd seen that nigga Pookie go. Nothing in me told me I was making a mistake, that I was just precious moments away from death's door. So when I spotted him in the corner of Dame's weight room jawing on the phone, telling somebody to catch Trigga once he came back through the gates, I didn't hesitate to let my presence be known.

Dame's weight room looked every bit as high-tech as the most modernly designed gym. Pookie was standing in the corner under the 50-inch flat-screen TV.

"What's up, Pookie?" I asked him, my voice laced with venom.

He turned around with a quick jerk. Then surprise registered across his features. Where Gina had sliced his face was still red and swollen with stitches. Now both sides of his face matched with cuts. She had cut his ass good, from the corner of his left eye all the way down to the corner of his mouth. He looked as if he had a Sicilian smile.

His annoyingly scratchy voice asked me, "Damn, bitch! You just gon' come to nigga pussy out, ready to fuck, huh."

I didn't have time to be making conversation with the nigga, so I crossed the room and walked up on him. I grabbed his dick in my hand and stroked it through his jeans, making him think he was about to get some pussy. He smelled like he had been smoking weed and running through a field of wild onions.

Yeah, a bitch was just about out of her mind, but I was focused. Even when his cold hands came out to grab my titties I didn't flinch. I kept my game face on, skinning and grinning in that nigga's face like his piece of dick was really what I wanted.

I opened my legs just enough to fool the dumb mutha-fucka into thinking he was really about to get some cut. He was so busy focused on sliding his hand between my legs, he didn't see the knife in my right hand.

I brought it around and stuck him right in his neck. "That's for Gina, you pussy-nigga!" I cried out then stuck him again.

I always heard my daddy talking about having niggas bleeding like a stuck pig. I guess this was what he meant. As he stumbled back into the wall grabbing his neck, I stuck him again, this time in his chest, but my knife got stuck.

Trigga had given me that knife just as he'd passed me off to Big Jake. I tried to pull it out that nigga's shoulder, but it wouldn't budge.

Pookie gained his bearings then shoved me back so hard, I rolled over my head and landed hard against a steel weight bench. "Stupid bitch! You gon' die tonight, ho," he growled out as he ran at me.

His words were gargled, sounded like blood was stuck in his throat. The knife was still in his chest, and blood spewed from him, but he came at me so fast that it scared me.

I kicked my feet out to stop him, landing a blow to his groin. It slowed him down, but not enough for me to get away. I tried anyway. Made the mistake of turning over on my stomach to try to stand, and he got on my back, pinning me down to the floor.

He grabbed a handful of my hair and slammed my fore-head into the floor, dizzying me, but not knocking me out.

"Uh, huh, I'ma show yo' ass what a real dick feel like inside of that monkey. A nigga been wanting to hit this shit for a minute anyway."

I could tell he was having a hard time breathing because of the wounds I'd inflicted, but I hated myself for not aiming high enough to end his life immediately. I was already naked, so it was nothing for him to slip about two of his fingers up my ass, his nails scratching and tearing my rectum on the way in.

I screamed out at that invasion. Not even Dame had violated that part of my body. Pookie kept shoving his fingers up my rectum then abruptly stopped. I could hear his belt buckle clinking as he pushed my head down to the floor as hard as he could. The shit hurt worse than any pain I'd experienced vaginally, but I was preparing myself for what I knew he would try to do next.

Even in Gina's death she looked out for me. She had been inside of that house so long that she said she often felt as if it was a prison. That's why she knew how to make weapons out of about almost anything. Before she'd died and on one of those days when Dame had left us locked in his room, she showed me how to make a blade with a cheap toothbrush, Saran Wrap, and fire.

"Wrap the plastic 'round the bristles real tight, Ray-Ray. You gotta make sure you do it good, so the shit won't melt off when the flames hit it."

I sat on my knees inside of Dame's closet while she sat lotus-style and watched me.

"Wrap it about a good ten, fifteen times then take the lighter and melt the plastic onto the bristles. Then take that brick right there and grind each side down like if you're sharpening a knife. Do it 'til the side with the bristles get sharp on both ends."

As I sat there doing what she said, she hummed and rocked back and forth. Her eyes would wander, and she would often use the base of her hand to beat herself in the side of the head mumbling that she had to get out of this place. Yeah, she was a bit off in the head, but she knew how to survive. That was why I knew how to insert the homemade blade inside of my pussy.

***

I knew Pookie could probably overpower me and that the first thing he would do was try to rape me. So it was no surprise when he tried to ram his dick up my pussy that he let out a yell that turned him into the bitch he was.

He fell back against the same weight bench I'd fallen against. Only, he picked himself up holding his bloody dick in his hand, legs kicking out, as sweat raced down his face.

I quickly turned over, opened my legs, and slowly but surely pulled the handle of the blade from my pussy, careful not to slice myself.

Once I did, I jumped up and charged him like a maniac. I sliced at his face over and over again. I may not have known how to use a knife, but the blade was my friend. As I sliced his face, nose, neck, and chest open, he threw his hands up not sure whether to hold his dick or try to keep me from gutting his ass like a fish.

In my blind rage and fury I saw I had sliced his chest open, and the shit was looking like Zorro had been there. I sliced until my arms were burning. I could hear somebody coming down the hall, but I needed to make sure this nigga was dead.

I moved over to the fifty-pound barbells sitting next to the wall. As Pookie lay groaning, his arms limp at his side, I struggled to pick up the weight, but I got it. Then I moved back over and stood over him, raised the barbell as high above my head as I could, then brought it down on the nigga's face. His shit split like a hard-boiled egg that had been cracked. That wasn't good enough for me, though; I brought it over my head again and repeated the process.

"What the fuck, Ray-Ray?" I heard Big Jake call behind me.

I glanced over my shoulder then dropped the heavy weight on Pookie's chest. "Told you it wouldn't take long," was all I said as I turned and walked past him.

I had never killed anyone before, but killing Pookie gave me sick satisfaction. Was that what Dame or Trigga felt like when they killed people? My heart beat slow in my chest, felt like the walls were closing in on me, spinning me around.

I stumbled down the hall, legs feeling as if they were about to give out on me. Flashes of Gina slicing her throat turned my stomach. I stopped to hold the wall. Pookie's brains leaking from his skull made vomit rise in my throat, and I threw up all over my feet.

A pair of arms that I almost didn't recognize picked me up. I could tell by the way my body molded into his chest who it was. Trigga had been the only nigga to pick me up or hold me. I immediately melted into his hold. It had always been that way since day one.

I was covered in blood, probably smelled like I didn't know what after having that nigga Pookie on me, but Trigga carried me to Dame's room anyway. Big Jake whispered something in his ear then ran back down the hall to where I had left Pookie. I didn't know where that big nigga had gotten a gas can from or what he was going to do with it, but him and Trigga were on a mission.

Once in Dame's room, Trigga dropped me on the bed then crawled in with me, caging me between his arms. I looked up into his eyes. He looked to be in killer mode, ready to end life. I didn't know where he had gone or what had been said to him, but cold hatred and evil danced across his features.

"We leaving here tonight dead or alive, li'l shawty," he said, his voice cold. "Understand?"

After watching Gina kill herself and smashing Pookie's brains in, I felt cold, like all my innocence had left me.

That crazy part of me that took over at times made me wrap my arms around Trigga's neck and nod. My breath probably smelled like hot slop, since I had just vomited in the hall.

"Dead or alive, I'm your Bonnie, you're my Clyde." I actually giggled after I said that lame shit. Maybe I was still geeked up.

Trigga didn't flinch though. He didn't even seem to care that I was naked. After he moved my hands and placed them above my head, he reached down into his pants and then placed a small gun in my left hand and another in my right.

"I ain't gon' tell you what to do with these because, when the time comes, you gon' know," he said. "I need to know you're really loyal to what the fuck is about to go down. Shit's about to change in a matter of minutes. Feel me, li'l shawty? And a nigga need to know that Dame ain't in your dome." He tapped a finger against his temple.

"Why you even asking me this? I told you what it was. You see me doing my part, so what the fuck you asking me this for? You planning to leave without me or something, nigga?"

I asked that with an all-new terror. I'd never thought about the fact that maybe Trigga was never going to take me out of here with him in the first place. My heart started to pound against my chest. My eyes gazed up at him with a new coat of fresh tears that had nothing to do with the high I was on. He was silent, too silent for my liking.

"Well, fuck you too! I don't need you to help me get out. I'll get the fuck out on my own. Fuck you, Trigga! You made me do all this shit just so you can fuckin' leave me here?"

When he still didn't respond, only stared down at me like he couldn't care less, I reached out and smacked him with as much strength as I could muster, but he didn't look like the hit fazed him at all. Didn't matter, I was livid. This nigga was going to leave me. He wasn't about his fuckin' word.

Fear of having to live in that house for another moment replaced common sense for a minute, and I lashed out at him again. Only, this time he grabbed both my wrists.

"Chill the fuck out and calm down. One, don't ever put your fuckin' hands in my face again, two, actions speak louder than words. I need to see if you true to this, need to see that you taking serious what we doing."

I didn't know what to say for a minute. What else could I do to make him see that I wasn't on some bitch shit? "What you want me to do, Trigga . . . short of killing myself? Anything else, I'll do."

He moved my legs apart and lay between my thighs. If I said having him that close like that to me didn't make me feel some type of way, I'd be lying. Yeah, Dame had pretty much fucked up the good parts of sex for me, but maybe if me and Trigga made it out this place alive, he could help me to try it all over again.

I could feel the huge bulge of his dick laying against my sweaty pussy. My shit was probably like an open road in Arizona— hot—but I didn't think I smelled. I was hoping I didn't. Still when he moved his hips in a grind like we were fuckin', I looked up in confusion at him. It didn't make sense, but I didn't care.

His locks swung around his shoulders, making strokes like a paint brush. When he pulled his shirt over his head, my eyes widened at the way his body was cut up and at all the new tattoos he had decorating his red clay-like skin.

I wanted to kiss him, wanted to know what it felt like to be kissed by a man who wasn't going to try to torture me at the end of the night, or who didn't repulse me. I rubbed my fingers through his locks and actually moaned out when he dipped his head to take my nipple into his mouth.

Even though I hissed out because they were still sore from Dame biting down on them like a crazed animal, I felt pleasure for the first time and didn't feel sick about it afterwards.

His name flowed from my lips so easily, and I was so caught up in that fairy tale show he was putting on, it never occurred to me that Dame could be in the security room with his eyes locked on the camera. I'd totally forgotten that there were even cameras, my mind was so lost on Trigga.

Trigga

Diamond's moans had a nigga's dick on a hundred as I moved against her. I was doing my best to be careful against her body 'cuz I could see the cuts on her silky skin, and she was still covered in blood from her kill. It was kinda sexy as fuck to see how she handled Pookie. She didn't know I was watching, but I had gotten into the house just at that time and heard that nigga's screams as she worked him up. By then, my mind was on working this shit out 'cuz it was that time. Now I know niggas would wonder what the fuck was jumping off with me in Dame's bed with Diamond under me, but the sound of the doors being kicked in, with that of guns being loaded, had me sliding off Diamond slowly, knowing that nigga would fall for the bait.

I whispered in her ear, "Do exactly what I say, shawty. Stay behind me and watch this shit go down like a fuckin' queen with a smile on ya face, because this nigga is done." I then looked into her big cocoa eyes.

She said nothing then kissed me. Her pillow-like lips made me feel like a king the moment we touched, and our tongues did what the fuck they do, touched and danced. Damn, she was a bad broad.

I pulled back from her as her fingers combed through my locks then ran over the back of my neck. I knew she got it. A smile played across my face where only Diamond saw it, and I ground my hips, working them against her on purpose to make her arch up and clutch the sheets.

Her sweet titties pressed right into a nigga's face, and I snaked my tongue out to brush her hard nipples then leaned up close to her to cage her.

I took my time sliding off her, keeping my head down, to sit on the edge of the huge white bed and play like I tucked my dick in my jeans. See, I had plans to actually fuck her, but after all the shit done to her body, was no way I could even get down like that. And, plus, it wasn't time.

"The fuck you doing touching my bitch?" Dame yelled, standing in the doorway of his room.

His face was red, and his eyes turned dark like the fucked crazy-ass demon he was. Nigga was so mad, his veins were popping out and, I swear that nigga shook like a dopehead.

Glancing up at the nigga that brought nothing but pain in my life, I leaned forward to rest my arms on my thighs then smirked. "Nigga, exactly what the fuck you see me doing—fuckin' what's yours and taking what's mine."

The sound of Dame's goons, Blackout, and one other nigga's groans had Dame turning around for a second.

As he turned to see his men snatched up, I pulled my Glocks out from under the sheets where I'd stashed them then went off. One round went purposely in each kneecap, just so he could turn around and look at me. As he did, I reached to tap Diamond on her thigh, while locking eyes on him. That nigga fell to his knees slumped over, slobbering out the mouth.

"Shoot that nigga that took from you, baby girl," I ordered her.

"Okay, Trigga. Bye, Daddy," Diamond cooed, waving good-bye to Dame, a smile on her face.

Dame tried to reach for his cane to unhook his Glock but was too slow due to the shot of his kneecap being blown off.

Diamond draped her arms over my shoulders and aimed for him, and several rounds went off, hitting niggas running up the stairs.

I reached up to aim her arms toward Dame and rounds went off, hitting his shoulders. Then I moved her arms again, aimed for each of his hands, and watched him fall over.

"Damn, just like that, shawty, just like that," I muttered to her then had her slide back.

I watched Diamond's titties jiggle out of the corner of my eye as she fell backwards then pushed off the bed slowly and walked toward that nigga Dame. Standing over the man who took from me then hurt my fam, I gave a smile then sent my Tims into his face.

The sound of bone breaking against my boots had a nigga amped up. Several of his teeth and blood mixed with spit flew from his mouth. I reached out as his neck snapped back then punched that nigga in his face. My grip on him switched, so I could push my fingers in his wounds just to hear that nigga scream like a bitch. Which he did.

Dame's deep yell filled the room, and he tried to swing at me, managing to hit me in my face.

I stepped back with a laugh then shook the blow off, bringing my Glocks out. "I let you have that, bossman."

"Nigga, you better end this shit, because your life is mine if you don't. You took from me, played me, nigga, huh? You..."

See, a nigga didn't have the time or care what the fuck he had to say, nor was I the type of nigga to hold a death back. So, as he spoke, I reached out, snatched him by the neck, and dropped my gun to pull out a blade and slice it across his throat.

The sound of his gargled groan made me smile. His blood spilled over my clenched hands like hot soup.

I looked that nigga in his light eyes. "Every nigga got a sob story, Dame, and every nigga got an agenda. You are mine."

My locks fell in my face as I stripped that nigga naked. The room felt hot as hell, as if the devil was prepping to send that nigga there in this moment. I let out a light laugh and heard Diamond shift against the sheets on the bed.

"Now I got shit to talk about." I took my belt in my hand and started to beat that nigga like I had seen him do plenty of broads in this house. "This shit is for my pops."

Whack! Whack! Whack!

"This shit is for my moms who you raped and fucked for a week before she and I took out some of your boys."

Whack! Whack! Whack!

I was sweating like a fuckin' slave in Mississippi heat, but I kept beating that nigga through his groans and yelps.

I then pulled out my blade again. "And this is for Gina, Jake, and Diamond." I pressed the blade deeper into his throat, and I saw his eyes darken, and then lighten in understanding.

"Yeah, nigga, it's me, homie, boo, nigga, boo," I mocked, reaching down to pick up his cane while dropping my knife. I pushed that nigga down on his side, slamming his cheek to the floor. I then rammed his precious cane right into his asshole, tearing through his rectum, just like he had done to the many young girls who had come through his world.

That nigga's gargled scream was so loud, I had to slap him to get his attention. That shit right there was for Gina and Diamond.

Pulling back to sit him up as straight as I could with the cane up that nigga's ass, my Glock was back in my hand pumping mad steel into his fuckin' dome. Streams of blood, pieces of his brain, and skull went flying, painting the doors behind him. "And that shit is for me. E.N.G.A., nigga."

Dropping his body to the floor, I turned to check out Diamond, and then I turned to pick up my knife. "Get as clean as you can, shawty, get your shit, and let's go."

Diamond jumped out the bed, pausing to look at Dame's dead body. "He's gone, like, for real. That punk-ass nigga is gone, just like that?"

I walked up to her, having gotten my shirt and pulling it back on. Pulling my hoodie over my head, I kneeled down and snatched that nigga by his head. "Yeah, he is. Check it, take my knife. Forgot I had to do something for the Nigerian queen."

"A'ight. What you gotta do that I need ya knife for?"

"Yo, take that nigga's head. That's the NQ's MO. They collect dicks or tits."

Diamond started laughing. "For real?"

Grunting as I moved Dame's heavy body, I nodded. "Yeah, do that and hurry up. We gotta go before the rest of those niggas come back. Jake is taking care of some of them, and I gotta string this nigga up while you dress."

"A'ight." Diamond moved quickly and didn't hesitate.

I kept my eyes on her face, as she pulled that nigga's dick out and cut his shit off as best she could. First, she tried to do a clean cut, but that didn't work, so she ended up sawing. Sweat covered her temple and her hair fell around her face.

It was crazy seeing how her eyes kinda turned hazel. I knew her moms was mixed, so I ain't ever notice the slight changes her brown eyes took. When she finished, she held up the dead flesh in her hand.

"A'ight, wrap that shit up and go get dressed," I said, motioning for her to haul ass.

I threw Dame over my shoulder and climbed that nigga's bed. DOA stared back at me as I looked at it. I wanted to spit on that shit, but then I thought of DNA.

The sound of gunshots going off in the house put me back on my game. Jake was doing that shit, and I could tell some of the broads I helped were holding him down, taking niggas out left and right.

The night was ours, and Dame's house was done. I pulled on the sheets and tied his body right under his code. Nigga's arms were spread out, his head slumped over his chest. Coating his blood with my fingers, I crossed out DOA then stepped back to empty my Glock. The gun I used traced back to Sasha, and my prints were nowhere on it, 'cuz I made sure to have gloves on my hands.

"Trigga, I'm ready. Niggas are dying like crazy, and Blackout and 'em are waking up," Diamond said behind me.

Shawty stood in Gina's pink-and-black Jordans and black shorts that showed off her ass and thighs. I gave a slight smile when I saw she had on a black hoodie with a bag in her hand. Walking off the bed, I dropped down to pick up the guns I had given her and then stepped over the pool of blood that was Dame's.

"A'ight, so check it. I'm taking you to the back. There's a car waiting for you. In it is a black bag. Take that shit, because it's got tickets outta the *A*, money, passports, and something I got from ya parent's home—your birth certificate. Let's go."

As I walked past her, she stopped me to take my hand then reached out to hug me. "Thank you, Trigga, like my bad for coming at you—"

"Ain't got time for that. Let's go, and it's cool, Diamond. Keep your Glock ready becaue we gotta move fast. Jake, my nigga, light this shit up!" I yelled.

"I got you, Trig!" Jake yelled from downstairs. "That nigga dead yet?"

As we ran down the stairway, I could see him taking down niggas left and right with ease. Some he would punch then shoot once they were down. Others he'd snatch up and break their necks with just the squeeze of his arm.

I pushed Diamond back to move her out of the way, so I could pump some steel into niggas who tried to rush us. We both moved to cover Jake.

Diamond took the lessons me, Gina, and Jake gave her. She pointed her guns to perfect her aim. She was still kinda shaky but good for her first time using a gun.

"You know where to go, shawty. Get there now!" I yelled at Diamond, keeping Jake covered and making a clear way for her to run to the back down by the kitchen.

Jake kept pumping iron then tilted his head upstairs.

I glanced up and saw Blackout and a couple of the niggas Jake had knocked out getting up then running down to where we were. Both of us moved further in the house, kicking furniture to trip niggas up then going hand to hand with them. My Tims landed on the chest of one of the new niggas we had been training. Broads, some naked, some dressed, ran around screaming as soon as glass went flying in the air and bullets rained around us.

Sweat in my eyes, I ducked down to jump over a table to get to the kitchen.

"I got you, Trig. You know what I gotta handle. Go get shawty outta here." Jake ran to the basement, where he had placed gasoline with trip wires to set off the lab Dame had down there as well.

"Hey, yo, don't hold up the process. Your big elephant ass betta be behind me, nigga. Don't make me come back for you!" I yelled, narrowing my eyes at Jake.

Nigga just gave me a smile and flipped me off. "I got you, fam. Let me do this last bit for Gina. I'm right behind you."

Checking back on that nigga, I watched him open the door to the basement, aim his gun and shoot off some rounds to start a fire. Turning, he held the trip wire in his hand then glanced to his side to set off some rounds.

I moved out, making it outside. I saw Diamond pumping off rounds as she stood next to my ride. The Trap was lighting up with fights. It was like everyone knew Dame was done. All the chaos kinda felt good. I turned to see if Jake was behind me. The sound of the back door opening with his big frame in it had me nodding my head in respect, but when he locked eyes on me, I saw a sadness on his face. I knew what was about to go down. Gina was that nigga's heart. He wasn't about to go anywhere. Death was about to be his escape. That had me pissed the fuck off, especially when he closed the door.

"Yo! Jake!" My eyes widened.

Turning fast, I pulled at Diamond as she screamed out Jake's name too. "Shawty, listen to me. Get in the ride. There's a kid in there. Tell her I told you to take you to the safe house. Once you get there, wait for your ride. You'll know who it is because don't no one know about the safe house but us and who I want to know. You get on that plane. No matter what goes down, you get on that plane. I'll meet you there, a'ight. I need to get Jake."

Diamond's doe eyes locked on me, and her nails dug into my arm. "You promised me you wouldn't leave me, nigga! You can't go. I ain't going. Fuck that shit!"

Anger had me yanking her by her arm and pulling her around the car to push her in the driver's seat. "Follow what the fuck I said and go! Damn, shawty! Don't fight with what the hell I'm saying. I'll meet you on the plane. Go!"

Slamming the car door closed, I yelled, "Ghost, tell her where to go, and remember what I told you. Ride out, Diamond, now!"

Diamond glared at me, tears falling down her cheeks. She rolled down the window and leaned out. "Wait!"

The sound of her voice quickly pissed me off, but what she asked next had me not cussing her out.

"What's your name? Tell me that at least, Trigga. I ain't leaving until . . ."

Annoyed as fuck, I glanced around, making sure we were alone, then narrowed my eyes at her. I thumbed my nose then dropped my voice for only her to hear. "Kwame Kweli. Ride out, shawty, and keep that to yaself."

Diamond stared at me then mouthed my name before saying, "I like that shit," and then she pulled off.

My eyes followed her ride until it disappeared down the block.

I quickly ran back to the house, my feet crunching stone from Dame's driveway. Guns were still going off. I pulled open the door and moved through the back, dropping low as I snatched the gun from a dead nigga's hand then aimed it upward at another dude that came my way. I could hear Jake's loud hollering as he talked shit and fucked some niggas up with his hands.

"Dis giant-ass nigga thank he's gonna get out of here alive and take us all down," Blackout's raspy voice echoed. "Fuck that Scarface shit! Nigga, dis ain't the movies, and you 'bout to die, homie!"

Jake had punched that dude in this throat, so every time he spoke, nigga would cough and try to get his voice back.

I stood hiding in a corner. Jake was now being held down on his knees over broken pieces of glass, his arms behind his back, and his face was covered in blood and cuts. His right eye was swollen shut from being fucked up.

Jake's shoulders shook up and down as he laughed. "Naw, nigga, we ain't homies. But I beat ya ass, didn't I?"

Blackout stood in front of Jake. "Fuck you did, nigga! You da one on ya knees. Ya da one in blood 'bout to die. You an' that dumb nigga Trigga fucked up. Can't believe you two turned on Dame! Where's dat loyalty that nigga always talk 'bout, huh? Where dat stupid-ass nigga anyway? I know he didn't thank this shit up. *A, B, C, D* ain't even in his vocab, ya dig." He laughed

"*A, B, C, D*—ya dead, nigga."

It only took one bullet from me to go through that punk-ass nigga's temple, exiting to take down another who stood next to him.

Moving from where I hid, I ran across the living room to get to Jake. Bullets ran down around us, and I flew backwards into the side of the wall, getting hit on my side and shoulder. I bit down on my lip as hot, sticky blood soaked into my hoodie and dropped down my body.

I gripped my side, glancing around the room, counting down all the niggas in it. I knew how many bullets I had left in my Glocks, and I could guess at how many was left in the guns I had snatched off some bodies.

Spitting on the ground, I pushed up and dropped my hood back, reaching into my pocket to pull out my cell. Then I texted my uncle and Diamond, before wiping out all the info then stomping on my cell.

Through the firefight, the niggas that held Jake's arms back were now on the floor. He slowly stood glancing at me. Nigga was covered in sweat and blood too, and the waves on his fade were shiny with sweat.

I told him, "Yo, Jake, why the fuck you couldn't just come, nigga? We brothers. You ain't have to die like this. I coulda killed ya in honor if ya had asked."

Jake then pulled out the shotgun he had hidden against his back. "'Cuz, nigga, I ain't feel like it. Plus, I knew you wouldn't."

So Jake and I moved in circles, talking shit to niggas we used to work and kill with, getting our hidden Glocks and knives ready. Now that Blackout was gone, them stupid fucks only had themselves to look after and ain't know what to do now.

Smirking, I rolled my shoulders then I dropped my bloody hand as I joked. "Well, nigga, now I'm shot 'cuz you wanna go down like a punk ass, when you don't even have to play yourself like that. You suppose to trust in a nigga, have my back. So damn, man, what you got to say about that shit, preacha? Huh, bro?"

Laughing, Jake glanced around at the niggas and broads that pointed their weapons at us. He shrugged. "All day every day, I got you covered. My bad for my mindset, just wanted to kill some niggas and to see Dame's dead body. Good look, bro."

"Shoot them niggas!" one cat whispered.

Inching away, some other dude muttered, "Nah, that's Trigga and Jake."

That nigga knew what was about to go down.

Jake held out his hand, and we slapped palms twice then three times.

"Oh yeah, though I walk through the valley . . ."

Pain dug into my side and shoulder while Jake spat out his Bible verses. Meanwhile, the new bloods started trying to figure out what to do before others came up with more Glocks.

As my eyes roamed the place that used to shelter me, I saw my moms and pops dressed in all-white looking down on me from the upper walkway of the entryway with pride. It look like they whispered, "Thank you," to me, while my pops glanced at my Glock and told me what to do.

Blood dripped in my eyes and made me blink, glancing back toward them. My baby sister stood between them, dressed in all-pink, bows in her hair. In her arm was a teddy bear, one that matched Gina's old bear.

I knew what was about to go down, and I welcomed it with a sharp laugh. "You know how I do it, but check it, we may die tonight, but you all coming with us. E.N.G.A., niggas!" I yelled

Jake let out a roar, pulling his guns and letting out rounds. "E.N.G.A."

We fell backwards, both of our Glocks aiming for every nigga that ever turned on us, every nigga that blindly followed Dame and hurt good people in this house. Then I glanced at Jake as he followed me to the back. I picked up the trip wire that lay in water, debris, and furniture, then chucked the deuces at every stupid nigga in the house that tried to fuck with us. Niggas had to learn—You don't take Trigga out, Trigga takes your ass out.

Then, like that, the Trap was on fire. Dame's kingdom was no more. Every nigga that was part of that house died where they stood as the house exploded then burned down while the sun rose.

Ray-Ray

"You gotta keep driving 'til you get to Exit 235, then you get off on the exit and keep straight, across to Frontage Road."

I looked at the kid sitting on the passenger side of the car Trigga had pushed me in. I couldn't really tell if it was a girl or a boy. He was dressed like a boy but at times had very girly features. I followed the directions the kid gave me, but the fear in my heart made my hands tremble against the steering wheel.

"If Trigga don't make it, you gotta say you my mama. You gotta say you twenty-one, and say I'm seven, but I'm really nine," Ghost said.

The words "if Trigga don't make it" kept playing through my mind. I could tell the kid had been schooled on this for a long time. There I was, a kid my damn self, responsible for another kid. At least for the moment I was.

Traffic was light, and I was thanking God that my high had come down enough for me to drive right. Didn't see a cop anywhere in sight at first, and when I did, I had to wonder if they were rushing to where we had just left.

"You know Trigga is my daddy? That bitch-nigga Dame killed my mama. I was hiding in the walls when he did it. Saw him do it. So, I'm glad Trigga killed that faggot."

My eyes widened. I looked at the little kid again. He didn't look like Trigga. Damn. Trigga had a nine-year-old kid? I tried to do the math in my head but didn't really know how old Trigga was to begin with, so I couldn't really count up the figures.

"You don't look like Trigga," was all I could manage to say, my voice still shaky from emotions and the tears.

"Well, Trigga is my new dad. Dame really my daddy, but Trigga be taking care of me and shit."

I glanced at Ghost then back at the road. I knew it was fucked up, but I was glad to know Trigga wasn't his daddy. And now that I really looked at the kid, he did look like his father. He had on a hoodie like Trigga, but those light eyes, that skin tone, and those thick lips were all Dame.

Ghost pushed the hood back from his head, and long curly black hair fell around his shoulders.

"I ain't no boy either, I'ma girl. But my mama dress me like a boy, so if Dame saw me, he wouldn't try to sell my pussy."

My eyes widened. He was a she and had seen way too much already at nine years old. I said a prayer that her mental wasn't too fucked-up, and that she could have a normal life. I couldn't believe Ghost's language. She was talking like she was a hood misfit just like me. And, really, she was. I didn't know what else to say to the kid.

My mind was all over the place. *Is Trigga okay? Is he alive? Is Big Jake alive? Would they make it on the plane with me the next day? How did I take this kid with me without any questions?*

I got off on the exit she told me to. The light was green at the next stop, so I kept straight across to Frontage Road like directed. The area looked familiar to me because my mama and daddy used to run down this way, Clayton County, Zone 3. Dame had control over Zones 1, 3, 4, and 6. I wondered what would happen to them now.

We passed the Farmers Market and a big billboard for a gun range.

"When you see the sign for Pink Pony South, you gon' turn in there then get out and close the gates behind you. Then you gotta park the car all way round the back in the big garage," Ghost told me.

I saw the big pink-and-white sign that said Pink Pony South. It had an actual pink pony on the sign. It was an old strip club. *Trigga's safe house is an old strip club.* It looked deserted. Weeds and tall grass made it seem inhabitable, and there were big cracks and potholes in what used to be the parking lot. The building itself looked like it was about to fall apart.

I turned in then got out of the car to close the gates behind me, just like Ghost had told me.

When I got back in the car, she said, "That's gon' let our contact know we in there."

Her soft voice told me she was just a baby, but her mouth told me she had been tossed into the wild and had adapted.

I moved the car around back and did just what Ghost said to do. She got out with me and showed me where and how to move the blue tarp so I could get to the garage. I was shocked at the big car shop/garage that sat behind the place. It showed that Trigga had always wanted to get out of the game and had been working toward it.

Once done, I parked the car inside, and Ghost walked me up a flight of rickety stairs that led to a door with the faded letters VIP on it. She punched in a code on the door and then used a key to unlock it.

While the outside looked like it was about to fall to pieces, the inside was the exact opposite. It wasn't extravagant, but it reminded me of the lobby of a luxury hotel or a loft. There was a kitchen with all-black accessories with a bar laden with liquor. A big 70-inch flat-screen TV sat against a brick wall. The floor was stained cement, and plush furniture with different earth-tone colors sat around. The stripper poles were still there along with the stages, but it just looked like a part of the décor.

Ghost hopped on the sofa, turned the TV on, and grabbed the PS3 Controller. She was comfortable, right at home, but I was scared shitless.

I dropped the backpack Trigga had left me and sat at the bar to look through the contents. I pulled out a silver box with my name on it and opened it. There was my birth certificate, social security card, cash, and my mama's locket that she had on the day she died. Inside was a picture of me, her, and my daddy. Trigga must have gone back the day they had killed them. Tears burned my eyelids.

I pulled out passports, one for Jackson Hawkes, and one for Chasity Orlando. I cast a quick glance at Ghost. Her real name was Chasity. Then I pulled out the one for Gina, and my chest got heavy. Her smiling face looked up at me and made me remember those rare occasions that she genuinely smiled in that house. She was supposed to make it out with me. We was supposed to run away from this place together. I was so pissed at myself, mad that I didn't rush to try to stop her.

"But who are you to try to take away her shot at peace and freedom, Ray-Ray?"

I looked up and saw my mama.

"Sometimes death is better than life. Some of us . . . we get tossed into the game and the only way out is death. That's our freedom, 'cuz we don't have to worry 'bout this shit no mo'. So you wouldn't have had the right to take her freedom away from her. Don't you see how she wasn't free with that nigga? She would have never been free without death."

I kinda understood what my mama was saying, but I wanted to tell Big Jake that it was possible Gina was carrying his baby, and never got the chance to.

I wiped my eyes and pulled out Trigga's passport. Kwame Kweli. I would have never guessed that was his name. He was a killer, so I just wasn't expecting a name attached to the motherland.

"Oh, God, please let him and Big Jake make it out. Please," I found myself pleading, in a muttered whisper, and crying.

I thought back to the way shit had gone down back at Dame's. Every last one of them niggas got what they deserved, even Sasha. As I was running through the basement to get to the car, I saw her fate. She was laid on top of a table, a pipe stuck down her throat and one shoved clear up her rancid pussy. I figured Jake or Trigga did that for Gina.

"That was for Gina, bitch!" I had said and spat on her lifeless body.

I was glad Pookie got his too, but nothing gave me more satisfaction than cutting Dame's dick off. He used his dick as a weapon, so I was more than happy to disarm him.

I didn't know how long I had been sitting at that bar praying and crying when I heard Ghost's soft voice.

"Ray-Ray."

I slowly looked up at her through blurry vision. "Yeah."

"Is Trigga coming?"

I swallowed hard, the lump in my throat threatening to choke me. "I don't know."

She looked down at her Jordan-clad feet then back up at me. "Will you make me something to eat? Can you cook? Trigga can. I like his fried bologna sandwiches best. Can you make me one?"

I smiled down at her and nodded. "Yeah, I'll make you one."

She smiled. Her smile was innocent. She still had that about her, and in that moment, I wish I had the same.

"Make sure you toast the bread like he do and burn the meat on one side, and don't forget the mayo," she said.

"Okay."

She skipped back over to the red sofa.

It didn't take me long to fix her sandwich. I made it just how she wanted it, and she ate it, saying, it was almost better than Trigga's.

For the rest of the night neither Ghost nor I slept much. After showering and nursing my wounds as best I could, I would doze off then jump awake at the slightest noise hoping it was Trigga and Big Jake. It never was.

I changed channels on the TV to see that the news of Dame's kingdom falling had already been reported. They showed his mansion up in flames and were reporting that there were no survivors. My lips started to tremble.

Ghost looked at me then dropped her eyes. In that moment I felt in my heart what I didn't want to accept. Ghost walked over and crawled on the couch with me. She pulled the covers up to her chin, and I felt her tears drip on my arms.

"Trigga coming," she said, her little voice trembling. "He said he wasn't gon' leave me and stuff, so he coming. You just watch."

I held her tight. She was a little girl, and so was I. The game had stolen everything and everybody away from us. We had no one. I didn't want to accept that, but my life was what it was.

The next morning Ghost and I woke up to a coded knock at the door. She skittered to the door and knocked in code to whoever was on the other side. Once she was sure it was safe, she opened the door, and in walked two females in black suits that hugged their curves. I knew who they were because I'd seen them with Anika.

"You two ready?" one asked, while the other one stood guard at the door.

Her voice was buttery soft. It didn't seem like she was anyone's bodyguard, but I knew she could kill a nigga with her eyes closed.

Ghost and I nodded and grabbed our shoes and hoodies. I made sure to grab the backpack.

As they led us to a black Lincoln MKZ, I looked at all of the cars and trucks passing by, hoping that Trigga would be in one. I even asked the guards to wait a few more minutes, trying to keep the last little bit of hope alive, but after fifteen minutes they said they couldn't wait anymore, that they had to take us to the airport.

For the first time I looked up and saw the big sign for the Airport Hotel, rooms twenty-five dollars a night and up. I couldn't help but think it was a ho trap. Dame's hanging body flashed in my mind, and I gave a slight smile through my pain. The devil was dead.

Once at the airport, I expected people to ask me more questions, since I knew I looked young as fuck, but nobody asked me shit. Ghost and I walked through security and to the Delta gate without as much as a glance from anyone, except the occasional dude looking at my ass in the shorts I had on, or someone glancing at the bruises I couldn't hide.

When the call came to board first class to London, me and Ghost didn't move. We didn't move until they made the last call for boarding, still hoping that Trigga and Big Jake would somehow show up. We finally stood and walked toward the attendant, and then Ghost pulled on my arms and pointed.

For a second we both got happy when we saw a guy with locks and a hoodie walking toward us. From a distance he looked like Trigga, but the closer he got, the more our reality settled in. The tears I had been holding in rolled down my face as I handed over our first-class tickets and boarded the plane.

Epilogue

Ray-Ray
Three Months Later

London had been good to me and Chasity, who still wanted me to call her Ghost because Trigga had given her that name. We were living in Dalston, in a borough called Hackney. It was one of the places Trigga's contacts had showed us, and I liked it right off the rip. I had even gotten a job at the café around the corner.

I was in the kitchen of our flat when Ghost asked me, "Diamond, can I go across the way to Joslyn's for a tea party?"

Ghost had made friends easily, while I mostly kept to myself. I really didn't know what the hell I was doing. I kept praying that everything was all a dream, that I would wake up free to be a kid again and not be an adult before my time.

It was hard. Every day was hard. My ID said I was twenty-one years old, but I was still just sixteen. Although I had more money than I knew what to do with, I didn't want to be flashy, still scared shitless that nigga Dame had eyes even over here. I didn't know who was still on his team and who wasn't.

This nigga haunted me in my dreams. Most nights I'd wake up screaming, seeing him in my bedroom. Everywhere I looked, even though I knew he was dead, I would see his scowling mug. One day when me and Ghost were at the neighborhood park, I swore I saw that nigga standing there plain as day. I grabbed Ghost's hand, and we hightailed to my job just so he wouldn't know where we lived. The nigga still had a hold on me even though he was dead. I could hear him laughing at me in my head. For the most part I cried when Ghost wasn't looking.

Me and Ghost were learning as we went along. For a while, neither of us would go outside unless it was to get some food, but I was smart enough to know people would start to talk if we both just stayed cooped up in the flat, so we started to go out more and sightsee. We always made it home before nightfall so we could lock up. I was paranoid. Didn't trust nobody.

"Yeah, I guess that's okay, but don't stay too long."

"Okay, I won't. Thanks, Diamond."

She had stopped calling me Ray-Ray about a week after we'd settled in.

"You're welcome," I told her, putting the last of the dishes away.

I listened to her lock the door after she left. I made sure she was gone before I grabbed the black backpack. There were times I would pull out Gina's, Big Jake's, and Trigga's pictures, and sit them all on the table and talk to them, just to let them know I hadn't forgotten about them. That day was one of those days. I never wanted Ghost to see me doing that shit though. I kept feeling that I had to be strong for her.

After I sat all of their pictures on the table, the backpack fell on the floor, and a cell phone fell out. I'd seen it before. Had kept it charged with the hope that one day Trigga would call.

I picked it up and looked at the screen. It vibrated in my hand, alerting me to a text.

Li'l shawty, just in case I don't make it, wanted you to know that you still got fam. The Nigerian Queen,

Anika. She yo' peoples. Ya aunt. Had been looking
for you since your folks got it, and when she saw
Dame had you, she started planning on ways to get
rid of that nigga. To make a long story short, me and
her hooked up because she's my uncle's woman. I'll
tell you about that shit later if I can. May not ever see
you alive again but needed you to know this.

I kept reading the message over and over, making sure I
was reading it correctly. I have an aunt? Anika? The woman I
had openly admired when I first saw her? The woman Dame
had beat my ass for because I was staring at her too hard? I
couldn't wrap my mind around it.

I would have been sitting there the whole day just
reading it over and over again had a knock not come at
the door. It was a coded knock, so I knew it was Ghost. I
knocked in sync three times, then four, then two, and she
responded in kind.

I snatched the door open a bit annoyed, because
she sometimes refused to use her key. Then my heart
stopped. Nobody was there. Only a happy birthday cake.

At first it felt like my heart slammed into my chest
again. *Happy birthday?* Somebody was playing with me.
My mind screamed, *RUN!*

Immediately I slammed the door closed, sprinted to
the couch and grabbed the gun I had hidden. "Shit!" I
remembered Ghost was still out.

I reached for the cell phone but dropped it as soon as
something fell in the back room. Keys jingling in the door
alerted me. When a smiling Ghost walked in with the cake,
I rushed over to snatch her in the house, kicked the door
closed, and locked it.

"I didn't know it was your birthday, Diamond," she
said, oblivious to my paranoia. Until she saw my Glock.

I knocked the cake from her hand and kneeled down in
front of her. "Remember what I said to do if we ever had
to run?"

She nodded. "Yeah. But why we running?"

"Just get your stuff, Ghost. Somebody knows we're here. I don't know who, but we gotta go."

She just ran for her room without asking any questions. I grabbed the backpack and shoved the passports back inside then ran to my room and looked in all of the secret places I'd hid money.

"I'm ready, Diamond."

Ghost was efficient. That's why I loved her. She always listened to me no matter what.

I abruptly grabbed her hand, and we rushed for the door. We didn't say anything to anyone.

To be honest, I didn't know where to go. I still had some info from Trigga's contact, so I decided I would call him when I felt we were at a safe distance. His name was Phenom. He looked like Idris Elba. No, he just reminded me of him. The accent, the way he walked, talked, all brought to mind the man my mama had said was finer than old wine.

Me and Ghost ran down the stairs so fast, we bumped into hella people along the way, but we were getting the hell out of there one way or the other. I didn't have a car because I had to get used to driving on the wrong side of the street. I moved past a group of UK niggas shooting dice and ran right through their game. Various UK accents mixed with Caribbean and African influences yelled out at me.

I was running so recklessly, a car almost hit us, but I still didn't stop. Ghost was right there with me. Horns blared, people cursed at us.

We took the back way down an alley, but something told me to stop when I saw a black car block that exit.

"This way, Diamond!" Ghost yelled.

We made a quick detour down another alley, but I didn't see the guy in a hoodie slowly making his way down the alley until I was right up on him. Dudes in this area always wore hoodies, so it didn't seem out of the norm to me. Ghost skirted past him, but I almost knocked his shoulder off as I ran past him.

"Damn! You gon' knock a nigga's shoulder off. You gotta pay attention. Learn your environment, li'l shawty."

Something clicked when he called me li'l shawty. My heart crashed into my chest just as I came to an abrupt halt. I stood there a minute with eyes closed, letting the words replay in my head. That down-south Georgia-boy slang sounded like a melody from heaven, but I could have been fantasizing. After all, I still talked to my mama and my daddy and they were dead.

Both me and Ghost slowly turned and looked at the male figure in front of us. He took his left hand and slid his hood back. I let out the breath I had been holding. His locks were longer, his body stockier with a more defined muscle tone, but that red tint to his skin was still there. And those light honey-brown eyes that looked like they were lined in kohl still looked right through me.

"Trigga!!!! I knew you was alive! I knew it!"

Ghost had taken off running before I could stop her. I still thought he was a ghost, thought I was dreaming as I batted away tears. I thought my mind was playing tricks on me again, until he scooped Ghost up in his arms and swung her around. She was laughing and happy.

My feet slowly made way in their direction. I was nervous, chewing down on my bottom lip the whole way. "You-you're alive," I stuttered out when I got close enough to him.

He licked his lips, propping Ghost on his shoulders, and then looked down at me. "Yeah, li'l shawty, a nigga alive."

I had dreamed of that moment for the last three months but never thought it would happen. My dreams tortured me with images of him and Big Jake going down in a blaze of glory. I saw their bodies riddled with bullets and the fire burning the flesh away from their bones. I had thought I was the only one to survive the omen that was Damien.

Part of me wanted to go ham on this nigga and swing on him for leaving me in a foreign fuckin' country to try to figure this shit out by myself. I wanted to scream that I was only fuckin' sixteen years old and didn't know shit about life other than what had been done to me. I wanted to know why he would leave a nine-year-old in my care, knowing I didn't even know how to take care of my fuckin' self.

But I didn't do any of that. I simply moved closer to him, stood on my toes, and wrapped my arms around his neck. We stood that way for the longest. Maybe later I would cuss, scream, kick, and yell at him, but at that moment I was just happy to see him.

I pulled back and asked him, "You put that cake by the door?"

He shook his head. "Nah. Ya girl did."

I looked up at Ghost.

"Not me," she said.

My gaze went back to Trigga, and he motioned his head behind me.

I turned around and saw that black car again. When the door opened, my curiosity got the better of me. I ain't have no girls, no friends other than Dominique, and she wasn't in London. When Big Jake stepped from the car, I laughed. He was alive too. That big nigga made it out alive.

Then another figure stepped from the car. She was slim and almost as dark as me, and she had long braids down past her ass. She looked like she could be Kelly Rowland's twin sister. Her big doe-like eyes were wide as she chewed on her bottom lip.

I shook my head, not understanding. "Gina?"

"Yeah." She nodded slowly, a white gauze wrapped around her neck.

I turned to look at Trigga then back at Big Jake. "I don't... I saw her kill herself."

"Naw, li'l shawty," Trigga said. "You saw what she wanted you to see."

"My mama a doctor," Gina said as she rushed to hug. "I know how to cut myself to make it look one way. I may be dense sometimes, but I'm a smart bitch when I wanna be."

I broke down crying like the baby I was. I still had a family. I still had my peoples, my makeshift family full of hood misfits.

I listened as Gina told me she'd slit her throat in a way that made it look like she'd committed suicide. Trigga had taken her body from Jake's arms to get her away from the house. He was going to make sure she got a proper burial, was going to go curse her mama out and threaten to kill her if she didn't bury her daughter the right way. Until Gina grabbed a hold of his neck to let him know she was alive.

Gina told me she was the one who'd killed Sasha. I was shocked again. She said, after Trigga took her away for those first few hours, she got stitched and cleaned up just enough to come back and see that bitch meet her end. Then she asked me if I knew it was really my birthday.

I looked around at them all trying to remember. It was August fourteenth. I was seventeen years old. "It's really my birthday," I said. "Didn't really think I was going to see it."

"I know that feeling," Big Jake chimed.

Trigga looked at him and smacked his teeth. "This big swolle nigga was gon' kill himself fa nothin'." Then he asked me, "You see why I had to go back, right?"

We all laughed as Big Jake and Trigga started clowning each other again.

I nodded. I had so many questions to ask. Needed a lot of answers about Anika and Trigga's uncle, but for now, all was well in my world. Our world. We were all so happy that we didn't see that Dame's ghost had followed us all the way to the UK.

Well, it didn't follow us; we landed right in its backyard.

None of us had noticed the steel-grey Mercedes parked just a few feet away. Inside was a man identical to Dame in every sense of the word, including looks. Only, he was the evil that his younger twin brother wished he could have been.

E.N.G.A. Every Nigga Gotta Agenda, and we had just become his.

Prologue
California, 18 April 1906

WHEN THE EARTH shook, the great houses on San Francisco's hills stood firm. Windows cracked, plates smashed and ornaments were broken. Nearer the water, on acres of badly reclaimed land, the poor in their shoddy homes sank into liquefying sands, and the residents of Chinatown were entombed in their collapsing tenements. When the tremors stopped, the silence was eerie and unnerving. Then the screams began, and the fires started to spread.

Across the bay in Oakland, the damage was minimal, except for a grand old house set high in the tree-lined hills. The first jolt woke the children and sent the little boy running from his room. He jumped into his big sister's bed, clutching his teddy, and buried his face in the pillow. A second later, the room shook. It was thrust up and spun round. The quake twisted the tall chimneys skywards and weakened the ageing mortar. They snaked back and forth and then the tallest leaned forward, suspended at an impossible angle for several moments, before toppling, at first in slow motion, and then in a torrent of bricks that smashed through the roof and into an attic room where

1

two maids had slept only half an hour before. The floor timbers broke under the weight, and the chimney crashed into the room below, driving the girl's bed down into the dining room, where it landed on the walnut table, snapping its legs instantly.

The roar of the quake died and the dawn sky was visible through a gaping hole cut through the heart of the house. Under a pile of bricks, rafters and floorboards, Ellie couldn't see a single chink of daylight. She reached out her hand. She felt the soft fur of her brother's teddy, and then his arm. He didn't move and she couldn't pull him closer because she was pinioned by a web of splintered wood. Dust and soot from the chimney coated the inside of her mouth. She could smell wood smoke, and she would have shouted for help if the weight of the bricks hadn't stopped her filling her lungs with air.

She whispered, 'Bobby.'

He didn't respond and his breathing was shallow. Stretching her arm until it hurt, she wrapped her fingers around his wrist. 'Bobby,' she said again.

He moaned but didn't move, and she began to cry. Dust, soot and tears clogged her eyes and made them sting. As she tried lifting her other hand to wipe them, the debris creaked, shifted, and settled more heavily on her.

Ellie listened to her brother's breath grow fainter.

'Bobby, don't go to sleep on me, you hear,' she said, trying to generate enough saliva to loosen the dry coating from her mouth. 'Pa is going to buy you a bicycle for your birthday. Mom told me.'

Bobby didn't stir, and gradually his breathing grew so shallow she thought it might have stopped. 'Stay with me, Bobby,' she pleaded. As his skin cooled slowly under her hand, she talked to him, and to God, her voice rasping, begging her brother to live. When the rescuers lifted them off the bed, she realised that no one had been listening. Bobby lay limp in a man's arms, perfect and untouched except for the dust on his pyjamas and the soot that turned his golden hair black.